PRAISE FOR *CHINESE TAKEOUT*

'One of the best books about the artist's life... A compelling read.'

Village Voice

'[Nersesian] has a talent for dark comedy and witty dialogue... Woven throughout...are gems of observational brilliance... A vivid tour.'

American Book Review

'A heartfelt, tragicomic bohemian romance... The hip squalor...takes on a mythic charge that energizes Nersesian's lyrical celebration.'

Publishers Weekly

'A witty tour through the lowest depths of high art... A fast paced portrait of...la vie boheme.'

Kirkus Reviews

'Unsentimental but romantic, stark but emotionally rich, chaste but sexy, *Chinese Takeout* compellingly brings together the whole sad and glamorous world of the young artist. A novel that rings with truth and beauty. A novel you don't want to end.'

Frederic Tuten, author of *The Green Hour*

'A definite achievement... Confirms Nersesian's literary artistry. His edgy exploration...is hard to put down.'

Booklist

D1321769

'Nersesian's feel for the maneuvering of the city...is what makes his city stories so wholly engrossing.'

Philadelphia City Paper

PRAISE FOR ARTHUR NERSESIAN

For *The Fuck-Up*

'Combining moments of brilliant black humour with flashes of devastating pain, [it] reads like a roller coaster ride... A wonderful book.'

Alternative Press

'Nersesian has a knack for making a descent into homelessness suspenseful. It's hard to stop reading.'

Time Out New York

For *Manhattan Loverboy*

'Funny and darkly surreal.'

New York Press

'Part Lewis Carroll, part Franz Kafka, Nersesian takes us down a maze of false leads and dead ends... Told with wit and compassion, drawing the reader into a world of paranoia and coincidence while illuminating questions of free will and destiny. Highly recommended.

Library Journal

'Nersesian...has become, though he may not relish the comparison, the poor man's Bret Easton Ellis.'

Toronto Star

For *dogrun*

For *Suicide Casanova*

For *Unlubricated*

Arthur Nersesian's other novels include *The Fuck-Up*, *Manhattan Loverboy*, *dogrun*, *Suicide Casanova* and *Unlubricated*. He has also written three books of poems and one book of plays. Nersesian was the managing editor of the literary magazine *The Portable Lower East Side* and has spent time as an English teacher at Hostos Community College, City University of New York, in the South Bronx. He was born and raised in New York City. He can be reached at ArthurNersesian@yahoo.com

Chinese Takeout

a novel by

Arthur Nersesian

MARION BOYARS
LONDON · NEW YORK

Published in Great Britain in 2005 by
MARION BOYARS PUBLISHERS LTD
24 Lacy Road, London, SW15 1NL

First published in the United States by HarperCollins Publishers in 2002

www.marionboyars.co.uk

Distributed in Australia and New Zealand by Peribo Pty Ltd, 58 Beaumont Road,
Kuring-gai, NSW 2080

Printed in 2005
10 9 8 7 6 5 4 3 2 1

A CIP catalogue record for this book is available from the British Library.

ISBN 0-7145-3111-1

To the memory of Tom Reiss,
teacher, artist, friend
(1957–2002)

Lonelier now, completely dependent
on each other, not knowing each other we don't
lay out paths that meander anymore,

we make them straight. The primal fires
born only in steam boilers now, heaving hammers
that grow stronger. While we weaken like swimmers.

—Rainer Maria Rilke, *Sonnets to Orpheus*

One

Twenty years after the subway accident, at thirty- three, I had two pieces accepted to a group show on lower Broadway. My financée, June, and I were late to the opening at Entrance Art Gallery. June dashed off to meet one friend just as the curator, Laura Vierst, grabbed me. She said someone had already shown interest in one of my pieces.

"Orloff," she whispered, "I want you to meet Barclay Hammel."

Laura pushed me toward the back of a small, younger man chatting with the gray-fox mogul Victor Oakridge. The short youth looked like a big yellow dahlia and smelled of roses.

"So few artists realize that patrons are their hidden partners," I overheard Victor pontificate to his partner in wealth. "People remember Michelangelo, but if Pope Julius II didn't toss him the Sistine Chapel commission or the *Last Judgment*, if the Medicis didn't throw him into their funeral tomb, he'd just be an obscure stonecutter."

"Listen, Or," said Laura, while we were waiting. "I got him to take your piece for half the price, and I think you should do it." In other words, instead of eight hundred, I'd get four, minus Laura's commission—still twice as much as I would get on the street. "Barclay's plugged into this whole dot-com survivor support group and I really think that if he takes this, we can move your other works in that crowd."

When Victor finally stepped away from the floral lad, Laura introduced us. Barclay talked about how much he liked one of my paintings entitled *East River Swimmer*. Done in acrylic paint, it was one of a series of four plywood square-foot panels. Each one was a different view of the swimmer. Although everyone complimented them, I had been unable to draw out all I wanted from them, and feared I had reached my artistic limits.

I wanted to work on the series longer and develop them into a solo show, but as usual, I desperately needed cash. I was hoping to rent a gloriously huge loft with June, so against my better judgment, I agreed to let Laura put the red dot next to it on the price list.

Delighted, Barclay shook my hand and went on about how great the work was: "I usually buy art as an investment, but your piece immediately grabbed me. You really feel the guy struggling. I intend to hang it in my bedroom so I'll never forget that life is a challenge." I had to sell my labors at half price to remind a millionaire that life was hard.

When his cell phone chimed, he excused himself and took the call. I was expected to wait politely. Art collectors were a despicable bunch who held artists by a short green leash made of nouveau cash. A year before, I had painted a series of collectors like pompous Victor Oakridge. I characterized them as purple and bloated Turks destroying Armenian artifacts, prissy and gray Nazis looting the Louvre, and sleek, pedigree dogs fighting over a bloody piece of meat. Ironically the cycle sold well.

Only the ongoing fear of starving to death drove me to put my work on gallery walls.

In a flash, the boy fascist was off the phone. Before he could cut the check and scram, I brought him to my beautiful girl, Junia, who I introduced as a brilliant young artist.

Described by one critic as "a photographic *ultra*-realist," June was apt both in landscape and people. She could immediately scale down a scene—no matter how grand—to the perfect ratio of a page, with nearly no revision. Her weaknesses were conception and composition. Her talent seemed to overwhelm her. She'd work quicker than she could actually think. To look at her work, you'd see it lacked thematic cohesion. Still, I was in awe.

I genuinely hoped Barclay would buy something from her, but truthfully my vanity was also at work; I wanted to show him the living beauty I possessed that money couldn't buy. After his eyes popped out and his jawbone dropped off, he asked if she had any pieces in the show. Of course she did. Colorful abstractions that looked like they had been composed by Rothko in a Spin-o-Rama, not her usual stuff. As he flattered her framed tie-dyed T-shirts, I saw another dark green jug of red wine having its black top unscrewed.

Klein Ritter got to it first. He was a shrunken, deviously mild-mannered man and the most venomous art critic on the scene. For the longest time he'd flatter me, come to all my shows, and perpetually promise to write an introductory essay in a major art journal. Eventually, though, I learned that he swore this to every good-looking straight male artist who crossed his crooked path.

When I started pouring the vino, he stood behind me and said, "So,

3

Or, how does it feel knowing you have the best piece in the gallery." He gulped down the drink.

"I only believe reviews that I read in magazines." I refilled his cup.

"Come on," he replied. "Who do I look like, Robert Hughes? Good reviews are no fun. Besides, success is the worst thing for young talent." Like a bad odor, he seemed to dissipate away.

"Body and Soul," whatever that meant, was the title and theme of the show. Inspecting the various works, I realized that Klein's compliment had unfortunate merit. Among the many tiredly shocking pieces, a conceptual artist had submitted a series of Polaroids of his solid waste, which he referred to as "Brown Carps." Next to them, splattered configurations of his seed spilled on a black page were labeled, "O man, Onan!"

When I looked over to point out the vulgarographs to June, I saw that she was still with Barclay. She giggled as he yapped and I couldn't be happier. He was obviously smitten by her. If her dark hair, almond eyes, and perfect breasts helped her shake a deal in the savage art world, so much the better.

I found myself falling in love as well. One particular work of neglected art, an incredible portrait of a little girl on a crowded street had completely enthralled me. It truly was *the* best piece in the place. The child was absently scratching the inside of her elbow with a lollipop. What the artist had captured was her amazing expression. While the girl's face struggled for a seen-it-all cynicism, her eyes betrayed her bewilderment turning toward terror. The crowd, too, was complex and conflicted. Although their faces were united in a sort of mass placidity, they each subtly dwelled on their own little drama. One man in the crowd looked like a drug abuser; another guy on the other end of the canvas was a wealthy uptown type. The field of colors, the precision and composition of shapes, the delicate irony of relationships — all were perfectly balanced. I stared at it so intently that I missed a breath and gasped suddenly for air.

Laura was in her office tenderizing a prospective buyer when I politely interrupted and told her I needed to know who did the piece hanging in the corner.

"In the far corner?" She smiled freakishly, obviously pissed at my imposition. "That's Bethsheba Argus's work."

"You're kidding," I remarked and dashed out to the crowd. The first time I ever saw this Australian artist, she was sitting naked on a table, modeling for seven bucks an hour at the Art Students League. With her stout legs, muscular ass, and large bosom, Beth was a sexy compact. Once, at an opening together soon after we met, she and I got soused and intimate. Over her years in New York her accent had completely washed away. Hopefully her artistic style was finally fading as well. She was known for her bland minimalism, but this new piece was nothing like that. It was gutsy and exciting, and that made her equally irresistible.

I circulated for about five minutes before I spotted her listening to some twinkie in a bow tie. I dashed over and gave her a big hug and kiss.

"That is one amazing fucking piece you did!" I cut right in.

"Wow! Thanks," Beth replied, clearly pleased. The poor geek with the pink-tinted glasses faded into the artwork.

"Where did you come up with that?"

"It's really pretty typical for me," she replied modestly.

"Do you know that little girl?" I asked pointing to the work.

"There is no little girl in my painting," she said, wrinkling her nose.

"Hold it." I led her to the masterwork.

"That's not mine." She pointed to the neighboring work. "That's my piece."

It was another rather boring minimalist watercolor.

"Well that's nice too," I stated calmly, trying to gloss over my obvious fuck-up.

"You know Adele Oreckle?" she responded. "She painted that."

"Is she here?" I asked.

"I didn't see her."

"I'm really sorry."

"It was nice being discovered, if only for a fleeting instant." She smiled demurely.

When June and I left the opening that night, we celebrated my cut-rate sale by buying a cut-rate bottle of white wine and dining out. While sipping down a pinot grigio over an Indian meal, June explained that Barclay had promised to pay her a studio visit in a few days.

"I described my three new works and he seemed interested," she said.

She had been experimenting lately, trying her hand at large abstractions. I didn't have the heart to reveal that they were too gimmicky and derivative. Her strength was in realism. Her early pieces were inspired. Ever since she was a teenager she had toiled at her craft, and she deserved a break.

True to his word, at the week's end, Barclay paid his first studio visit and June came home waving a thousand-dollar check. Instead of the half-baked abstractions she was hoping to sell, he had bought five pedestrian charcoal sketches at a premium price.

"I can't believe he didn't go for your oil paintings," I replied. Those were her best.

"Maybe I'll show those to him next time," she added. "We're going out for coffee next week."

"Why?" I asked nervously.

"I don't know. He wants to be my patron."

Over the next month, she'd casually mention that Barclay had called. When June finally said that he was interested in seeing yet more of her work, I found myself combating incipient jealousy. *She loves me*, I'd assure myself. *She loves me not*, all my inadequacies kept whispering back. But how could I have any doubts? We were, after all, engaged to be married. Lately she had been talking about having children.

What my jealousy actually amplified was my very inadequacy as a provider. Over the past year, we had eked out a joint existence in our cramped hovel. More and more, June had been talking about the squalor we dwelled in, the mice and roaches, the used furniture, and the bad smells in the hallway. I didn't mind austerity as long as I could paint. But for June, poverty was traumatic. During her childhood, June had hopscotched throughout the archipelago of low-income projects along the East River—the Lillian Wald, Baruch, and Jacob Riis Houses where her extended Dominican family lived.

A few months before this we had lucked out, subletting a summer work space nearby. That was around the time I began the East River Swimmer series. Each day, we'd take turns neurotically painting in the claustrophobic studio, a classroom in a former public school on Suffolk Street. During the late morning, while I sold used books on the street, she'd paint. In the afternoons and early evenings, while I used the space, she taught ESL for a labor union.

Although our classroom sublease was ending, a dear friend, Shade, was supposed to rent out his villa-like loft in Chinatown while he went away on vacation. During those late September days while Barclay was calling her, I hoped that the luxury of working in Shade's marvelous space would miraculously curb my growing suspicions.

"What's your problem?" she finally screamed at me in the middle of an eerily wordless dinner one evening.

"You know what I've been thinking?" I asked delicately. She didn't respond. "That maybe we should have a baby soon. I mean we're not getting any younger and you want a kid, don't you?"

"How are we going to feed it? What's he going to wear, paint? No way am I putting a kid through the hell I went through."

Of course she was right. A baby was the last thing I could handle, but I was terrified of losing her.

After the meal, when she was sketching, I finally made a wooden effort to allay my anxiety by bringing my jealousy out in the open. I explained that I found her friendship with Barclay slightly unnerving.

Instead of reassuring me that there was nothing to worry about, she threw it back in my face: "Hey, when I saw you kiss that cow in front of everyone at Entrance Art, I didn't say a word."

"I wasn't kissing *her*, I was kissing her *art!*" And it turned out not even to be Bethsheba's piece that I loved.

She chuckled over her sketch pad. "You are so pathetic."

"Just say you're not . . . *seeing* Barclay!"

"I'm not seeing him," she mimicked my whiny tone. "Now stop!"

THE DANGER OF BEING a representative artist is that it's all on the page. The sketchbook never lies. About a week before we were supposed to move into Shade's loft, instead of squeezing my oil worms of paint onto the palette, I flipped through June's many drawing books. Endless 18" x 24", 70 lb., acid-free pads. No recycled newsprint for her. She was a compulsive sketcher. While watching TV, or eating dinner, sometimes while on the toilet, she'd sketch. At times I wondered if she even knew she was doing it. Images, places, animals were all caught by her nimble fingers.

Finally, after three hours of frenzied searching, I found the evidence. A sketch pad with page after page of nude and interlocked bodies. An encyclopedia of sexual positions. Forbidden acts we had never dared perpetrate. The male model sported an erection brutally unlike my own. I felt my heart beat so articulately just below my thin layer of flesh that I had to close my eyes and catch my breath. With a ringing in my ears and a silent cry shooting from my throat, I had confirmed that my girlfriend had been cheating on me with a vengeance. I began tearing the images from out of the pad, digging through the book. How could she?! My volcano had only started smoking.

I pulled down her three latest works that she had propped against the wall. The stark feeling of betrayal translated into pure rage. Grabbing a palette knife, I slashed across her large-framed works-in-digress.

Still inflamed, I reached up to the overhead space above the doorway where she had her early autobiographical pieces neatly stored away. Yet as I looked at her early images I was humbled: a portrait of her grandparents, whom she had painted while visiting Santo Domingo just before they had perished in Hurricane Hugo; a sketch she had done while still in her teens from her bedroom window of a nest of rats; a mother suckling her pups in the unweeded and littered lot next to her old home. Eight patiently painted panels of bombed-out brownstones with their sheet-metal windows and cinderblock doorways. These abandoned buildings made up her neighborhood before they had flowered into high-priced condos.

I placed these works back in the overhead space. She would have killed me if I had destroyed them. Though I was still pissed, what I had done seemed like a fair response.

I folded up my own artwork and supplies and piled them into my van downstairs. Then I raced home and shoved my clothes, along with a few other personal effects, into two old pillowcases. I took a final glance at the packed apartment we had moved into just a year earlier. I loaded up the rest of my things and headed downtown.

That was the first time I ever regretted being an artist. I knew that if I were some nine-to-five wage slave, able to provide basic comforts, I wouldn't have lost the great consolation gift of a luckless life: my future wife, the mother of my unborn children.

TWO

Before moving in with June, I had lived for a while out of my banged-up Chevy van. I initially bought the old jalopy from a plumber who had framed it with girders to support the toilets and bathtubs that he would carry on its rooftop. He had also customized it to withstand theft and burglary: padlocks on all the side and back doors, as well as a gated rear section, made it a rolling fortress. The windows were one-inch Lexan set in welded, reinforced tracks. It even had a kill switch, which prevented anyone from hot-wiring it, not that anyone would ever steal the hunk of junk.

Like all glorious things, it was dying. It was a 1980 model with over two hundred thousand miles on the odometer. Not even the constant layers of graffiti tags stalled the cancerous advance of body rust. Because I sold and painted on the street, I kept my books and artwork packed in the back. On top of them was a large piece of plywood, upon which was an inch-and-a-half-thick square of old foam rubber that served as my bed. After accumulating ever more stuff, I was able to tunnel only a narrow corridor to sleep in.

As the city became increasingly expensive and unfamiliar, downtown seemed to be slipping further and further down. Without even knowing it, my generation had come full circle. We were inhabiting the same filthy streets as our refugee grandfathers. South of Houston, the same old, grimy tenements were now obscenely priced as they inescapably awaited our occupancy. Stanton, Rivington, Delancey, Broome—to me these streets sounded like the names of internment camps. A dark, shuttered neighborhood from Allen to the East River was creaking back to life almost against its will.

Smack in the bottom of this area was my bar, still too out of the way for the nitwit weekenders who mobbed the Village. It still bore the sign of the former enterprise: The Good Will Barber Shop. It was on Orchard between Canal and Division, and I always found some of my good-for-nothing cohorts there, artist wanna-bes, street booksellers, and pleasant drunks. Parking a few blocks away, I tried not to think of June as I headed to the pub. Once there, I sat at the bar and downed three tequilas in five minutes before happy hour frowned away.

Cali levitated over. She was a large, beautiful woman with a strikingly angular face and broad, dramatic features. She had come a long way from the wild parties and celebrated lovers of her youth. Now she allegedly ran a small gallery around the corner, the Colossus, but she no longer had openings. She seemed to divide her time between the saloon and her huge salon. An exotic, maternal figure, Cali was the one who got me my first solo show.

11

"How's it going, Calliope?" I asked tiredly. The gallery owner had been in a financial slump lately, and I knew she was suffering from general depression. She handed me a postcard she had received, a call for new "representational works." A friend of hers was putting together a group show in Portland, Maine. I thanked her and slipped the card in my sketchbook.

"I'm selling my van," she stated with her slight, sexy trace of an accent.

"Really? Your '94 Ram van?" I confirmed. It was a dream to ride and seemed twice as big as my own.

"How much?" Shaughanessy, a Scot with an Irish name — my part-time mentor and future sublettor — who was commonly known as Shade, came over with a glass of white wine for her and a scotch for himself.

"Three grand. Just enough to pay off some people."

"You mean me," Shade replied.

"Three thousand is way below market value," I said. Her van could easily fetch twice that price.

"I was waiting for a collector to buy some new prints but he's not buying and I got to raise some cash quickly," she explained.

"If you're really worried about money," Shade suggested, "sell one of your de Koonings." Among her art collection were several portraits painted of her by the great abstract expressionist when she was his young lover nearly forty years ago.

"I'm in a funk," she said, and wiped her beautiful brow hidden by her thick, black lockets.

"Me too," I concurred, but I didn't want to recount June's painful betrayal.

"You both need a swift kick in the ass," Shade replied and slammed his empty dram down on the counter, slightly spilling our drinks. "You're completely missing the point!"

"There's a point?" I inquired.

"It's not about being giddy or not being fascinated. Of course you're depressed! *You're supposed to be depressed.*"

"I just meant I was having trouble selling work," Cali said, then smiled a bit, "but why are we all supposed to be depressed?"

"Why *shouldn't* you be?" he instantly retorted. "Are you rich? Young? Famous? No. You don't have a family or a proper career . . . so what do you have left? You're supposed to be artists!" Cali had recently tried her hand at painting, then she attempted photography, but she didn't show much aptitude or interest in either.

"Occupational therapy," she replied, painting the air as though she were in the dayroom of Bellevue.

"Your brain is a workshop, isn't it? It's a studio and gallery. Like a piece of garbage, we're tossed into this life. We have a couple of gasping breaths, that's all! You have to throw that work onto that canvas before death's quick snatch."

"So *that's* what we're supposed to do. Thanks for the encouragement," she said glumly.

Fresh drinks were placed before us, causing a silent race to see who could get the glass to their lips swiftest.

"I'm not saying I don't get depressed," the Scot resumed after putting his scotch down, "but for me depression is a sign that I'm not working hard enough."

"Do you ever fear that it's all for nothing?" I asked.

"Hey, I'm turning seventy in a few years," Shade replied. "When Renoir was my age, he had brushes tied to his hands so he could still paint." He paused. "The possibility that I'm going to get discovered in my lifetime is pretty slim, but that doesn't take away from the belief that my work has meaning—even if only I see it."

"You're deluded," Cali responded, then rose wobbily and wandered outside into the void of a Chinatown night.

I excused myself, headed to the bathroom, and took a long piss, my most joyous sensation of the evening. In the filthy yellow light of the smelly stall, a green "Vote Nader" sticker glowed. Near it I read a mailing label containing the latest "powem" that my friend Pablo had fastened there: "Enchanted red ribbon of embers. Enters would rather think, not toward . . ." Although he was part Puerto Rican, and referred to himself as "Nuyorican," his precious poems were neither ethnic nor, for that matter, clear. They usually were little more than a few words. I preferred profanely scribbled potty humor to language poetry any day.

When I returned, Shade had grabbed a table. He was drinking alone before the red glow of the bottled candle, squinting at a filthy plaster mold of a nicotine-brown cupid hanging on a far wall. There was something eternal about the Scottish artist. He was a giant of a man with a long salt-and-pepper beard. His head of hair was so shaggy that snapped-off teeth combs from decades gone by must still be harpooned in its tangles.

Shade first came to America over forty years ago and used to hang out at the old Cedar bar with the now overly celebrated abstract expressionists of the '50s. Not that any of them, upon gaining fame and fortune, ever helped him. Like the vast majority of artists, he was poor and an unquenchable drinker.

For Shade, everything was about the art. When I was first introduced to him, he dismissed me with a snort. But when Cali later showed him some of my paintings, he suddenly took a shine to me.

As I came over, he lifted the candle at the table and asked, "Ever read Kipling's *Light that Failed*?"

"I missed that one."

"I'm not afraid of dying, but I'm terrified of going blind," he said, and as though reciting a poem, he blurted, "As the daylight dims, more and more of the underworld comes pressing in."

I ordered another drink. He ordered another drink. We drank. Then he ordered another drink and I ordered another drink. He must have sensed that something was wrong with me, because for the first time I was actually keeping up with him.

"June cheated on me," I volunteered.

"Usually it happens the other way," he tried to comfort. "Guys usually two-time, don't they?"

"Well, this time it's the girl."

"So another pecker poked her, big deal. Forgive her and move through it."

"It's too late."

"Oh, don't say that." He looked at me gravely. "You didn't kill her, did you?"

"'Course not."

"Thank God. I still remember Carl and Anna." He finished his drink with a second sip. He had mentioned them before, a South American couple who were both artists. In the 1980s, it was the O.J. Simpson case of the New York art community. Their relationship had been going sour, and one day Anna either fell to her death or was pushed by Carl from their high-rise apartment building on Waverly Place.

"I slashed three of her canvases," I said to Shade after finishing my drink.

"You didn't!" He froze.

"They were three lesser, abstract works. They weren't even finished. I mean, she should have stuck with realism."

He nodded his head, started chuckling, and said, "Realism from an idealist."

"I'm no idealist."

"Where are you sleeping?"

"In my van, why?"

"It's late. Come along," he said, putting down a twenty. I paid the balance and followed him out the door to the adjacent building.

The S. Jarmulovsky's Bank (est. 1873) on the southwest corner of Canal and Orchard is the biggest building in the neighborhood. A monstrosity of large grayish stones illuminated by eleven stories of

flourescent lights, it consists mainly of clothing sweatshops for undoc-
umented Chinese workers. On the ground floor an "Enternet" café had
just opened.

Shade's studio was on the sixth floor in the rear of the building. He
moved in when New York real estate was still a land giveaway, but he
never revealed the rent. We took the rear freight elevator up to his loft.
There he flipped on a switch. Half of the dozen or so flourescent bars
didn't even go on.

"How can you stand this lighting?" I asked, squinting irritably.

"Don't be such a wuss. In the days of yore, when artists painted at
night, they had to do it by the flicker of candles." He had a point.
Ruined eyesight might be the best thing for modern art. Most of the
cardboard squares that clipped into the metallic, drop-ceiling frame
had vanished, leaving exposed electrical wiring, water pipes, and joists
from the building.

Despite the large space, the loft was crammed with crap. In fact,
his actual living quarters seemed tighter than my packed van: a Formica
table, some wooden folding chairs, and what he referred to as a trundle bed. An old wooden easel positioned before the window with one
small canvas on it was all I could see of his work space.

Most of the massive loft was strangulated by gray metal shelves. I'm
sure it was a fire hazard. What little I could see of the floors and walls
was splattered with a thousand layers and colors of dulled paint. At one
time the huge room must have been all work space, but as Shade's pro-
ductive years turned into art and the art had no takers, the canvases
became cocooned in bubble wrap and stacked on the spreading
labyrinth of shelves.

"There it all is," he said, answering my thoughts. "A lifetime of
painting."

"You're kidding," I replied. There must have been a thousand canvases of all sizes. "You haven't sold anything?"

"Oh sure, some here and there. A few every year. I sold three pieces to various museums. Last year Cali sold two to a Rockefeller for fifty thousand apiece, but my output has always outpaced my demand."

"What the hell are you going to do with all these?"

"Donate them to the New Goo," he joked. That was his nickname for the recently proposed downtown Guggenheim Museum, which was supposed to be built only blocks away and was projected to be ten times bigger than the original one uptown.

"Can I see some of your work?" I asked, wanting to believe that I was in the presence of a modern-day Rembrandt, unjustly neglected in his own lifetime.

"That's why I brought you here," Shade replied. He led me to the back wall, where he flipped through a stack of canvases and finally selected one frame of sofa-size art that was wrapped in cellophane.

"Here it is," he said, bringing it under a bar of light.

"What's this?" I asked.

He carefully tore the masking tape and removed the wrapping.

"This is where I was born and raised." He revealed a complex and vibrant painting: it was a row of squalid cottages set against a green, rolling hillside. Two guys who looked like farmers were examining the distant rain clouds and the older children in a group were looking at their elders. The painting consisted of several small components working together—as you stared at one part of the work you were transferred to another until slowly you moved through the entire piece. The composition and details were flawless. The colors, original. The children in the foreground, though small, had studied and engaging faces. Signed articulately below was the name Shaughanessy. The only problem with the work was running right down its middle. Robbing it of all tranquility was a pair of old tarnished zipper teeth sewn right through the canvas like a Frankenstein scar.

"This painting was my first great work," he introduced it slowly, proudly. "A day before finishing it, I got a modest offer from the local lord. It would have been my first real sale."

"Really?"

"Oh yeah." Then as though I had missed the zipper, he pointed to it and asked, "See that? My first wife took a knife to it after I came home drunk that night. She accused me of whoring."

"You could have taped it together in the back." If a painting is cleanly slashed, it can easily be taped and touched up with a good chance of full recovery.

"Don't you think I knew that?! The little wifey repaired it."

"Why?" I asked, inspecting the heavy zipper.

"Who knows? The next morning when I saw she had stitched the zipper onto it, I went nuts and hit her," he said, collapsing across his bed like a fallen oak. "She moved out after that. And I came to the 'mericas."

"So you brought me up here to tell me that cutting up June's paintings was awful? Well fuck her, I loved her and she cheated on me."

"That happened over forty years ago," Shade replied. "I don't know what became of Sheila; wouldn't'a known it if I passed her on the street. I only brought you up here to tell you that June might forget what you look like, but she'll never forget what you did. And you'll never forget that you loved her."

"And she me," I assured him.

As soon as I lay down next to him he passed out. I had trouble sleeping as I recalled the sound and feel of ripping through June's three newest canvases. Images of injured art dominated my dreams. Flowers spotted with abrasions and bruises, a frame trickling with blood. The work faded away, but I remembered its heaving gray contours and jaundiced yellow complexion. Its edges were crusted with purple blood. I awoke with tears in my eyes. Shade was snoring.

I remembered one evening when June came home in agony. She had spent several days up in Harlem painting a row of beautiful old brownstones. She was almost finished when some motherfucker appeared and told her she had to pay him to paint on his block. When she patiently informed him about the laws of public domain, he scoffed.

"It's my block, pay if you want to stay."

"Fuck off!" she shot back.

The guy knocked her to the ground, grabbed her canvas, and just walked off. She screamed for help, but no one came.

No one ever does.

Three

Shade's seismographic snoring blocked my reentry into
sleep, so I rolled out of bed and stumbled to the bathroom. As I peed, I
stared down Division over the recently cleaned Arc de Triomphe of the
Manhattan Bridge. The beautiful old dome of the former East River Sav-
ings Bank peeked out, a huge financial leftover from the Gilded Age.
Now, it was the Hong Kong and Shanghai Banking Corporation, or
HSBC. Nearby was a large red high-rise. Vegetable dealers filled the
street during business hours. Chatham Square, a major hub of the neighborhood, was empty. In the square was the Kimlau memorial, named

after a Chinese American soldier who was killed during World War II.

Long before Chinatown, when this was still the eastern edge of Little Italy, it was divided by Italian gangs that grew into Mafia families. Before then, Irish and Native American street gangs warred here. Going back nearly two hundred years, this area was commonly known as Five Corners or Five Points. It was America's first real slum.

Feverishly I watched cars appear and vanish. Feeling tipsy, I realized I was still partially intoxicated. I cupped my hand under the bathroom faucet and sucked down about a gallon of rusty tap water. Then I carefully reinserted myself back onto my quarter of the lumpy trundle bed without waking up Shade and thought about June.

I had met her in a class at the Art Students League. Her work, like her, was immediately fetching. When I complimented it, she thanked me, but she never stopped working or even looked up from her painting.

"What do you paint?" she whispered.

"Lately I've been drawing people," I replied.

We talked a while. Her voice was as soft and tender as a paintbrush in my ear.

I invited her out for coffee, and soon after she met me at the studio I was subletting. I showed her nude sketches I had recently done in class.

"These are fabulous," she cooed. Coincidentally, they were of Bethsheba, who had happened to be modeling. June critiqued, "You really made her a lot more beautiful than she is."

"I couldn't possibly do that for you, but I'd love to try."

"In the nude?" she presumed.

"If you don't mind," I replied, although that hadn't been my intention.

Without batting an eyelash, she pulled off her heavy wool sweater and unsnapped her black bra. Out tumbled a pair of breasts, much larger and firmer than anything I had ever fantasized. She added that she only had an hour before she had to leave. I positioned her lying down and tried to sketch, but couldn't catch my breath. I found myself growing dizzy. I was trying to draw, or at least pretend to draw her, but I knew she'd eventually insist upon seeing the work. I put down my charcoal and silently walked over to her. She looked up at me and leaned forward. We kissed at the same time.

All day and night we frantically made love until exhausted, we finally fell asleep. We resumed early the next morning and for endless days afterward. Usually a smitten couple gets a honeymoon period that lasts a matter of months. For us, we screwed like wild animals for two years.

With a sudden force of will, I pushed all the memories aside, focusing on the dreamy blackness. I drifted back to an empty sleep.

Shade woke me around noon.

"Come on, boy, more than twelve hours sleep and you're inviting bedsores," he said. It had been more like five hours.

I groaned and rose. Sitting next to me in his torn boxers, he handed me a fresh pint of scotch. "Dog of the hair."

"If I have any more, I'll cough up a fur ball." I rose feeling a chill and held a small wool blanket around me.

Shade dressed in the same outfit he wore yesterday, black flannel pants dotted with spills, a grayish yellow shirt that was once white, and a torn brown vest. I too donned yesterday's clothes, but still cold, I kept his old blanket over me like a shawl. He led me down the crowded staircase, overly used during the day by the building's many businesses. We slowly walked the few blocks down Division. I kept my eyes catatonically ahead of my feet, and for the first time I realized that the sidewalks were completely blackened with filth. During the daylight hours, these streets were converted to crowded loading docks where oils and other food stock dripped and littered the pavement. Shade and I had to dodge old Nissan and Toyota forklifts that elevated wooden pallets balanced with stacked and wrapped goods.

We crossed Allen. Shade led me past Triple Eight Palace, the fancy dim sum house, down a side street to Delightful Garden Restaurant, one of the grittiest, dingiest dives I'd ever set foot in. A sign on the wall actually stated, "No Spitting." As we waited our turn at the counter, I rubbed up against a Formica table where a corpulent man belched. A waiter cleared a short stack of dirty dim sum plates off his table as the plump patron reached onto the top of his passing cart and grabbed two steamy dishes that looked like a pair of fried crow's feet.

Shade finally gave two orders to the dehydrated ancient obscured behind the old cash register. The old dim sum cashier fed the request into a grease-caked intercom, then commented in Chinese to Shade, who replied in the same language. Both snickered.

"You speak Chinese?" I asked tiredly, pulling the wool blanket around me tighter.

"You pick up phrases over the years," he replied. In a moment the cashier put a brown paper bag on the counter. Shade paid and we left.

As we walked a few blocks away to the Happy Lucky Pastry Shop on East Broadway, Shade explained that he never ordered dim sum too late in the afternoon because "bacteria from the street migrated in and festered as the day progressed." We bought two thick, overly sugared Vietnamese coffees—coffee syrup with heated condensed milk. Then he led me to his outdoor breakfast nook on the Allen Street Mall. This was a stretch of broken benches on a traffic island that ran up the entire length of the street. Old newspapers and other garbage was strewn around the eroded concrete bench supports and rusted iron gates. This strip somehow had evaded Mayor Giuliani's golden age of urban renewal. We parked ourselves next to a group of junkies who were propping each other up, tiredly socializing the morning away.

"Hey zomb-boys," Shade called out to them.

"Hey Shadito," the nearest one shouted back.

"Who are these organ-donor rejects?" I softly asked.

"This is a needle exchange site," Shade explained. "They come here three times a week."

"Gosh, they look scary," I uttered, still tugging the old blanket around me.

"That line of faces is right out of a page of the old masters," he muttered as he thumbed over toward the recidivist drug users.

"How do you know them?" I asked.

"Oh hell," he exclaimed just above a whisper, "I knew the whole lot before they fucked their lives up with the needles." He nodded his shaggy head toward one unidentifiable creature. "See that one, I remember when she was one fine-looking lass, and that one I knew when she was still a he." He nodded toward a group of mastodons who all looked older than Shade. "I remember when those two lads were kids. They're brothers. The last two in a family of seven Gonzalez boys. All the others died one by one: Vietnam, drugs, shanked in prison . . ."

"Sounds like hell," I commented before finishing the last sugary grains of my java.

"They make reliable models," he pressed on. "They just nod off and you can paint them all day. You know, they'd make perfect angels to your demons paintings."

"What demons paintings?"

"The art collectors."

Shade had declared I had talent as a painter when he saw my Art Collectors paintings. At the time, when I had finished the series, I joked that I needed some angels to round out all the demons. Now they had long since been sold or given away.

"Who'd pay to see these monsters?" I asked, despite my own visual inclination toward the infirm and grotesque.

"I'd pay," he replied. "In fact, in exchange for the great deal I'm giving you on my place, I want you to do a portrait of my little domain—paint these clowns. Is that fair?"

"Oh God!" I groaned. I was never good at doing commissions. The paranoia of trying to fit someone's expectations into my work always hindered me. I pulled the blanket over my head.

"Hey, everybody!" Shade called over to them, "This is my buddy, Orloff. Or," he pointed from left to right, "this is Bobby, Andy, Lucy, Donna, Ramone, Kenny, and Kid. He's going to paint you!"

One of the droopy-lidded seven dwarves waved back. The others didn't seem to notice, especially Lucy, who was fast asleep with her drooling lips parted, revealing her missing front teeth. Her eyelids were also slightly open, showing the ghoulish whites of her eyes.

As I carefully surveyed the grotesque Mount Rushmore, it was evident that they rushed no more. Slow moving objects, that's what the police called older addicts.

Over the years, I had seen and known my share of them. Some hid it well and were fairly preserved, but this group by far was the hardest looking lot I had ever seen. Their ailments were etched right on the surface like medical charts: Hepatitis B, liver cirrhosis, renal failure, bronchial and lung ailments. It wasn't all due to narcotics. Alcohol, poor diet, and no exercise all played a role. Their ravaged faces were painfully unique.

Shade split his pre-scored chopsticks in two, opened a napkin over his filthy shirt, and splashed the tiny plastic cup of soy sauce onto his limp dim sum. I did likewise. As I thoughtlessly flung the warm pasta jacket of soggy shrimp into my foul morning mouth, Shade mused, "You know, I had an apocalyptic dream last night—a tumult of angels. It was an epiphany, really. Right out of the Book of Revelations."

"Go on."

"I did battle with the double-headed dragon. Sword but no shield. And I slew one head—its neck collapsed to the ground—but then I was clenched in the jaws of the other head. The beast tore my arm off. It didn't hurt me, but I looked down and saw my socket and bones, my nerves and veins were shooting blood. My chest was bare and sweaty but I didn't stop my fight."

"What do you think it means?" It sounded like a trailer for *Conan the Barbarian*.

"It can only mean one thing," he summed up, with the sudden insight of a C. G. Jung. "I have to slay the second head."

"What do you mean?"

"I used to wonder how I was going to die. Wonder, wonder. Still don't know, but . . ." He looked off pensively and swallowed a dim sum. "It means on my trip to Scotland I should hunt down Sheila, apologize for cracking her jaw, and accept her apology for slicing my masterpiece."

"She apologized?" I didn't know he had broken her jaw.

"'Course, why else would she stitch a zipper into the painting?"

"I had this strange dream about a dying piece of art," I replied.

"She was the dumbest thing on two chicken legs." Shade ignored my mention of the guilt dream. "Marrying her was the kind of mistake that only a horny nineteen-year-old kilt-wearer could make. Don't misunderstand me, I was glad I broke her jaw. Unlike my art, the mandible healed. It was all for the best, really. I would have had to spend my entire life hand trucking that useless twit around. I would have had to give up my beautiful brushes to be hamstrung with a gang of half-wit kids, each one stupider than the next. Trying to teach them survival skills so they wouldn't starve. I would have bloody martyred myself to the ongoing propagation of mediocrity and hypocritical bourgeois values. Six billion boring people spreading toward sixty billion."

"Well, I ought to be getting on," I said, anxious about my van. Although the windows were gated and the doors padlocked, vandalizing vehicles was done as much for sport as for profit, and all my belongings were inside.

"Hold on now," he stopped me. "I'm not fooling kid, you've got to paint this lot if you're going to occupy my loft."

"I've actually got to talk to you about that."

"Don't tell me you're not renting my studio any longer," he asked.

"See, I was going to do it with June. I want to rent it, but I just can't afford to do it alone."

"Hmmm," he replied pensively. "Tell you what we'll do. Seeing that you're a savage Caravaggio, the last of the Ashcan Artists, here's the deal. I'll chop a third off the rent if you give me a painting of this bench bunch that is so good, it knocks me on my ass."

"Okay," I said hastily before he could retract.

He then looked at his watch. "Meet me here tomorrow at one and we'll talk about the rental."

I agreed, we bade farewell, and I walked a few blocks away to Grand between Allen and Eldridge. I was amazed to find that no one had even tried to break into my van.

As I drove along Washington Square South, I saw that all the good spots along Fourth Street were already taken by early booksellers who lined the street. Between today's hangover and last night's heartbreak, I lacked the stamina to even try. I found a parking spot in the East Village, took out my folding bike, and began a search for cheap used books. The first place I hit was down at the Delancey Street Goodwill where I had once purchased a turn-of-the-century edition of *Leaves of Grass* for fifty cents. I later sold it for a hundred and twenty dollars on Abe.com. Then I slowly zigged and zagged, hitting a variety of thrift stores as far west as Lafayette Street and as far east as Avenue B. An hour and a half and twenty-five new books later, I finally concluded my merchandise drive at the row of three thrift stores located side by side up on Twenty-third Street between Second and Third Avenues.

Heading back downtown to my van, I bumped into Pablo leaving the Saint Mark's Church in-the-Bowery. He was tacking a flyer on the Poetry Project bulletin board advertising his group's reading entitled, "The Emperors Have No Powems."

"You've got to come. KGB Bar. Day after tomorrow at six." Then he paused and added in excitement, "And tonight is the Green Party rally at Madison Square Garden! Only ten bucks."

I told him I'd think about the rally, and promised I'd go to his poetry shindig if he didn't bug me about it.

Later, I remembered that the "Body and Soul" show at Entrance Art was over and that I was supposed to pick up the one unsold Swimmer painting that I had loaned to the gallery. I called Laura Vierst's office to say I would be coming by later that day.

"No need," she replied breezily. "June took it."

"What? When?"

"About an hour ago, when she picked up her piece."

"Oh, shit!" I exclaimed.

"What's the matter?"

"We got into a big fight. She slept with that collector you introduced me to."

"You're kidding! Barclay?" She shrieked his name with disbelief. "He's not like that."

"Well, he was with her." I paused and confessed, "I lost my cool and destroyed some of her work."

"You did what?"

"I shouldn't have, but I did. So my guess is she destroyed my piece."

"Oh, Orloff," she sighed. "How could you? What were you thinking! Why didn't you call me . . . I'm so sorry." Rebuking me one moment and being sympathetic the next came easily to her. "It was such a wonderful piece."

"I know it was," I replied angrily, and slammed the phone down. I marched around lower Manhattan until I felt dazed. When streetlights started popping on I realized it was evening.

That night I bought an aluminum tin of rice and beans from a local cuchifritos joint, and squeezing down the narrow corridor in the center of my parked van, I unfurled my sleeping bag and started on my dinner. After a few bites, though, a growing anger displaced my appetite. I tried to remember and sketch my savaged Swimmer until my hearing focused on a scraping sound. It almost seemed like it was coming from inside my head. Then I realized it was underneath me—a rat. They occasionally crawled up into cars to keep warm next to the engine blocks. I whacked the floor of the old van, but the scratching continued. It sounded as though it were gnawing on my wiring or maybe a brake line.

Angrily I threw open the door of the Chevy, got out, grabbed my easel, unscrewed its legs, and set it up under a bank of light. I wanted to redraw the four Swimmer panels from memory.

Painting one: a naked muscular swimmer, reddish pink. Stepping timidly and uncertainly into the blue flow, rippled by dashes of white. I had painted just the back of the young man, his strong arms, muscular buttocks, and powerful thighs. A slice of a river.

Painting two: a long view of the swimmer three-quarters submerged. Only his shoulders, arm, and head are showing. The river is wider, faster, bluer, more formidable. The distant ribbon of gray highway and the emerging skyline is visible on the far shore.

Painting three: the focus is tighter on his concentrating face. His right elbow is pulling back a little too soon, out of sync with his left arm. He is struggling. Skyscrapers loom clearly before him.

When people drown in the ocean, it's frequently because of an undertow or a rogue wave that sweeps them away. Drowning in a river is different. It's more of a miscalculation. The swimmer believes he's stronger than he is and that the river is easier than it appears.

In painting number four, I had hoped to convey possibilities. Doubt, fear, uncertainty are all subtly visible on the swimmer's face. He holds his head up too long. His reach is shortened. He is trying not to panic. He can still make it to the other side, but then again, he might not.

The last canvas shows the swimmer rising up on the sands of all-powerful Manhattan Island. Its mighty towers seem not so much built on earth as to come down from the heavens. The swimmer has reached the farthest shores, unvanquished.

At the Entrance Art show I had entered the first two of these works. Instead of painting them again on plywood, I stretched a clean canvas onto a wooden frame, nailed it, and quickly sketched out the first image I was going to paint. I filled in the background, the color of the water and sky, and then I let the work dry on the roof of my van. Tomorrow I'd finish it.

While moving boxes around to make room to lie down, I discovered a portrait I had done of Mayor Giuliani that I had been intending to install for a while now. Exhausted, I squeezed onto my sleeping bag, intending to nap for a few hours. I would mount the portrait late tonight.

Over the past six months, I had harvested pointless street signs that explained the obvious: "Don't Honk" or "No Right on Red." These were the canvases for my agitprop art project.

Nowadays good art was not enough. To get discovered you needed more than talent. Gimmicks, sensation shows, publicity stunts. From the graffitied subways of the '70s to Basquiat's SAMO, and Haring's doodles in the '80s, "agitprop" had been a staple attention grabber. One had to go out and steal a slice of the neglectful public's attention on the gallery of the streets, so I painted portraits of ironic moments in the lives of New York politicians.

I had posted three works in high-gloss, waterproof acrylic. The first one was of Ed Koch wearing the judicial robes from his stint on *The People's Court*, bungee jumping off a bridge. I hung it at a bus stop on Forty-second Street and Fifth Avenue. The second painting was of Al Sharpton in a jogging suit, eating a large piece of lemon meringue pie. I hung this up on 125th Street near the Apollo Theater. Now I had a painting of a dwarfed Giuliani making mocking gestures in front of a podium as his son was trying to give an inaugural speech. This was a reversal of what actually had happened.

Around four in the morning, I got up, unfolded my yellow bike, slipped the portrait under my arm, and pedaled down Broadway to

Chambers near City Hall. I found a plastic milk crate, which I propped up against a green metal signpost. Then I took out the portrait. I had already belted two pipe clamps with a screw lock around it. I quickly scanned for cops before I hopped up on the crate, speedily slotted the metal pieces together, and tightened the two screws.

I biked back uptown to my van. It was still dark. I was soon spread out on my narrow little sleeping bag. In a few hours I had to be up to sell used books, yet the thought of June in Barclay's large, warm bed, and my Swimmer painting on his wall, made it difficult to drift off.

Four

I awoke just before it was time to feed the meter, eight o'clock, and I drove over to Fourth Street in front of the NYU library. They were all out today: Crazy Ike, Meaningless Mike, Hairy Larry, Pablo the Poet, Crackpipe Bob, and others with screwy, pejorative nicknames that everyone else called them behind their backs. I really didn't know most of them and could only wonder what others called me.

The Loeb Student Center had been knocked down, but NYU was erecting a new, taller one. The Elmer Holmes Bobst Library was on the next block east, then Leon Shimkin, the Stern School of Business, and lastly Tisch. Across from those recently constructed halls of academia, aluminum folding tables were lined up upon which we hawked our used books. Pablo, wearing a "Vote Green" T-shirt, flagged me down for a tight spot next to him. He helped me unload my boxes. Then we unfolded my table and flipped it over.

"You missed the Nader rally at Madison Square Garden," he said.

"Oh, I forgot," I replied as I organized my books into different groups and slipped in the category cards: Fiction, Nonfiction, Biography, Poems, Plays, Occult, Mythology, and so forth.

"Bill Murray, Tim Robbins, Rage Against the Machine. It was a real blast and—"

"June cheated on me," I interrupted his renewed hope in American politics.

"No!"

"She slept with some rich cocksucker."

"No!"

"I destroyed a bunch of her work."

"No!"

"Yep," I replied calmly. Maybe even psychotically.

Pab's face was horror-stricken. His shattered innocence seemed to make the betrayal even greater. I considered trying to mitigate my actions by explaining that her work was abstract. But he was a language poet, an abstractionist of the written word.

Pablo had been around since my courtship with June. He liked her and regularly flirted with her. He knew her work and even posed for her, though not in the nude as she had requested. As he stood there shaking his head in disbelief, I nervously wondered for an instant if his shock signified that he too had slept with her.

"I thought of you guys as a perfect couple. I can't think of one of you without the other. I mean, this shakes my very faith in love," he said poignantly.

"I feel miserable enough."

"So what are you going to do, Or?" I looked into the endless expanse of blank blue sky but found no answers.

"Weren't you living together?"

"Yeah."

"Where are you living now?"

"In my van, but I have another place lined up."

"Oh, Flake's place." He spun the Scot's name so it more aptly fit his character.

"I can't believe she did this to me," I replied, too tired to reprise all five acts of my played-out rage.

Some cute chick was flipping through Pablo's out-of-print, slightly battered copy of *The Destruction of Lower Manhattan* by Danny Lyon. First published in 1969, it was a photo-essay of the buildings that made up Radio Row, the area that was demolished for the Twin Towers. At a hundred and fifty dollars it was his most valuable book. Pablo drifted away. I wasn't sure if he liked the girl or was worried about the book, but both details took precedence. Business was business. And sympathy, sadly, was an unaffordable luxury.

I asked Pablo to keep an eye on my table for a minute and drove around until I found a parking spot. Four quarters every hour. Then I dashed to a corner deli for a tall cup of boring coffee, a poppy-seed bagel, and twenty dollars in change.

For the first hour or so, Pablo and I talked as we cleaned our most recent acquisitions. A quick Windex wipe was done on glossy book covers. We went through the pages, unfolding dogged ears, erasing whatever marks we could, and finally we finished with the pricing. A sharp pencil mark on the top of the first page, right-hand corner, dark enough to be read, faint enough to be erased by the buyer.

I rarely found any collectible hardcovers, but Pablo always did. These books he covered in Mylar wrap and priced accordingly.

Like most booksellers, I kept an itemization of everything sold, and by the middle of that morning the list was short. The still waters of time that passed on the busy street were marred by several curious ruffles. One was a wispy, older lady who looked like she had been painted by the late pen-and-inkist Ed Gorey. This willowy ghost visited about once a month always looking for *Loving*, a novel by the British writer Henry Greene. She didn't want the new Penguin edition, which I had along with two of his other books. She was in search of the old Anchor edition, which was long out of print. Worse still, she always explained that she wouldn't pay any more than three dollars for it.

Next, two black teenagers approached trying to sell me blue bags of M&Ms at twice their price, allegedly to raise money for uniforms for their inner-city sports team. The only other interruption of the day was when an undercover detective flashed his gold shield and asked if at approximately two o'clock yesterday I had noticed a large Italian dashing down the street, possibly holding a handgun.

"He was probably sweating and his shirt might have been drenched in blood."

"Is this a murder investigation?" I guessed.

Somberly, he explained that it was.

"I didn't work yesterday," I confessed.

He sighed and asked the other booksellers on the row. I spent the time trying to draw some of the other night's dream about the dying work of art—the guilt dream brought about by destroying June's paintings. No matter how many drafts I made, I just wasn't getting it right. My hand couldn't see what was in my head. Slowly, passersby surveyed and occasionally bought my books. By noon, the list was still pretty meager:

Kamikaze Lust	$6.00
Memoirs of a Revolutionist	$3.00
One Flew Over the Cuckoo's Nest	$3.00

Wisconsin Death Trip	$12.00
Dharma Bums	$5.00
This Life (autobiography of	
Sidney Poitier) (signed)	$20.00
Horse's Mouth	$4.00

At one, I suddenly remembered that I had to meet Shade about his sublet. Pablo again offered to watch my table for a while. I jumped on my bike and pedaled down to Chinatown. Shade was sitting on the weathered green benches in the same spot I had left him. I was about fifteen minutes late.

The needle exchange administrators hadn't yet arrived, so the benches were filled with the usual suspects.

"I thought you vanished on me," the Scottish artist said, "which is all right if you want out."

"No, no, I'm in."

"I'll need three months of rent up front," he said as if reading my fears.

"How much is that?"

"Five hundred a month times three—fifteen hundred." I interpreted this sudden financial request as an effort to dissuade me from taking the deal. "Can you swing it?"

"Yeah," I replied. Although I was cash poor, my credit cards were still healthy.

"I'm leaving in a week," he said.

"I'll have the money in three days." I was sure he realized his sublet offer was too generous.

While Shade rambled on, listing details I'd never remember about maintaining his apartment, I watched as the volunteers from the needle exchange program arrived. They looked like bedraggled Peace Corps workers.

One of them, a girl with a shiny face stood out among the lackluster needle users. Her eyes and face grabbed me all at once. Although she wasn't stunning and her scalp was recently shaved, she carried herself fearlessly, like a young goddess.

"So we got everything squared away?" Shade checked, shaking me from my obsessive staring.

I told him that it was and said I'd see him sometime later at the bar. He gave my shoulder a squeeze and left. A moment later, the skull-shaved babe approached me.

"I'm Rita. You look familiar. Have we ever meet before?" And at that moment, I realized that I *had* met her somewhere before, but I had no clue where. I worried that I might frighten her if I mentioned it, so I didn't ask her.

"I don't think so," I replied, and I let her believe I was just another needy needler. I extended my hand for a shake. "My name's Or."

"Like either/or," she kidded. "what's your ethnicity—ambivalent?"

"Actually my last name is Tanzarian." I explained nervously, "I'm Armenian."

"Sure, the genocide." This was the reason I felt uncomfortable mentioning my heritage. From 1915 to 1923, the Turks brutally butchered roughly half the Armenian population and pushed them from their ancient homeland, yet the Turkish government still denies it to this day. With our pain unresolved and our land robbed from us, we were permanently locked as victims.

"So is Or an Armenian name?" she asked.

"No, I was born during Vietnam. My father was drafted. My mother protested and they named me after that antiwar poem by e. e. cummings."

"'I sing of Olaf glad and big / whose warmest heart recoiled at war: / a conscientious object-or,'" she casually rattled off the line.

"Oh my God, no one ever knew it." I was amazed.

"But cummings's character is the Swedish 'Olaf.' I thought you're Orloff."

"My parents Russified me," I replied.

"Ever use the clean needle exchange before?" She snapped back to business.

I shook my head no. "Do you know about how to clean the works and stuff?"

"I don't think so," I replied, staring into those big, earnest blue eyes of hers.

"So you're not registered?"

"Right," I said, still trying to place where I had met her.

"We're funded by the city. The clean needle exchange swaps about three million needles a year with about thirty thousand registered." She talked at me for roughly twenty minutes about all the dangers of using drugs, and she listed various programs that would help me escape its clutches. Then she pummeled me with half a dozen questions, which included my mother's maiden name and my birthday. Enigmatically based on those two details, Rita gave me a secret code.

"You get ten new syringes. We'd like you to bring in your old needles and give that code," she explained. She gave me a pamphlet that listed other locales where I could swap needles. I thanked her.

"Here." She took out a cellophane bag filled with stuff and opened it up. First, removing a small container, she shook it and said, "This is bleach to clean out the needle." She took out another small sealed vessel. "This is pure water to cook your heroin with." She put it back in the baggie and removed some tiny packed pieces of cotton. "Use these to filter out any impurities." She also showed me what appeared to be a metal bottle top, which, with a little water, I was supposed to boil my drugs in.

Finally she located a square of gauze and said, "Use this to clean where you inject. Promise me you'll do it."

I did and located a condom at the bottom of the little baggie. "What's that for?"

"That's a balloon for being a good boy," she said with a smile.

"So where's the heroin and the needle?"

"This isn't a start-up kit. Heroin's illegal. You buy it wherever. And you have to wait for your spike." She pointed to the corner. Guarded by another member was a cardboard box lined with a green plastic garbage bag that read, "Biohazard Medical Waste."

The guard counted out new syringes as one of the old mastodons deposited his old needles into a small hole on the top of the box.

"I know this sounds really cliché, but can I paint you?" I asked her before she could dash.

"I have a big, nasty boyfriend who might object."

"You can bring him. I'm not trying to pick you up."

"What? I'm not pretty enough?"

"No, you're beautiful."

"So he finds me attractive!"

"I just—"

"Relax, I'm just playing."

"Hey, Rita," a needle exchange administrator called out. "Can you take care of Carl?"

"Let me think about it," she replied to me politely and was instantly off to serve and inform another IV user. I jumped back on my bike and cycled north to my book table near NYU. Only about a half an hour had passed since I had left.

As I whipped my bike around Mercer and sped down Fourth, I couldn't believe what I saw. My table had collapsed to the pavement. The aluminum poles holding it up and the quarter-inch cardboard surfaces were all mangled and snapped. All my books were on the ground. Some of them were stacked. Pablo was talking to a customer, trying to hustle a hardcover version of *Flowers of Evil*.

"What the fuck happened?" I asked as I coasted up.

"It was an accident," he said, taking a short break in his sales pitch. "June came by and she was waiting for you. For an instant she leaned on the table, and it all came down."

"I'm sure it wasn't an accident."

"It was, I saw it with my own eyes. But she is pissed. She said she didn't cheat on you, and wants to talk about it. She kept people from stealing your books. She stacked them."

"Is this book the variorum edition?" some old guy asked him. Pablo turned back to his sale.

I spent the next fifteen minutes loading my books back in boxes. My table was old and had been slightly rocking, so I begrudgingly gave June the benefit of the doubt. It would cost at least seventy-five bucks to replace it.

"Give her a call," Pablo pushed. "I bet if you apologize—"

"Fuck her! She cheated on me," I yelled back. To go into greater detail still felt too humiliating.

He nodded dolefully. I dumped my busted book table and finished packing. As I headed down to Chinatown, passing Houston Street, I thought I saw Rita, the exchange worker, stick her head in a car chatting with someone. I didn't get a good look at the guy but he had a New Jersey license plate.

I dropped seventy-five bucks for a new table, and as I lugged it back to my van, I considered my predicament with June. If Pablo was correct and she did accidentally destroy my book table, maybe she had come down to try to straighten things out. I tore up some of her works; perhaps she regarded stealing my piece and flattening my table as evening up the score.

Much as I hated to admit it, I felt a genuine physical ache in losing her. She had cheated on me and now my choice was simple: I could either forgive her and try to reconcile, or I could break up and never speak to her again. I decided right then and there to forgive. At a pay phone on the corner of Divison and Allen I dialed her number. When the line proved busy, I realized that she was the one who cheated. She really should be the one to initiate the reconciliation. Then I could be the one to forgive.

Five

That night, I headed down to Mekong Delta, a Chino- Viet joint on Allen, and ordered some cold sesame noodles from the Buddha-bellied cashier. Then I parked over on Hester and Norfolk, where there was a live electrical outlet behind the metal plate at the base of a lamppost. I ran a heavy-duty extension cord out the rear of my Chevy and was able to plug in and watch my crappy portable TV while gobbling down the noodles. I didn't mind living nomadically in a moving bread box if this was the price I had to pay for making art, but it bothered me that until I had a studio space I could only paint small frames. All the real six-figure sales came from the monstrous wall-size canvases beginning at twenty feet. Upon moving into Shade's spacious loft, I hoped to remedy this with some larger pieces.

Early the next morning I was awakened by the approaching hum of the street sweeper. Naked, I jumped into my torn vinyl driver's seat and barely drove off before the meter maid could slap a big, lime green "This Street Was Not Properly Cleaned Because of This Vehicle" sticker on my window and write me up another fifty-five-dollar ticket.

My burnt-out engine barely had enough power to putter from parking spot to parking spot. It cost twenty-five dollars to stick the van in a lot where at least I knew it wouldn't be burgled. My life was now a race. I had to pay off my mounting ticket debt, and try to buy Cali's van before this one conked out. I was always worried about the City Marshal's mobile unit. These barracudas periodically drove down streets and typed license plate numbers into their dashboard computers. They would undoubtedly tow my little van away, leaving nothing between me and the street.

That day started late. I drove back to where I worked yesterday. Pablo had taken the day off. While the light was still good, I took out my sketch pad and tried to draw various textures of the rapidly flowing river. Experimenting with different tubes of paint I had in the van, I attempted to mix colors to match the tone of the East River during the early afternoon.

During the late afternoon, I inspected various photography books of New York's shorelines. From them I made background sketches that I might use for the swimmer approaching Manhattan. By the end of the day I didn't even clear sixty bucks.

Depressed, I loaded my van and headed east where I found a parking spot on the southern edge of Tompkins Square Park. Then I walked over to the confining space of KGB Bar, where I caught the last of Pablo's "Emperors Have No Powems" reading.

"Vote Ralph Nader, because there's no difference between the

Republicans and the Democrats," he said, concluding the evening.

"Only a Republican could have thought of that," Cecil, a lawyer turned bookseller, called out.

Everyone politely applauded, and I drank down my second beer.

"Look who's here." One voice pulled me back onto the undried fresco of the moment. I put down my sudsy mug to see Micah, a watercolorist who lately had been painting on old hardcover books.

"I heard you recently broke up with June," he said. I didn't bother to explain that I had decided to forgive her and was waiting for her to call. "I saw her last night at a big black tie at the Guggenheim." The watercolorist was a caterer by day.

"Swines wearing pearls," I commented. "Did she seem very depressed?"

"The only pressing thing she showed was her cleavage. Her dress must have cost her at least a grand."

Though I didn't let on, this bothered the hell out of me. Now that June's been with Mister Moneybags, how was I going to ever compete? Though I stayed for another hour or so, I simply wondered how I could generate more income. Finally drunk and anxious, I thanked Pablo for the glimpse at the future of poetry and rode my bike back to my van, where I stripped and flopped into a checkered sleep.

Early the next morning, the van didn't start at all. I got out and searched for a place to pee. They let me use the bathroom in the back of Blackout Books, an anarchist bookstore on Fourth and Avenue B. I bought a bagel and chewed it down in Tompkins Square Park, then I walked up to the Stuyvesant Post Office. It was my first visit there in weeks. My little PO box was nearly unopenable, bursting at the hinges, mainly with art calenders and junk invites to every opening over the next six months in the Northern Hemisphere. This was the reason I never got hooked up with e-mail. It would just be another sewer duct for unwanted offers and mass invitations.

Browsing and tossing, I found two rejections, coupled with returned slides of my artwork. I constantly had a rotation of slides on submission to grant foundations and galleries in the tristate area.

When I first started submitting my work, I used listing guides like *New York Contemporary Art Gallery*, which broke down the different galleries in the city and described the types of art they accepted. That was how I first learned about the various categories of art spaces, like vanity galleries that seemed to take advantage of young and foreign artists. They rented out viewing space, packing as much crap onto a wall as it could hold, without selling a single piece. I preferred co-op galleries. When first starting out, several times I got together with a bunch of artist friends. We would each pitch in money and time to curate a space, then we'd each take turns showing our work. But what every artist wanted was to get into a private space—where some rich Chelsea gallery director would pay for everything and present your art to the top collectors in one of those luminous cathedrals along the Hudson. The 50 percent commission was a bargain at their apoplectic prices.

Among the solicitations and bullshit offers I got in the mail was an invitation from Ned Tanner. He had sold assorted canvases of mine over the years, earning me a few thou, tax free. According to the postcard, his latest show would be opening tomorrow night at P.S.1. I felt obliged to attend.

Toward the bottom of the postage pile, I also found, to my amazement, I had two gallery acceptances. John, the manager of the Astor Place Starbucks, wanted two of my Swimmer paintings. Unfortunately, both were the recent casualties of "Body and Soul." Another pair of my paintings were accepted for a group show entitled "Crossing Styx," by Persephone Miller, who true to mythological association had named her Brooklyn gallery the Pomegranate. Unfortunately I only had one left. It was the last of a small cycle of paintings: Latin fishermen along the East River who I had painted last summer. One of the men had appreciated his portrait so much, he asked if he could buy it, but he was broke. Of course I didn't want to give it up, but it seemed greedy. Millionaires have portraits commissioned but they rarely pose for more than a minute. Considering all the time these anglers had given me, it seemed unjust that all their paintings would go to rich cocksuckers. He ended up giving me his old radio/cassette player for his portrait. The submission deadline for the last fishermen piece was tonight.

As I walked downtown, I heard someone yell out my name. I turned to see Bethsheba waving from across the street. She barreled across five hazardous lanes of First Avenue traffic. Just as she reached the last one—*bam!* A small black VW slammed on its brakes while striking. She flew onto the hood and bounced up about five feet before she landed on her sinewy ass.

"Holy shit." I dashed over. She struggled to get up. "Stay down!" I kneeled to the ground, holding her.

"I think I'm okay."

"Stay down, you can get a great settlement from the insurance company."

"Hey," she said, getting up. "Just 'cause I'm poor doesn't mean I'm a crook." She jumped to her feet. The small Asian woman driver got out. There was a huge dent in the center of her shiny hood.

"Get a new pair of glasses!" some East Village type called out from the small crowd that had gathered on the sidewalk.

"Leave her alone," Beth yelled back. "It was my fault."

"Are you okay?" the driver asked. Her cell phone was at her ear. "I'm calling an ambulance."

"Please don't, I'm fine," Beth said. "I'm sorry. I should have watched where I was going."

"Okay." The lady closed her flip phone, and taking out a pen and scrap of paper, she scribbled something down and handed it to Beth. "This is my name, phone number, and driver's license. Call me if you feel any pain later."

"Thanks," Beth said. The driver got into her vehicle and rode off.

"I can't believe this," Beth said calmly. "First I see June then I catch Or."

"Where'd you see June?" I asked, still nervous from her accident.

"Just a few minutes ago. Over on Thirteenth Street. You can still grab her if you want."

"We broke up," I replied.

"When did all this happen?" She asked, with a twinkle in her eye.

"You remember that night, at the 'Body and Soul' show? She met a richer body with a more corrupt soul." I felt like too much of an idiot to explain that I had introduced them.

"I'm so sorry." She radiated a big, warm, space-heating smile.

"So what are you doing on this side of the river?" I asked, knowing she lived in Fort Greene. "We don't want no stinking Brooklyn artists here."

"A few errands, wheels, and deals, then I'm off to the new improved East Village—Williamsburg."

"You're kidding, I'm going to Williamsburg tonight," I replied, without further explanation. I liked her, but I didn't like her enough to tell her about a group show.

"Great, I'm going to be busy all afternoon. Give me a lift. We'll go for dinner," she commanded more than requested.

"Meet me at five o'clock at my book table over on Fourth Street between Mercer and Greene," I explained.

The Aussie minimalist went one way and I the other. A half a block later I was feeling profoundly alone. My mind began to race. Years ago, when I was twenty-one, still in the Art Students League, just being conscious was enough. I didn't need anything else. I was entitled, endowed, and selected. My voracious intellectual appetite seemed to be a promise that I'd eventually get all the treasures that life had to offer. I read a lot, studied my craft, and saw as much art as I could roll my eyes across.

I quickly digested the various histories of art movements and could identify key works splattered, dripped, smeared, and brushed over the past two thousand plus years. But, very soon after, just knowing wasn't enough. I needed to *do*. I had to leave my mark before twenty-seven. That seemed a make-or-break age; all bona-fide geniuses proved themselves by twenty-seven. I worked my ass off. I made a study of my one great terrifying moment—the subway accident. And the following year, at twenty-five, thanks to Cali, I had my first solo show in Chelsea: the Subway paintings. I sold some work and got three decent reviews. It was then that I first realized that I was not as great as I thought I'd be. But that was all right; I could still be a good journeyman painter. Although my work might be just a footnote to others, I could still turn out a body of diverse and fascinating paintings so that I could one day have my own goddamned retrospective and a fat hundred-dollar coffee-table book with my name on it.

Eight years have passed since that first solo show. In that time, hundreds, maybe thousands of canvases and sketch pads later, I've learned my craft and struggled to constantly challenge my abilities, turning out ever more difficult works. But the struggle has only grown harder. Now at thirty-three, after having produced and undersold a corpulent corpus of art, I'd come to a reckoning. It wasn't enough having done the works. Who had seen them? Who had sought them out? Where was the fame and fortune? Just as old goals had been modestly attained, new and more complex aims had replaced them. Although I didn't write myself off as a complete failure, all the illusion and romance was gone. I was no longer able to inflate myself; I had already disappointed my own expectations and was genuinely worried about dying on the streets.

By the time I drove down to Fourth Street and unfolded my table and lined my books up, it was only eleven o'clock. The bygone best-seller, which had long since lost its buzz, and the wrongly neglected masterpiece that had steadily found a growing niche of readers, all sold at their own pace. I also took out the two swimmers I was boldly re-creating, the ones I had lost at the Entrance Art show. I used the passing hours, nervously working and wooing the image out of the canvas.

"Those really are wonderful works," a middle-aged woman in a pressed gray pantsuit said, startling me. I restrained the impulse to shout, Fuck off.

"They're for sale," Pablo jumped in, never missing a beat in his natural salesmanship.

"No they're not!" I shot back. I was trying to break the habit of underpricing myself. Besides, these works weren't real. They were funereal art, designed to help me get over losing the originals.

"You sure you wouldn't take a hundred dollars for one?" Pantsuit asked. With her butch cut and power outfit, I immediately recognized her—a demigod from the underworld of the semi-rich.

Pablo started chuckling. "Go on, Orlofsky, a hundred bucks is more than Picasso ever got at your age."

"Lady," I said, standing up slowly, exercising my long-unstretched muscles. "You want to know how long I worked on these paintings? You want to know how much pain and loss went into—"

"Fine," she replied. "I prefer abstracts anyway."

"I'll take five hundred for both," I called out. They were imitations, and instead of reminding me of the genuine articles, they only brought to mind the two people who had robbed me. I was still intent on redoing the Swimmer paintings, but they had to be altogether rethought.

"I'll give you two hundred." The auction began.

"Lady, that wouldn't pay for the paints," Pablo told her. She turned and started walking away.

"How about two fifty?" I whined in a slightly pathetic tone. Now the thought of having the paintings for even another moment repelled me.

"You'll take two fifty?" she confirmed.

"Don't do it, Or," Pablo said, inspecting them. "They're beautiful paintings."

"I need the cash," I clarified. Books weren't selling, and after I cleaned out my credit cards to pay off Shade tomorrow, I'd have about twenty-five bucks to my name. The demon head in the catalog ensemble vanished to some corner ATM machine and in about fifteen minutes returned with the all-powerful dollars.

"If you ever do any abstractions, I'd certainly be interested in seeing them." She slipped me her business card. Ms. Camilla Hennessy, the card proclaimed without shame. It didn't reveal her profession, either. She gazed into her two new paintings. I could only wonder what she was seeing.

"What's your name?" she pushed. I hadn't signed the works.

"Or Trenchant," I replied. "I'll call you with some splishy-splash abstractions, but you're not going to get them as cheap as those."

She assured me I was "with talent," grabbed a cab, and was gone with my hasty reproductions.

"I got an abstraction for her," Pablo said squeezing his gonads.

Although I made a little over a hundred dollars in book sales that day, I was still glad I had sold the paintings. Three hundred and fifty dollars was not much of a safety net, but it was better than nothing.

Bethsheba showed up twenty minutes later. I had her watch the table as I returned with the van, then she helped me load my books into the back. We drove downtown and up onto the perpetually reconstructed Williamsburg Bridge.

"Do you remember that painting at Entrance Art that I thought you did?" I asked with a smile. I felt slightly embarrassed about it.

"What about it?"

"You know the artist?"

"Yeah, Adele."

"What does she look like?"

"I don't remember." She paused. "Which probably means she wasn't pretty."

"I think she's beautiful." I sighed and asked, "Did you ever speak to her?"

"Once, we just exchanged words really. All I remember is that she has a loft in Dumbo. Why are you asking all these questions?"

"No reason."

"You have a crush on her painting, don't you?" She hit the nail right on the head. "Don't be ashamed. I had a crush last month at the Armory show. Remember that cyber-landscapist, Gunter?"

"Oh God, his piece was so large and bloodless!" I replied as I drove. "It was like a giant tic."

"God, Gunter me any day," she swooned.

We were only about halfway across the bridge when I began to feel it. Something awful was happening in the depths of my sickly transmission. The power of the engine was surging out from under me. In another moment Bethsheba picked up on it. "What's going on?"

"We seem to be experiencing slight technical difficulty," I said, downshifting as cars behind us started honking. The van dropped down to about ten miles an hour. I was praying that we would reach the hump of the bridge where it started slanting downhill. As we went slower and slower, both of us silently swayed our bodies back and forth as though we were rocking in a giant swing.

"What are we going to do?" Bethsheba asked as the van gradually came to a halt.

"You steer," I said, hopping out. The car behind me was a mighty pickup truck. The driver, a sporty-looking lad in a Mets cap, gave a look of complete disbelief as I put my shoulder to the bumper and started pushing the van up the gridded incline.

"Get in," he called out in a *Semper Fi* tone. He brought the bumper of his truck up against my old clunker. I dashed back to the van, and took the wheel from poor Bethsheba. The pickup pushed us the last few feet to the crest of the bridge, where we started coasting. I angled into the exit lane. In a moment, we were snaking down the old ramp. The engine seemed to miraculously get well, and I drove down and over to the Pomegranate Gallery on Bedford Avenue.

"God, first I get hit by a car, then I stall in one. You're bad luck, Or. Next time I see you I'm wearing body padding and a parachute," Beth said.

We were both relieved to make it over the river.

"So where can I dump you?" I asked.

"I thought you were going to feed me."

"Can we pass on that, I'm under a little pressure."

"Fine. Just over here," she said and got off a block away from my destination. I gave her a peck on the cheek and drove off to park.

Before locking the door, I grabbed my last remaining portrait of the Latin fishermen along East River Park and headed over to the Pomegranate Gallery. Inside, who did I see handing over her frameless minimalist sketches to the curator but Bethsheba.

"What the hell are you doing here?" I was shocked.

"Oh my God, are you in this show too?" she replied and started laughing. She turned beet red. "What a pair of bloodsucking bastards we are!"

"Neither helping the other," I completed her rapacious observation. The curator, Persephone, took both our pieces. She asked us if we were insured. Beth was, I was not. Persephone had us sign contracts. She explained dates and financial arrangements, and then we left.

A few blocks away was a small Mexican joint. It was a nice night, so we walked over. There we ordered two pork burritos to go and a couple bottles of Corona. Bethsheba led us a few blocks west and some blocks north, through empty, arid streets, passing occasional twenty-something stragglers. On the last block, paralleling the river, we walked, carrying our bagged dinners past truck bays and desolation. I started getting a little antsy.

"Why don't we just eat in my van?" I suggested.

"Trust me," she replied as we came up to a rip in the bordering hurricane fence. Bethsheba pushed it back. We squeezed through and hiked across a stretch of pulverized concrete. It looked as if it had once

51

been the foundation of some behemoth warehouse. In the middle of it was a large metallic sculpture of a monster that some uncredited artist had welded together. Its head was a television set.

A couple of Mexicans were camped out on the abandoned ground. They were washing themselves. Bethsheba led me right up to the gentle lapping of the East River. There she took a seat on the rotten wooden remains of an old pier. She opened her bag and took out her burrito and beer. I sat next to her and did the same. While eating, I enjoyed the view. The more I looked across the river, the closer Manhattan seemed. The East River was actually not a river at all but a "strait" connecting Long Island Sound to the Narrows. I kept thinking that I could easily span that small stretch of water back to Chinatown.

"I'm a strong swimmer," I declared to Bethsheba, "and the river is pretty calm. About five years ago, I competed for the Gallagher Cup. It was an open-water swim around Manhattan, twenty eight and a half miles around Manhattan Island, starting at Battery Park. The race was about fifty times the length of this distance and that was on a windy day, with waves at times over four feet."

"You're kidding."

"Hell no. I registered to do it again two years ago, but they only select about a dozen and I didn't get picked."

"Weren't you worried about having all that filthy water buggering all your holes?" she queried.

"It's not that dirty anymore. Chelsea Piers is creating a sandy beach on Twenty-third on the Hudson River."

"With my luck, I'd probably get hit by a Circle Line," she replied, "or I'd freeze."

I put my hand in the water. The temperature felt about 60 degrees.

"It's not cold at all," I assured her. "I used to swim as late as November. I swear I could swim right to Corlear's Hook." I looked across.

"Where's that?" she inquired.

"See where the land dips in," I pointed to Manhattan. "That's called Corlear's Hook."

The beans, rice, and chicken were fine. The hot sauce wasn't too hot. There was a soft breeze. In the distance we could hear a radio playing "Bizarre Love Triangle."

As we finished our takeout feast, we watched the sun slowly set. The sky seemed to vault. The sunlight caught in the clouds created a prism of colors ranging from a bright seashell to a powdery pink. As our mountain-carrying, ocean-bearing planet spun counterclockwise at 1,000 miles per hour with us on it, the invisible pillars holding up our arched ceiling seemed to sink. Faint blue tinged toward violet as the day died. I tried to imagine that final day when the skyline would vanish and the sun would nova, billions of years from now.

"I'd die to paint with those colors," Bethsheba said. She was right. Not even the greatest artist could mix colors anywhere near as beautiful as the sunset that evening.

When the light show ended and dark blue filled the limitless void, Bethsheba pushed close for warmth. I reached around, holding her in my arms, and started nestling up against her.

"You are such a naughty boy," she said as I slipped my hand along the front of her billowy shirt. I ran my lips against her soft neck. She turned toward me and we were delicately kissing. After about twenty minutes, exhibitionist that she was, she unzipped my pants, rested her head in my lap, and started going down on me.

"Let's go back to the van," I suggested, not quite as uninhibited as her.

We took our garbage with us. In fifteen minutes we were back at the van. But it took another half an hour to rearrange all the boxes and crap. I finally freed up enough space to roll out the foam mattress. We lay down and started tonguing and touching again. Her hair, or more specifically, the aroma of her shampoo, smelled like freshly cut Granny apples. I couldn't kiss her enough. She pulled her tight jeans off and there on the right cheek of her wonderful pear-shaped thighs just below a small cupid tattoo was a huge blackish-blue bruise.

"Holy shit! Is that what the car did to you?"

"Yeah, but it doesn't hurt much," she replied. I gave the discoloration a delicate peck and we took off from there.

At one point we heard a group of kids walking by talking, and Bethsheba had to suppress a giggle. When they passed, she whispered, "Sounds like they're right in here with us."

"If you want, I could drive to a more secluded spot."

"Oh no! I like it here."

In another moment, we were into it, banging and a-bouncin', testing the springy old shocks on the van, bumping up and down. We heard more footsteps and voices outside, but that didn't stop Beth from screaming at the top of her powerful lungs, *"Fuck me!"*

Then we lay still, under a film of sweat, letting the semi-cool Williamsburg air chill us. It was a wonderful glow and I knew that this was the greatest joy of youth. I ignored the millions of people whose lives were probably better than mine and considered the billions more whose lives were worse, who would've envied me at that moment.

"What's that?" Beth interrupted.

"What?" I asked. She pointed up to a painting of the undercarriage of a train that I had done on my ceiling one drunken night and wished I hadn't.

"Bottom of a train," I explained succinctly.

"A choo-choo train?" she asked.

"A subway train," I replied tiredly. I didn't want to go into it.

"Oh that's right, that's the . . . You're . . ." She stopped herself. She remembered what she had heard and knew I didn't want to hear it. She looked up at me, probably to see if I was pissed or suffering from some sort of post-traumatic stress disorder, but I wasn't. She hugged me and, reaching down, she started playing with my penis. In another moment we were at it again. This time, instead of racing toward orgasm, we slowly screwed for about two hours before we finally picked up the pace and both came. Then she pulled the sheet over us. I thought to myself that if June had simply called, I wouldn't have done this.

Six

It takes two qualities to make a serious artist: an interesting aesthetic and a blunt trauma. The first is a method and the second is a reason to paint.

Ever since I was a small, scrawny kid, I liked art. I had gotten accepted to the High School of Music and Art when it was still up on 133rd Street and Convent Avenue, before it migrated to midtown.

One morning, during rush hour, I was standing mindlessly on the crowded platform heading to school when I saw the two little headlights of the express train. The number 2 IRT train was approaching. I don't remember thinking anything until my singular body was suddenly ejected from out of the countless limbs and torsos of like-minded commuters. I was propelled forward and roughly four feet down. Flat on my back, framed between two luminous rails, I was right in front of the oncoming train. At least a thousand people on both the uptown and downtown platforms saw me. Now I wish I had seen the motorman's face. What's the expression of knowing you're about to crush a boy to death? Arms, legs, body parts everywhere. I've tried to paint that view from every angle. The one detail I remember most clearly is the terror. Looking up from the tight little gutter of filthy water that baptized my body, I saw the greasy steel underbelly of the train shooting over me. I remember the first car. Then the next. Then another. Then another. Wondering when that infinite train was going to end before it finally screeched to a halt.

Yells, shrieks, and fitful screams.

"Oh my God! Oh no! My God!" Then, "Where the fuck is he? Who sees the body!"

"It's under there! Down there!"

Bodies scrambled down onto the tracks.

"Oh God! He's moving!"

"Are you alive?" I heard. Some guy was on the adjacent tracks, peeking at me between the steel wheels. I later learned that each wheel alone was seven hundred pounds.

"Yeah," I whispered.

"Just lie still! Don't budge or move a muscle, you could still get electrocuted."

A stream of foul water flowed down the center of the filthy tracks. I didn't even know that I had wet myself.

Carefully, slowly I was extricated from that nineteen-inch cage of electricity and steel.

"Did someone push you?" some stocky guy with a walkie-talkie asked. I shrugged.

57

"You didn't try to kill yourself, did you?"

"I don't know," I replied, shaking.

"You don't know what?" another guy asked.

"I don't know if someone pushed me. I was pushed, but I don't know who did it, or if it was an accident." I couldn't stop trembling.

"Just take it easy, kid. Breathe slowly. You're in shock."

A cop came over, talking into his radio. A big guy in a white shirt and blue parka made me sit on the blue wooden bench and cleared everyone off the platform. All service was suspended. An ambulance came and I was strapped onto a gurney and hauled off to the hospital.

I found out later that the train had nicked me. Some part of it tore a gash across the bottom of my belly. My collarbone was also broken, but the doctors believed that this was caused by the fall.

For a while I'd bolt up with nightmares of the train passing over. But at the time that it happened, while looking up at the wheels and axles of that gargantuan machine, I thought it felt like I was being swallowed, passing down the ribbed esophagus of some steel leviathan. Perhaps the closest we can come to meeting God in our lifetime is in the very belief that we *will* meet. And at that very moment as the train was passing over me, I thought, God was nigh.

That image of the undercarriage of the subway train, which had been branded into my brain, and I had painted a decade later, was my first great work of art. I developed the series on long, narrow canvases and had hung them on the wall like a string of subway cars.

Cali actually saw them first. Someone had introduced us and she came to my studio. She in turn introduced me to an influential friend who referred me to a top dealer. He put them in a big Soho gallery. That was about eight years ago, before the last of the great galleries evacuated to Chelsea. They sold for three thousand dollars a car. A few days before my opening, a woman was pushed to her death in front of the R train by a crazy homeless guy, which generated a burst of mainstream publicity. Subsequently, I also got coverage in every major art magazine. "A bold, haunting view of a mechanical hell," was how Rodney Helix described the work in *Artful* magazine.

Everybody read about me, the artist who got run over by a train and lived to paint about it. When your first show is a big success, a fraction of people expect great things from you, but I learned that most are just waiting for you to fall flat on your ass.

Although I believed I did other solid works of art, nothing was ever as catchy or topical. Therefore, nothing was as well received as my first show. When I did my second and third shows, only a few pieces sold. I lost my hot solo gallery and got an awful loser stigma. Returning to my original source of inspiration, I did a pathetic show on aspects of trains: a spike, a tie, train lights, tunnels, crowds waiting on the edge of a platform. But the originality and urgency was missing. Nasty reviews accurately described my work as a self-caricature.

A few years ago, I discovered that one of my subway cars had been resold to a corporate law firm for ten thousand. At the time I was piss broke. That was when I angrily copied the piece from memory onto the ceiling of my van. It was my Sistine Chapel—my only recollection of anticipating God.

Lying in the van, with Beth sound asleep next to me, I knew I was perched for "a comeback." I just had to prove it to everyone else. As I looked at the underside of a train above my head, I realized that that first show had fucked me up. How could I ever hope to paint something so exuberant and fearful and authentic ever again?

Late the next morning, around nine thirty, Bethsheba woke me up. She was already dressed and sitting up on the mattress next to me, ready to leave.

"I'll drive you," I said groggily.

"Or, if your van is a-rockin', I'd love to be the one you're a-knockin'," she joked, "but there's no way I'm driving with you in this oversized go-kart again."

"But usually—"

"The G train is just a couple of blocks away." As she crawled out, she asked, "When will I see you next?"

"This weekend is the Dumbo art fair," I suggested. "Let's go out there together?"

"Great, give me a call toward the end of the week."

She kissed me tenderly on the lips and headed out, down Metropolitan Avenue to the G. What I silently hoped, though, was that June would call. I'd forgive her and would be compelled to cancel my outing with Beth.

This was the day of the rent-for-keys handoff with Shade. I drove the van around Williamsburg a while to get my engine's courage up, then I zoomed up the ramp onto the bridge. The little engine chugged, but it didn't protest too much. As I reached the pinnacle of the bridge, I nervously glanced into the East River. A strong tide was rushing downstream. Between a southward barge and a northward tug, I thought I glimpsed the bobbing head of a swimmer struggling with the current. I could imagine him very clearly, kicking and stroking between boats, heroically gliding over the rough waters toward the great city.

A sudden blast of car honks made me realize I was weaving. At least the transmission was still going strong.

The van seemed fairly healthy today. Going downhill, even when I put the pedal to the metal, it never went above 33 mph. In a matter of minutes, I parked, withdrew all my cash, and was sitting among the addicts at the benches of the Allen Street Mall.

Inspecting their haggard and drawn faces, I remembered that I had loosely consented to paint several portraits of these visages. Their bodies looked pulverized by drugs. Heroin and other intoxicants had zoomed them up until their own mortality slammed on the brakes. Everything about them seemed flung forward as though through a windshield. Bellies and thighs, at first thin, eventually turned into blobs of fat. Their lips were scarred and bloodless. Teeth were missing. Eyes and cheeks were sunken in their skulls. Their skin, pasty and wrinkled, seemed to permanently secrete a profusion of sweat.

Finally a group from the needle exchange showed up and set up shop. The undead lined up. Users gave their magic codes and dropped their old syringes in a box for new ones. Out from this hell, I saw the vision come alive—Rita of the Blessed Needles. Tall, wide-eyed, and luminous, she seemed to be growing more beautiful with each sighting.

She was indeed a latter-day angel. Her skin shined. Her scalp had a growing stubble of blonde hair. Her body was tall and lean. I watched her dispense her little drug prep kits.

"Thanks Rit, you a real sweetie hon," I could hear one of them saying to her. All she needed to do was anoint their wounds and they were instantly healed. One of them softly mumbled some question.

"Luke," she yelled out, "what are the times of this week's NA meeting at Twenty-third Street?"

"I don't know," a pimply associate yelled back. "I think Sam has a schedule."

Her nonnative innocence and tentative smile was almost apologetic for her being so perfect. Periodically she gave a "Hey I'm just one of y'all" giggle as she talked to these dismal creatures. The whole scene was sad and a bit amusing. Then she called out, "Hey, the Armenian Painter. How's it hanging?"

"Fine. Have you thought about posing for me?"

"You know, I see a lot more con artists than real artists out here," she said, coming up close. "Show me some of your work and I'll think about it."

"It's a deal."

All the needles were soon exchanged and the do-gooders were preparing to leave. Like Santa's little elves, they scurried on to the next site. Rita was the last one to dash across the street. She barely missed getting clipped by a truck. It was at that instant that I remembered how

I knew her. I had seen her at a party a few years ago. She was with that son of a bitch Victor Oakridge. It was at some banquet benefit. She had striking long blonde hair and was wearing a strapless evening gown. She even had long white gloves that climbed up her elbows. She looked completely different then, a society debutante. What the hell was she doing here?

When Shade showed up moments later, he gently grabbed my lapel and led me to his building.

"Where are we going?"

"I have a job for you."

On his landing, stacks and stacks of canvases, cardboard boxes, and other junk crowded his hallway. He pushed open the door. Inside was a gutted, hollow space. Most of the metal shelf units had been broken down. Only the paint-splattered floor and the partially opened ceiling remained.

"What happened to all your work?"

"Stacked in the hallway," he explained. "I want you to toss it out on the day you move in. Bulk disposal day."

"Now why would you want me to do that?" I asked, suspecting that he was kidding.

"My young friend, there comes a point in life when you just got to 'fess up to what you are and what you aren't. I didn't throw everything out. I still have my best work, but up until now I had kept everything, thinking that one day, when I got discovered, someone would want my entire archive. But who's kidding who? I'm cooked. I'm not sure how I'll be regarded, but whatever I am now is all I'll be."

"You don't know," I tried to console him. "Who of us can judge ourselves?"

"No, no, it's not a bad thing," he explained. "I'm not depressed. I'm not going to off myself or anything, but look at all the space that was being used up by hope. Hope became my abusive lover. I know I'll still make art and sell pieces, but I decided to trade in all that vast hope for a great loft that I hadn't seen in years. It'll make my life much easier."

It was a sad but genuine exchange. Unlike Shade and his generation of artists, I could never afford to sustain a cheap and permanent space. Vehicularly homeless, I was only able to keep my sundry artworks rolled up in my van.

"Shade, I want you to know how grateful I am that you're letting me have your place for the season."

"Just don't take advantage. I still have all my earthly possessions here. Make sure they're all here when I get back." I told him not to worry and took out the cash.

"Now I don't have to extract some additional deposit from you for the phone and utilities, do I?" he inquired.

"Absolutely not," I assured him.

"You've always seemed straight up, Or," he remarked, "so I don't think that I have to say that if you fuck me over, I'll find you and snap your neck." He clamped a massive hand on my shoulder, reminding me of his Herculean strength.

"You don't have to say that," I answered him. Throughout my life, other than poor June, I've only fucked myself over.

He gave a couple of telephone numbers to call in case of emergency, then explained that I had to collect his mail downstairs and put it in a cardboard box near the door. He was waiting for a letter from a dealer and checks from a couple of collectors. When the phone and electric bills came, I had to pay them pronto.

"Most of the other residents in the building are Chinese," Shade went on. "They don't look or talk to you. You don't look or talk to them." Then he led me down a hallway and we passed a Chinese couple. The guy looked about fifty and had thick black hair, meticulously slicked back. He was tall, thin, and seemed mean. His young girlfriend couldn't've been older than twenty. Her eyes were fixed to the floor.

"That's Hong Kong Don Juan," Shade said after they passed. "He's got a different chickety every night. All of them in their teens."

"Maybe he can give me some advice."

"He's actually a nasty little prick. Don't say a word to him."

In a moment we reached an outdoor stairwell, a reinforced fire escape.

"About the garbage. You have to throw it in this can back here, and always keep the top on because this neighborhood has more bloody rats than grains of rice. They say there are nine times as many rats in this city as people, but in this neighborhood, I think there's probably a hundred times per capita." The Chinese, he explained, never reported rodents, so the pest population was always booming.

As we dashed down the metal outdoor staircase, I noticed a big gray monolith of filthy stone on the bottom landing. It looked about four feet tall by three feet wide and four feet deep. Scratching through years of soot and layers of dirt, I realized it was a chunk of white alabaster. I was never good at math, but the stone had to weigh at least a ton.

"Someone gave that to me thirty years ago," Shade commented.

"Do you sculpt?"

"I once did. Little pieces when I was younger. I was going to try my hand at it again. Still have the mallet and chisels upstairs," he said. "The fella who dropped it off gave it to me as a payment for sculpting him something."

To have such a piece quarried and hauled here would cost at least two grand. I had taken a sculpture class in college. I enjoyed chipping one abstract form out of another abstract form.

"So why didn't you do it?" I asked.

"I tried," he groaned. "It's fucking hard."

I saw that several ancient chisel notches had been made in the cube. Michelangelo's *David* had been cut from a piece of marble that had originally been discarded by another sculptor because the stone was too tough.

Shade led me out the front door. I thanked him and drove up to Fourth Street, where I squeezed my book table between an immigrant eastern European hot-dog vendor and an immigrant African incense peddler. Between food and aromatics, literature was completely lost.

For every hundred people that came by, one lifted a book and checked the price, and from that pool, it seemed, about one in ten actually bought something. I sketched various perspectives and images of bodies swimming across the East River: sidestrokes, backstrokes, breaststrokes. Finally I found a perspective that seemed to work and I began outlining my painting on the canvas. After a moment, though, I found it difficult to concentrate.

Watching a flurry of young coeds pass by, I fondly remembered Bethsheba last night. Her tight, curvy body was perfect, but Bethsheba always had a distance. Even while screwing she maintained an emotional aloofness.

With June, lovemaking was a kind of desperate physical act. It seemed like a way to get ever deeper into the very mystery of our existence. For hours after intimacy, I'd find strands of her long black hair in my mouth and taste her, a sort of musky chocolate that would linger on my tongue. Somewhere in all our sexual friction our love must have burnt out. How else could she have cheated on me? How could she have invested so much into me and then blithely withdraw it?

I was losing patience waiting for her fucking call. Throughout the afternoon I considered calling her, yet I kept remembering those profane sketches she had drawn. Lean, faceless bodies linked in unspeakable acts. Tight images of him invading her.

"How much is *A Hundred Years of Solitude*?" a solitary middle-aged man asked.

Tears came to my eyes as I said three bucks. Slowly, sadly, books sold.

By five o'clock I had made just over a hundred and three bucks. NYU, that brain-pressing assembly line for Long Island youths, had been turning out a lackluster product lately. The students were simply not as curious as they had been last year. I usually tallied about twice as much by this time. Today, however, was disappointing.

The Forsyte Saga	$7.00
The Cat in the Hat	$6.00
One Flew Over the Cuckoo's Nest	$3.00
Great Expectations	$2.00
The Brothers Karamozov	$6.00
At Play in the Fields of the Lord	$4.00
Picasso	$8.00
The Decline of the Roman Empire	$4.00
Catch-22	$3.00
Slaughterhouse-Five	$3.00
Even Cowgirls Get the Blues	$3.00
The Alienist	$5.00
War with the Newts	$3.00
Collected Poems of Thom Gunn	$8.00
Flashman	$5.00
The Year of the French	$3.00

Thinking about my plans for the night, I remembered the colorful invitation postcard from Ned that I had gotten the day before. Secretly I hoped that perhaps June might show up and we could finally reconcile, but I didn't want to seem too eager. Around six o'clock, as the crowds were heading home, I packed, folded, and loaded up my stuff.

A parking space on Fifth Street between First and Second near the Ninth Precinct opened up and I pulled in. In the bathroom of the Astor Riviera Diner, I gave myself a quick sink shower and a shave. I pulled on my art-opening clothes: a white, button-down shirt, black slacks, and a dark blue blazer with shiny brass buttons. Then I waited for the F train at Second Avenue. I pitched pennies at a large rat scurrying along the tracks, until the train finally arrived—it was the last pleasure a cent could afford.

Seven

P.S.1 was a defunct grade school. It was designed like
all the Depression-era public schools I had ever seen in the city: wide
hallways branched off into the renovated gallery classrooms. Passing
all the black-shirted teens, the place appeared to be a job program for
the many inner-city kids who served as tacit ushers.

In several scattered glass bowls were a few damp pretzels and bruised
grapes. The three designated one-gallon-size bottles of chilled white
wine were already empty. All the usual vegetables were in the salad.

Quickly surveying the crowd I saw no sign of June. Aside from wealthy collectors who Shade called "the chug-and-thug contingent," there were the kooky dealers, the fruitcake artists, a few loony critics, and oddball camp followers. The older ones looked absurd enough, wearing any wrinkly secondhand garb they could pull out of Goodwill donation bins. The younger attendees, though, were downright scary. Ten years ago they all used to don the obligatory black. Funerals had more variety. I remembered attending Chelsea openings where I was the only one not wearing a charcoal Agnès B.

Colorful mix and match was the order of the day now: strange buzz cuts with vibrantly dyed head and facial hair. Tall Kabuki theater hats bobbed alongside red felt fezzes and African skullcaps. Surplus Mao and Nehru jackets fraternized as their namesakes never did. Billowy parachute pants paralleled horse-riding tights. Men were typically fey—or they were reactionary macho. Pixie cuts and bangs were in for women. I always wondered how these crackpots made it to these openings without being torn apart on the fashion-angry streets of our uncivilized city. A guy wearing a T-shirt that said, "Most Modern Art Is Boring" served me a warm glass of flat ginger ale.

The guy's shirt was right. Most modern art was boring, but so were most films, most literature, most TV shows, most meals, and most people. Why shouldn't art reflect that? I made the rounds and looked at the mediocrity on the walls: a photograph of a tired airline stewardess, her hair bunned up, pulling her little tote bag across a rainy New York street; a pixilated cartoon à la Lichtenstein; an overly intellectual black-lettered message, after Barbara Kruger (but not succeeding); a photo of a pigeon taking flight—all were subtly ironic and not at all afraid to be boring. Shows like this made me nervous: Did my art, which seemed so important to me, actually suck this much? Was it so vapid? So imitative? So absent of any originality and power? How many of my paintings made people stop and really look?

I surveyed the room, looking for Barclay the boy billionaire, but I only spotted mild-mannered, multimillionaire Victor Oakridge, the collector who had recently purchased a clock-tower loft in Dumbo. I decided to ask him about Rita the mystery girl. As I approached him, he joshed, "Don't worry, Or, you might get cold this winter but your paintings will not."

Like Barclay, he too had purchased some of my works of art. He actually bought two large, framed subway cars at my first show. A cell phone chimed and a pocket of people paused as everyone tried to detect if it was their own ringer. It was like watching mother seals trying to recognize the baying of one of their pups. It turned out to be Victor's phone. I was put on hold while he spoke.

Some time ago, during a heat wave while he was away in Paraguay, he generously let Juny and me spend a three-day weekend at his octagonally shaped beach house on Fire Island.

It was the one time when I got to see how the rich truly lived and, frankly, I was disappointed. I went through his closet and surveyed his wardrobe. It was predictably nice, but not stunningly nice. I checked out his fridge. He had frozen Omaha steaks, but he also had Kraft American cheese slices. In his pantry were Lay's potato chips and Pepperidge Farm cookies. Worst of all, his CDs and video tapes were all mainstream tripe.

When he flipped his phone closed, I asked, "I know this sounds a little fuzzy, but do you remember a couple of years ago, I saw you at a benefit and you were with a beautiful blonde girl."

"Benefits are my business," he alliterated. "Blondes are my pleasure. You'll have to be a lot more specific."

"Her name is Rita," I began and then took pains describing her. He listened for about a minute before he finally said, "Or, I have no clue who you're talking about—I'm sorry." Then, he vanished into the crowd.

"Did I hear correctly that you were renting Shade's flat?" whined the diabolical voice of critic Klein Ritter.

"Subletting for the season," I clarified.

"This piece would turn a hyperactive into a narcoleptic," Klein said, criticizing some canvas. Then, flipping back to me, he replied, "I'd love to have a look at his Highlands hideaway."

"I promised I wouldn't bring anyone upstairs."

"When did you have your first show, Or?"

I told him. He then asked me a wide variety of other biographical questions before making inquires about my art, the major series I'd painted, my influences, my big collectors, how much I had sold various pieces for.

"Why are you asking me all this, Klein?" I suddenly became nervous about his inquiries.

"I'm putting together a catalog for someone," he replied. With anyone else, I would've been doubtful, but the man was a busybody and a know-it-all. When he finally asked, as was expected, how June had influenced my work, I winced.

"So I heard your woman hooked herself a swordfish," he tore right in, tipping the long-stemmed wineglass to his bloodless lips but not drinking. He had white wine and I knew that he'd hold that half-full glass of warm liquid all evening, if only to show that he got here ahead of everyone else.

"She's just going through a phase," I assured him.

"You think it's just a phase?" He grinned mischievously behind his drink.

I shrugged. He saw that I didn't want to talk about it, so he felt compelled to continue.

"I know you loved her . . . dearly. I could see it in your eyes," he tortured. "You two seemed inseparable."

I don't think Ritter did it voluntarily. He seemed obsessed by the sensation of pain. It was some kind of neurosis. When he sensed a soft spot he just couldn't contain himself. He had to slowly apply pressure to the bruise.

"You brought out the best in that Latina." His voice was so soft and teeny tiny that it seemed almost telepathic.

"That's enough." I really wanted to forget all about her, and put her out of my head, if just for that night.

The paradox about Klein was he was an open sufferer. Twice he had wept in my arms for one dumb reason or another. Perhaps he was irritated that no one else demonstrated their anguish as freely.

"I don't think you heard the news, Or," he went on.

"They went on a few dates, so what?"

"Or, you poor fool, don't you know that your exotic beauty is getting married?"

"What the fuck are you talking about?" I yelled, enraged, and without intending to, I reached up and grabbed him by the throat and shoved him against a wall.

"*No!* Please! It's true! We all got invitations!" He splashed the wine all over his white shirt.

I let go of him. He chuckled and panted, rising slowly to his feet.

I walked away from the cruel little arachnoid and stood in the corner. She had gone and done it. It really was all over. I stared off all alone until Ned came over.

"I would've broken the news to you myself. I thought you knew," Ned said.

"Apparently I'm the only one that doesn't know," I replied.

"I don't want to hurt you, Or, but frankly I'm surprised that you feel this way."

"How am I supposed to feel? The only girl I ever . . ." I couldn't say anymore.

"She told me what you did."

"What *I* did? She had *sex* with this clown and—"

"That's not what she said. She said you destroyed her pieces because she was the better artist."

I let out a chuckle that sounded more like a gasp. "Did I also push her to marry her benefactor?"

"Or, I don't want to get in the middle of this, but she told me—"

71

He suddenly stopped, as though he was saying too much.

"Do you think she'd be marrying him if he didn't have money?" I asked. He didn't respond. "Come on, let me have it. What'd she say?"

"Well, she could be saying this just to get back at you," he disclaimed.

"I'm sure that whatever she told you, she was hoping it'd get back to me, so go ahead, let it get back."

"She said very earnestly that she didn't sleep with Barclay. At least she didn't before you destroyed her work."

"Oh please." I grinned angrily. "Come over some time and I'll show you her sexual confession. They were all freshly drawn."

"Like I said, she could be lying, and I really don't want to put you through any more than necessary . . ."

"But what? Just say it all!"

"She said she did those sketches a few months ago, before all this. She said they were pictures from some porn novel or something she was reading."

I froze at the possibility that I might've been wrong, but I couldn't remember her *ever* reading a porn novel, much less any novels at all.

"Look, I was wrong for what I did," I replied assuredly, "but she's fucking with you."

Ned had to dash because a painter of the foppish variety was bitching to one of the staff about how his work was "misoriented," or hung upside down. I congratulated Ned on the fine show and escaped back to the city. Once in Chinatown, I bought a fifth of Stoli and found a parking spot on some dark street under the roaring traffic of the Manhattan Bridge. It was a warm, humid night for early October. As I lay down on my sleeping bag and stared up at my painted image of the train pouring over me, I could hear a light rain falling on the roof of my van. I drank down the vodka and feared that maybe June hadn't cheated on me. Could there be any truth to it?

It was more likely that she had set me up. She knew from my telling her that I was jealous. I already had suspected she was sleeping with the son of a bitch. That way, I would accidentally stumble across the incriminating images and go crazy. Then, she could deny that they were anything but provocative sketches. Subsequently she could leave me for him—and marry him—which she was going to do anyway. Only now, she was able to tell everyone what a monster I was, and how I had pushed her into a relationship with Barclay.

The Stoli started spreading through my body, giving me hot flashes, so I opened the back of my van. As the drizzle continued, I felt as though I were on fire. The street was totally empty. I stepped outside, naked with my bottle of vodka, and sat bare-assed on a stoop. The rain came down and I felt unsure of everything.

Initially I thought about all the possible causes and fuck-ups: her poverty, my poverty, and this guy's riches. Then I started blaming myself: If I had only confronted her with the pictures initially and let her apologize, if I had only seen her when she came to my book table or just called her afterward. Soon slightly intoxicated, it crossed my mind that if this were a painting—a heartbroken man sitting naked on a stoop holding a half-empty bottle of vodka—it'd be a sappy cliché of melancholia. Ironically, despite losing my girl, feeling mildly drunk, and covered in cool rain, I actually felt pretty good.

Eight

The next morning, I awoke to the jolt of something bumping my van. It wasn't a big hit, just a thump, from the front. I jumped up to see that a tow truck had backed into me. The operator was getting out his chains to hook me up. In my drunkenness, I had forgotten that I was parked in a morning tow-away zone.

Stark naked, I jumped into the front seat and fired up the engines. The fucker furiously tried sliding under my van, hoping to hook an axle. I heard him curse me as I zoomed away. I still had the fifty-five dollar ticket on my windshield. If he had hooked me that would've been the end of it.

With that auspicious beginning, I drove over to Fourth Street and got a great selling spot right in front of the Bobst Library. Today was my day. I dressed and unloaded six crates of books. Strangely, no other book-sellers had arrived yet, which meant there was no competition. But it also meant no one else would watch my books so I couldn't park my van yet. Still, business was brisk. I sold six books before even unpacking.

After about a half an hour, when my table was neatly rowed up with titles, I saw the first gray clouds rolling overhead. I hadn't bothered to check the weather report that day, always a mistake. At least no meter maids puttered by. After about fifteen minutes a fine mist started. I unfolded my plastic drop cloth and draped it over my table. This was why the other sellers hadn't come out. Soon, the rain pissed down. My luck was out. Large drips splattered and made little puddles on the ruts and hollows of the plastic covering my books. Fortunately, I hadn't moved my van yet. I huddled inside my mobile cave and waited for the rain to let up. I had once made the terrible mistake of trying to pack up during a storm. I ended up losing about a hundred bucks in drenched books.

The longer I sat there the more I was forced to think about June's surprise marriage. Like all great traumas, the longer I mulled over this, the further I found myself moving away from my own hurt. While reviewing details of things she said and did over the years, I realized that although June always enjoyed art, home and family were ultimately her goals.

An ocean had been poured through a giant sieve. Soon New York's gutters were so overwhelmed they were troughs of water. The corner sewers were triangular ponds.

After another hour or so of rain, I had an epiphany that our rela-tionship was actually the source of my own growing guilt and insecu-rity. The simple fact was that although I had hoped I could, I never fully did believe that I would be able to give her what she wanted and still be a serious artist.

Around four o'clock, five hours after the rain began, it was still falling. Indians in New Delhi must have been staring at their blue sky wondering where their monsoon went. It wasn't about to stop. But I finally reached some conclusions about June: The greatest test of love was, ironically, the willingness to sacrifice it, rather than destroy that person's own ultimate happiness. Though I still didn't *feel* this way. I decided that this was something I had to work toward.

I could lie to myself and say she was despicable and I hated her, but I loved her. I didn't think I could ever really be happy for her, but I simply had to work at forgiving her. Otherwise my own love for June would have been nothing more than selfish. With this thought I finally decided I had earned the right to leave that wet fucking van.

The parting insult from that loathsome day came only after I loaded my last box of moist books and folded up the table—the rain finally stopped. I drove up to Utrecht Art Supplies to search for a shade of yellow I needed for the new Swimmer paintings. It was an obscure amber hue that I had first seen in a nineteenth-century painting. It was reported to have originally been made from the urine of camels that were fed mango leaves. They only had the color in the more expensive artist-grade, which I couldn't afford. I dashed around the corner to New York Central Art Supply to look for a tube. They had a color that was almost like it in an unknown cheap brand, which I settled for.

Cold, wet, and nearly broke, the only good thing was that I didn't have to spend the night in the fucking van. Shade's loft space was finally available for me. I drove down to the old bank building on Canal and Orchard and parked in front of the service entrance. I piled all my belongings onto my hand truck and headed upstairs. Through the cluttered hallway lined with discarded canvases, I rolled my necessary belongings into his empty living room.

I clawed out of my wet clothes and took a nice long, scalding shower—my first in days. I shaved, dressed, and searched for nooks to store my things in. Off in the corner of the huge room, I spotted the small stack of what Shade must have regarded as his greatest hits. I knew that I had better not touch them.

Every artist has their own strange concept of what they think is their best art. If I had died today I knew that my Subway paintings would most probably be regarded as my finest. But my own greatest work was yet to come—it was going to be an intensely ambitious and sprawling project that I hadn't even begun yet. While in art school, I had initially conceived of it as a fresco, but it had evolved. Although it was impossible to fully and clearly describe—partly because I hadn't completely thought it through—it would involve a hierarchy of modern-day angels, devils, and the divine system of justice that we all must eventually suffer through. Of course I had borrowed from Dante.

I would need a large, open space roughly the size of Grand Central Terminal—and not just the ceiling, but the walls and floor. At its most ambitious this work would require grants totaling millions of dollars just for the supplies alone. The more I mapped it out, in various notebooks and sketch pads, the grander the design grew. This, after all, was where ambition should unravel to its most absolute. Fully realized, I'd have to hire computer programmers, video operators, a full classical orchestra, and a modern dance company. Indeed, the work would transcend the visual. It would be part musical, part theatrical, and part performance art. It would require at least five years of my life. I'd also need a team of assistants. Ultimately it would facilitate a new and holistic way to consider art. Every great artist, to some degree, must try to transcend the conventional form. Only then can man's perspective be constantly enriched.

When I began writing out the first grant proposals to NYSCA and NEA, June read them and said they sounded like a practical joke. But I was not to be deterred.

It all made me return to the original question of what greatness really was. At that tired moment, I only had Shade's works to respond to this vital query. I grabbed an old paint-caked palette knife and carefully sliced open the tape. Then I tore open the bubble wrap protecting one of Shade's smaller canvases. The painting, dated 1963, was a single circle inside a clean and precise black square. In the foreground a series of eight distressed and washed-out colors divided the sphere into nine parts. Shade was a wonderful colorist but the shapes were cliché. I opened another of his canvases and saw a full-size portrait of a bald, middle-aged man grinning. His skin was olive and pockmarked. Under a single dark, arching brow, the subject had a pair of cold, narrow eyes. His muscular arms were securely wrapped around the soft, inviting shoulders of two young women on each side. Their faces were partially cropped, suggesting that they could be just any girls.

The bald man was so smug, so utterly abhorrent. Soon I had to stop staring at him because I found myself getting angrier and angrier. He struck me as the man who got everything. He stood in the way of every solo show I ever wanted. He blocked all grants, all applications to colonies, all major deals. He was probably even the traffic cop behind all the tickets I had ever gotten. He seemed to be smirking at every disappointment in my life. I angrily ripped open another bubble-wrapped painting. This one was a simple black square. But it wasn't just black. It was so dark nothing escaped it. The work seemed to eat light. Upon a touch, it felt like ice. The paint appeared to be painted with a mixture of tar and laminate, possibly Bakelite. The backdrop wasn't just white, it looked like the glistening white of the North Pole.

I tried to figure what it was about Shade that defied success. His work was both powerful and sacred. When I opened another painting, I saw a simple nude portrait of a beautiful girl. There was something strange about the portrait. While the painting of the evil man was boldly brushed, this painting didn't betray a single stroke. On the back was a date showing that the painting had only just been done a few months ago, yet there was something old-fashioned about the girl. Her hair style, her posture, maybe it was her face, which placed her in the '50s. More subtly, there was something about the painting that made it seem like a recollection. An old artist reaching back over fifty years to the precious memory of a young lover—that's what I sensed I was looking at. Then I realized this must be Sheila, the wife he had divorced, who after so many years he had finally forgiven for ruining his first real masterpiece.

The painting made me sad, not because of its content but because one day, ten, twenty, forty years from now, I'd look back at this particular *now* with all its vigor and urgency and it would be gone forever and forgotten. It would be replaced by a whole other now, a wiser, calmer, more peaceful now.

And just like that—although I had intended to spend the evening working yet again on my new Swimmer paintings—I picked up a sketch pad and started sketching June, her nude body with all its sensuality, while it was still fresh in my mind. I usually did drafts before rushing right in, but at that moment, I felt such confidence and power. I knew exactly what I was looking for. As I drew her, tears started coming to my eyes. Feelings and memories rose from me. Closing my eyes, I could hear her voice in my ears.

As though she were dead, her ghost enwrapped me. Looking again, I realized that the sketch pad was too small and flimsy. I only had one small canvas and several rough pieces of lauan. I dashed out to the hallway and grabbed three of Shade's used canvases, each one four by five feet long. Even though much of his rejected work seemed rather insubstantially abstract, they actually made great backgrounds. Successful artists frequently had their assistants paint their backdrops, so I didn't feel that using his reclaimed backgrounds was unethical.

I propped up the three canvases. Then carefully I traced June's entire body, head to foot, standing naked before me, just as I did when she first posed for me. When I was done with the first canvas, I leaned it against a wall and began a second. In this one I positioned her sitting up, her face half hidden behind her knees. She did this the very last time we ever made love. On the third canvas I had her lying sideways as she would when I'd first see her every morning. Finally I

79

opened up an easel box filled with little cakes of dry paint. Squirting in some water and mixing it, I decided to do these in watercolors. All I had were nine colors, the same number of paints Michelangelo had when he did the Sistine Chapel. For roughly an hour, I experimented, blending different quantities of paints trying to capture her exact olive shade. When I was done, I delicately brushed in her form. With each of the three paintings I tried to create an entirely different mood and tone.

I grabbed a fine-tipped sable brush and filled in her eye color and the thousand strokes of hair, eyebrows, lashes, and finally pubic hair. By the time I was done, five hours later, I was completely exhausted and covered with sweat. I felt like I had survived an exorcism. Looking at the image of her that I once so totally loved, I felt as though I had separated it from the real her—she, the liar, she, the betrayer. At that moment, perhaps because she had been reduced to so many intimate yet signature postures, I felt as though I had completely painted her out of my system.

From the hallway, I located and lugged ten large, reusable canvases back into Shade's apartment. Most of the rejected canvases were either too old and brittle, or too small and sculpted with thick swirls of oil paint. I took the unsalvageable ones downstairs and leaned them next to one of the metal carting garbage bins. Perhaps someone might fall in love and take them home.

The only place in Chinatown that was still open was the greasy Chino-Viet takeout, Mekong Delta, around the corner on Allen. Whenever I ate there, I either ordered cold sesame noodles or the Buddha Delight, sauteed oriental vegetables and a tiny carton of white rice. Cheap, simple, and I could eat them cold.

The cashier was a sexy new girl who I had never seen before. She looked to be in her mid-twenties and although she made quick eye contact when I gave my order, she didn't speak, smile, or even look at me again.

I took one of the few seats in the tight waiting area and stared through the big filthy restaurant window onto the dissolution of Allen Street and a filthy brick warehouse across the way. In the reflection of the greasy glass, I slowly discerned that the beautiful Asian cashier was staring right at my back. When another guy came in and placed his order, I discreetly turned around and watched her.

She mechanically prepared the outgoing order, tossing soy sauce packets, an envelope of chopsticks, and napkins into the brown bag. Then she folded a menu over the top, and stapled it shut. Looking at me again, I saw her battling back a grin.

I approached the old worn-down Formica counter with a smile. "Order not ready," she returned, looking to the floor still smirking.

"So what's your name?" I asked.

"My name?" she asked in a choppy accent.

"Yeah, me Or, you . . ."

"Me Lynn," she replied, then giggled and looked away again.

"Lynn, you live around here?" I leaned against the counter.

"I eat fish," she replied happily. "Hmmm. Fish. Good."

"No, no, where do you live?" I asked carefully.

"You funny American man," she said and covering her mouth, she let out a titter. "You so funny."

"No, no," I tried to explain and pointing to her, I started again. "Where do you live?"

"Not that it's any of your business," she said all too plainly, "but I live in Flushing."

"I saw you . . . look at me," I said slowly and pointed to her eyes. "I couldn't help but wonder why."

"All right, enough with the charades." She spoke in an emphatic American idiom. "What do you want?" She was obviously pulling my leg with the no-speakee-English bit.

"Was I being paranoid or were you staring at me?"

"Even though you're probably the most handsome man alive, I was actually staring at all that shit on your face."

Looking in the glass door, I could see that my cheeks were still dappled in June's flesh tones. I looked slightly insane. In a moment my dinner was ready. As I paid she asked what I was working on.

"Portrait of my girlfriend."

"Girlfriend, huh?"

"Ex," I corrected.

As she bagged my carton of Buddha Delight, I wanted to tell her how the bitch left me for a hoity-toity art collector, but I didn't want to come off as pathetic. I paid, thanked her, and headed out. The street was empty in all directions. For the first time that season, I felt a chill in the air. I was grateful that I had found a home for the winter. I could live in my van seven months of the year and be fine, but by the last week in November the vehicle was like a meat locker.

Even so, I had learned to tolerate the cold more and more. Each person's definition of cold varied. I had read that cold was a learned thing. In 1800 a boy was found living in the French forest of Aveyron. He had managed to survive nearly naked in the freezing cold. It was described how he could bathe in icy water without even a shudder. I too had tried to adapt to general depravation. I frequently took icy showers, but I didn't tolerate hunger as easily. Inasmuch as America was all about getting a lot of cheap food quickly, I didn't think I would ever have to worry about starving.

When I returned upstairs with my Chinese food, I opened up my heavy loft door and looked at the first nude portrait of June. It was the most sensual one. As I ate, I realized it looked different now. The paint had dried and the shimmering wet uncertainty that brought it to life was all gone. Now she was harder and colder. The wet painting had possessed everything I found sexy about her, but in that brief trip downstairs the colors had darkened. The shape was transformed. She looked more aloof, as life had shown her to be.

My vision started blurring so I brushed my teeth and stripped down, and for the first time in six nights, I jumped into a non-vehicular bed.

The next morning I was up at seven. I scouted Fourth Street: there were still holes in the wall of vendors near the NYU library.

I used to make nearly twice as much money in front of Astor Wines. But last year, even though bookselling is protected in the city charter, the police decided to crack down exclusively on used book vending there. They didn't touch the hot-dog guy; they'd bypass the honey-nut roaster and the new art book dealers, and I suspected they were getting gifts from the porn tape reseller. So, for the most part, I sold books on West Fourth Street. Last week, though, another bookseller, Jake, set up in front of the black cube, right on Cooper Square. He reported that the cops didn't even slow down. He also said he had cleared fifteen hundred bucks over the weekend. Driving past Ninth Street and Third Avenue, I saw the block wasn't as policed as Astor Place, or as oversold as Fourth Street. An alcoholic comic book peddler who I knew from the area, Comic Book Jerry, was already out there selling old comic books on a foldout TV tray. I parked next to him, unloaded my books, table, and other items, and asked Jerry to watch them for me as I drove around looking for parking.

Then I raced back over to my books and started setting up my aluminum table. Legally we were required to sell books on tables that stretched no more than six feet across by two feet in depth. Only once, a few years ago, had I been ticketed by one cop who actually took out a measuring tape and found that my table was three inches over the prescribed limit.

Before I finished categorizing all my books, I sold three old art books to a well-dressed man with a broad-rimmed hat. Each book was thirty, so I made ninety dollars in the first ten minutes. Considering I found all three books stacked on a garbage can, it seemed as though the gods were smiling upon me today.

"Is this book really five dollars?" asked one goateed revolutionary who looked like Trotsky in miniature. He held up a small hardcover copy of Isaac Deustcher's biography of *Stalin*.

I checked the first page where I had penciled in the price and nodded yes.

"It says here," he said, pointing to the list price printed on the upper right corner, "that the book is $1.95."

"Just like you," I explained, "that work has inflated over the years and—"

Sensing someone behind me, I turned around to see June standing there. Her face looked completely taut and for an instant I thought she was going to smack me.

"Where's my seventy-five bucks!" I yelled first.

"What the hell are you talking about?"

"For the table you broke!"

"Are you forgetting that you destroyed three of my paintings?"

"You fucking cheated on me!"

"Look, even if I did cheat on you," she said calmly, "do you really believe for an instant that that justifies what you did?"

"I found those sex pictures you painted, sucking his dick! Fucking him!"

"I did those sketches with you! When you brought that porn tape home!" A crowd slowly gathered watching us.

"What?"

"That tape you rented."

"What?"

"Your fucking tape!"

"You're a liar!"

"Rent the fucking tape and look at it, you'll see the same exact scenes," she cried. Ned had said it was a porn novel, but it was a *tape*.

"I was with you all night and I didn't see you sketch any fucking—"

"You passed out, you idiot!"

"How the hell could you sketch all those moments from a film?"

"I pushed freeze frame, asshole!"

"You're lying!" I shot back. "How else could you have gotten your ass engaged so quickly?" But I had this awful feeling that she was telling the truth.

One evening, long ago, after we had dinner out, we stopped in Kim's Video. Not finding any films we liked, we wandered into the Adult section. Still in the exploratory stages of our relationship, we rented a porn flick. When we got home, I guess I did pass out, because now I did remember her mentioning a desire to sketch the carnal images. Still, this was all a little too convenient.

"I don't believe any of this!"

"This is your entire problem as a person and artist. You're completely unable to trust anyone or feel anything beyond yourself."

"I fully understand how you feel," I replied angrily. "The seventy-five bucks I spent on this new table was all the spare cash I had. Now pay up."

Unexpectedly, with all her might, she kicked one of the legs from under my book table and walked off. The table wobbled a moment. I leapt forward trying to catch it, but down it went, and so did I, hitting my face against the concrete. I lay on the ground holding my cut cheek amid the pile of fallen books.

The goateed guy with wire-frame glasses who had witnessed the whole drama asked, "Can I just pay for *Stalin* and leave?"

"Keep it," I concluded painfully to get rid of him. Then I sat there until the pain and bleeding subsided. My new table had snapped down the middle. Comic Book Jerry, who also had seen everything, watched me rise slowly and walk away.

"You want me to watch your stuff?" he called out.

"Yeah," I replied absently. Completely decimated by the encounter, I soullessly headed to Shafee's Hardware on Seventh Street and First Avenue and mechanically bought a brand-new aluminum picnic table for seventy bucks. So much for the ninety-dollar gift from the gods. The Indian clerk politely brought to my attention the fact that my face was bleeding. I thanked him, removed the table from the box, and heaved the cumbersome item back to my spot on Ninth and Third. On the corner, next to the full garbage can, I disposed of the mangled table and unfolded the new one. Then I started restacking my heap of books. I also realized that the outlined canvas I had made of the swimmer, which was under the table, had been inadvertently destroyed.

"You know," Jerry yelled as I created order out of the biblio-chaos, "you should have stacked them before you left. People tried stealing some."

"My life has always been free for the pickings."

Soon I was back in business. The day was still young. My facial lacerations had stopped bleeding and I was still in debt. By one thirty, I sold four more books, earning twenty-two dollars. By four o'clock, I had sold another fifteen books and was up a hundred dollars. My fresh facial scabs seemed to attract a welcome pity. I sold a few more books than usual. By six P.M. my total was $182. I optimistically decided to stay until I reached two fifty. No sooner did I resolve this, though, than I hit the horse latitudes. I drifted in still, uncommerced waters unable to even give away anything for the next hour and a half.

Initially my thoughts, like pulses in an electrical fence, repeated variations of the same message: There was *no* way she could have painted those images from that porn flick. Gradually, though, between my recurrent mantra of disbelief, her story gained in credibility. She probably did draw those images that night, and as I came to believe this, I hated myself all the more. I had fucked up big time.

My silent wrath was finally interrupted by a cop who came over and asked to see my tax stamp. This was a small document issued by the Department of Taxation that book resellers were required to have. I wouldn't have shown it to him if the punishment was death. But it was only a fine, so I tiredly flashed him the document and he vanished.

By eight o'clock, Jerry announced that he had pocketed a hundred bucks and was heading to the bar. I asked him if he could watch my table a minute and I dashed off to get the Chevy.

As soon as I got back he left. I spent the next forty-five minutes stacking and packing.

Nine

As I drove home I remembered the great Austrian painter Egon Schiele. He was put on trial, accused of painting pornography. As a punishment, the judge had his wonderful works burnt before his youthful eyes. Schiele would die of pneumonia at twenty-seven, leaving the world his great yet scant collection. For years I thought about how despicable that judge was, depriving mankind of Schiele's genius. Now, after what I did to poor June, was I any less culpable?

That night, too tired to unpack my books and other belongings, I parked in a lot on Allen Street, stopped at Mekong Delta, ordered a

Buddha Delight, and collapsed into an old chair near the counter. Lynn, the deceitfully American-speaking cashier, gave the order to the tiny cook in the rear of the place, then said, "Last time you were here you were covered in paint, what's this?" She had noticed my scab-covered face.

"I walked into a door and fell down a flight of stairs," I replied, not caring to embarrass myself further by telling about my fuck-up.

"Oh my God!" She suddenly awoke to the fact that I had fresh facial scars. "Did someone beat you up?" she queried just above a whisper. "There's nothing to be ashamed of."

"It's a long story." Surprisingly, she came out from behind the counter with a wet napkin and carefully dabbed around the cuts on my face.

"Ow!" I winced after growing comfortable enough to show my pain.

"Poor guy," she replied earnestly. I was genuinely touched by her tenderness. "I got . . . hurt too. Last summer."

"What happened?" I asked.

"Door and stairs," she replied.

I nodded, sensing her desire for discretion.

"So how's the painting going?" She changed the subject.

"I'm going to try to do some now," I said tiredly.

"I'm too exhausted to paint at night," she remarked.

"What kind of stuff do you paint?"

"Ink and brush work."

"Oh, I saw a great ink and brush show at the Met a while ago."

Before the conversation could get too far, some husky bus drivers popped in, unbuckling a variety of orders from column A, column B, and column C. A few minutes later, Lynn gave me my hot little carton of eastern delights. She smiled politely while counting out my change and said, "Go home and heal. We'll talk about art some other time."

"Looking forward to it," I said and yawned.

"Hey," she added, before I could escape, "let me know if you hear of any affordable studio space."

"Will do," I replied tiredly, and stumbled home.

In a few minutes I was upstairs showering. Then, still naked, I put up Shade's much larger easel and placed a small canvas on it. I turned on the radio to perk me up and tried to think about the painting. I had been intending to start the new *East River Swimmer* all day, but the meeting with June had destroyed all peace of mind. I sketched the basic charcoal marks for the new first painting. Instead of having the swimmer walk into the water as I did before, I worked on a close-up of the swimmer's focused face. The Manhattan skyline on the horizon looked like the multi-tiered teeth in a shark's jaw.

I squeezed various dabs of paint onto a palette and started gently mixing them, but as I looked at the colors melting into each other, I found it difficult to focus. I flipped on another light and felt the slight vertigo common to exhaustion. Still, I was eager to get the image up before I lost it, but I had to sit down for a moment. I rested my head and closed my eyes.

I awoke exactly nine hours later. I turned off the lights and radio, which had been on all night. The canvas was still on the easel. The paints, like vividly colored worms, were dried on the palette. The Buddha Delight was cold and unpacked in the bag where I had left it. Details of a day unfinished.

Today, I was sick of being an artist, but like a head cold I'd get over it.

A few years ago, when I turned thirty, I tried giving up painting. I resolved to go to law school instead. Make a salary. Build a life, with a working wife and obligatory children with whom, as though forever trapped in an elevator, I'd grow old. Admittedly, I wasn't after a job or family. I was searching for a different kind of pain, one with less fiery creativity and more monotonous security. I wanted just one winter hot and one summer cool, a sense of permanence that a vehicular home couldn't give. I was claustrophobically bored of the whole poverty shtick: used clothes from thrift stores; seasonal visits to free clinics and food pantries; relentless hours of exhausting work that were almost never compensated. But then I remembered that there was really nothing else out there.

One of the few memories I had of my father was walking through a cemetery as he ranted drunkenly that if these headstones were honest, they'd have chiseled what failures people really were.

"If these fucking stones could talk, you'd hear, 'Had hopes of writing,' 'Couldn't cut it as a filmmaker,' 'Didn't have the balls to be an architect'." He regarded nine-to-fiving as a resignation of all real dreams. He behaved as though he was forced to get married, take a job, and have a child. His only rebellious and arguably creative act was killing himself. His entire rant and ultimate self-destruction contributed to my choice of vocation.

Now here I was—the glamorous alternative.

Late the next morning, as I walked up Allen, I spotted the youthful outreachers of the needle exchange offering a swap with the narcotic habitués. My first instinct was to dash home and grab one of my sketch pads. I desperately wanted to show Rita my works to convince her that I was a real artist, so that she'd pose for me. Looking through the mix of people, though, I didn't see her.

Pablo had mentioned that there was a big book sale at the midtown library. I headed up there to peruse the "removed" books, and spotted several other sellers in the crowd. I ended up selecting a box of decent, thumbed-through paperbacks then drove to the same spot as yesterday, right next to Comic Book Jerry. I set up my new table and used books, as well as my paints, brushes, and a new canvas: the valiant swimmer, take four.

I looked over the outline I had made on the first canvas, the swimmer's focused face. I had just finished sketching in the basic lines and shapes when a group of NYU freshmen girls tumbled out of their purple NYU cable-car bus. Tight denim, loose hair, and heavy on the eyeliner, they started turning my pages and badgering me. How much is this paperback? Do you have *The Bell Jar, The Fountainhead, One Flew Over the Cuckoo's Nest?* And other books off their first-year curriculum list. Those were the books I was forced to read in my junior year of high school.

None of them bought anything, but they knotted up about twenty minutes of my time before I was able to start shaking some shapes out. I drew for about fifteen more minutes until I was aware of a homeless guy looking over my shoulder at the canvas. Being watched no longer bothered me, but most spectators were lonely bores who would try to make small talk: "Are you drawing a kitty cat? 'Cause I like cats," an elderly lady once asked. Yeah, a cat—now take your pills and nighty night.

By the time I finally started making some book money, about an hour into my day, I was too fidgety to paint anymore. I washed off my palette, put my sable in a jar of water, and just sat there waiting for the dying breed of book readers that grows more precious every year.

Books slowly sold, and I was able to sketch a bit more but not much. By four o'clock, when the first trickle of raindrops fell, I had totaled $106. I threw a plastic drop cloth over my table, asked Jerry to keep an eye on it, and dashed over to the Stuyvesant Post Office where I checked my box. A packet of slides that I had submitted to the Spectacular Gallery in LA had been rejected.

Upon taking them out and holding them up to the light, I realized that it was good they didn't want them. I no longer had most of the canvases. In fact, after painting countless works, I only had a handful left, mainly orphaned pieces left over from larger series. Like children from an irresponsible mother, I had a blind faith that they were all somewhere out there. Even most of the unsold ones were in foster homes. Of the three Manhattan in the Rain paintings that I had done earlier that year, only one remained unsold. It was on loan to a friend in Forest Hills, Queens. In his bathroom he also hung the last of four paintings I had done of crime scenes. Over the past decade, I had also sold works in galleries, on streets, and through the mail. Others I had lost track of were rolled up in the van.

Going through my slides, I slipped six images into an envelope and addressed it to the group show up in Portland, Maine, which Cali had told me about. Then I put four slides into a second envelope that I sent to a dot-com millionaire in Summit, New Jersey, who, I had been informed, collected small street scenes of New York.

On my way back to my book table, I bought Comic Book Jer a tall-boy Budweiser. The rain had stopped a while ago, and when I returned, I discovered that Jerry had removed the drop cloth from my table and had sold eight books—he didn't know which ones—earning me sixty-two dollars.

I thanked him and offered him a fiver since I had been gone for nearly an hour. He said it wasn't necessary, which made me wonder if he hadn't made more money and was holding out. With over six hundred used books on a table, no one ever took an inventory. If Jerry sold another five books and pocketed twenty-five bucks, I'd never know.

After another hour or so and twenty-three bucks later, I got my van, packed up, and drove downtown. I parked in a delivery zone, toted my boxes upstairs, and raced back down before I could get ticketed. It defied me how a couple of years ago a woman got raped in midtown during rush hour, yet if you illegally park a moped in the most remote part of Staten Island, you'll still get a fucking ticket within minutes.

By the time I walked home, it was about eight o'clock. I wanted to see Lynn the Vietnamese scrollist, so I popped in and ordered a spring roll.

"Get any painting done?" she asked after I gave my order.

"Oh yeah, I'm getting more of it on the canvas and less on me," I replied. "What are you up to?"

"I'm on a bit of a culture kick," she admitted with a smirk and then amended, "I'm actually supposed to be finishing the last of a group of parade paintings."

"A group?"

"Yeah, I still have three to go: the Mermaid Parade, the Gay Pride parade, and the upcoming Halloween Parade. I'm supposed to have a show in late November and I have a grant to paint in Vietnam for one year."

"My father fought in Vietnam," I replied, free-associating.

"I hope he wasn't killed."

"No, he committed suicide about twenty years ago."

"Sorry," she said after an awkward silence. "So what's your breed?"

"Half Irish Setters and half something else."

"What else?"

"Armenian long haired," I confessed. When her eyebrows knitted in uncertainty, I simply said, "American. So how long have you painted?"

"All my life."

"Where did you study?" I asked.

"RISD. How 'bout you?"

"ASL. Have you been in any shows I might've seen?"

"I've had two solos in the last two years," she revealed.

"You're kidding, where?"

"Cho Gallery."

"Wow!" Cho was one of the hottest galleries in Chelsea. "Any reviews? Sales?"

"Sure," she said modestly.

"So what are you doing working in this dive?"

"Excuse me," she said indignantly, "but this happens to be my cousin's restaurant and since I was staying in the city, I figured I'd bone up on my Vietnamese and make some money before going over there." After a pause, she further explained, "I was born there. My father was a colonel in the South Vietnamese Army. We came over just before the fall of Saigon."

"Do you regard yourself as Vietnamese or American?"

"My name is Lynn Nguyen and my family has been in Vietnam since the dawn of time," she said in a perfect California accent. "So I guess I'm Vietnamese."

My spring roll was ready. The dispossessed princess of Vietnam bagged it, put in packets of different colored sauces, and handed it to me.

"I know I mentioned it last night, but if you hear of any loft spaces around here, I'm desperate for a studio," she concluded.

"How much are you willing to spend?"

"I don't know, six hundred."

"For how long?" I asked.

"I'm going to Vietnam in a month and a half."

"How much space do you need?"

"Around five hundred square feet with southern exposure and a fire-place would be fine," she kidded delicately.

I pursed my lips pensively and pondered it.

"Do you know of anything available or are you just teasing me?"

I liked living alone and knew that Shade wouldn't want anyone else in there. I also knew that anyone who lived or worked with me for too long usually disliked me, which would mean if I subletted to her I'd probably kill any chance of ever sleeping with her. On the other hand, I didn't get any vibes from Lynn, so I didn't think I had much of a chance with her anyway. And Shade's space, at two thousand square feet, was far more than I alone could use. If I charged her six hundred a month, I wouldn't have to spend every chilly, non-rainy day stand-ing on the street hustling used books.

"I know a place," I confessed. "Six hundred a month."

"Where is it?"

"Around the corner. On the sixth floor of the Jarmulovsky's Bank."

"Above the Enternet café?" she asked excitedly.

"That's it."

"You're kidding."

"No, but I better warn you that I live in there, even though it's not a living space."

"You're not one of those guys who have yellow fever?" she asked with a smile, referring to men who were obsessed with Asian women.

"No."

"Are you a sex offender?"

"Not convicted."

"Have you ever molested women in a crowd?" She sounded serious.

"I've offended women with my bad taste."

"How big is the space?"

"About two thousand square feet. You'll have your own area, but this isn't a living space." Shade didn't have to tell me, but I knew he was one of many living in a loft space that had no certificate of occupancy, a legal document that was required for a New York residence.

"I'm staying in Flushing, which is a little out of the way," she replied plainly. "When can I look at the place?"

"When do you get off?"

"I can dash out in a moment for about ten minutes or so."

"I'll see you then," I said, and told her where to meet me.

I walked home, went upstairs, and straightened up until the buzzer rang. She came in and inspected Shade's big cave of a room. It was actually the perfect art studio. All rough and ready. No place for fun or games.

"My God! How'd you score this?" It was love at first sight, but not with me.

"A friend. It's six hundred a month, for two months." I led her to a clean, well-lit corner and said, "This will be your work space."

"Are these yours?" she asked politely. Looking at the nudes I had painted of June, she commented, "I like these."

"They're not really done, but if you want to buy one . . . ?"

"You can send slides to my curator."

"That's kind of you." Artists rarely offered up their curators for solicitation. "I'm holding off until I get enough for a show, then maybe I'll take you up on it."

"You know, I really love your back images." She carefully examined Shade's abstraction behind June. "Is this an acrylic?"

"Probably," I said, visibly deflated.

"What's the matter?"

"I didn't do the backgrounds," I explained.

"Well, I'm not saying I prefer it to the foreground. Don't be so sensitive. It just has this aged look."

"That's 'cause it was done years ago," I clarified.

She was right, I was too sensitive. To last as an artist one had to feast on neglect and guzzle down rejection, because those were the only two things you were guaranteed. I thanked her and agreed to meet her around dinnertime tomorrow at Mekong Delta for the rent-for-key exchange. The space that I was supposed to share with June was instead being rented to a cute Vietnamese takeout girl who I didn't know from a hole in the wall. Fate's shell game both conned and rewarded in the most unpredictable ways.

Ten

Since I broke up with June, that mangy yet loyal mutt, depression, was never too far away. Still, I had vowed not to go on pharmaceuticals until I hit forty. Controlling my mood was at times a moment-to-moment struggle, but that night—probably due to the unexpected transfusion of sublet money from Lynn, or maybe just from talking with her—I felt an unfamiliar ease. It was as though I had been awarded a MacArthur genius grant for an hour. It temporarily restored a belief that maybe my work had not been produced in vain.

I headed down to Good Will Barber Bar, where I bumped into

Pablo, who was wearing a T-shirt that said "Let Ralph Debate!" He was drinking with his latest beauty, a Tibetan girl named Twit or Tirt. Between kisses and gropes the two were collaborating on some poly-gotted love poem.

"Kaleidoscope seems a little out of it," he commented, referring to Cali. She was sitting alone at a table staring dead ahead. Her attractive diamond-shaped face and mysteriously dark features had not really aged over the years. However, like Dorian Gray's portrait, her hopefulness seemed to have come apart at an alarming rate. Lately, whenever I saw her, she was dragging and inebriated on cheap white wine. I sensed she missed Shade, so I joined her.

"You know I'm going to your girlfriend's wedding in a few weeks," she initiated conversation.

"Can we talk about anything else?"

"How's art?"

"Enjoy doing it, just can't move it."

"That'll all change," she said in a haze. "I've been making big plans for you, my son. You're going to be a big success."

"What kind of plans?"

"I don't want to jinx it," she said, and seemed to slip into a mini-coma. She closed her eyes and slowly bent forward. I was about to sneak away when she suddenly hit her forehead on the tabletop. As she sat back up, the whack seemed to set off a sad reverie: "I remember being a skinny, wide-eyed girl with a great bod. In the summer months I'd take the ferry to the Peloponnese Islands. The rest of the year I'd spend in New York. Every week there was a wild party somewhere and a new gorgeous guy." The aged doyenne smiled. "People seemed so much bigger and unusual back then. You'd meet wacky characters. People reading protest poetry and folk singers and endless cute boys with their facial hair just sprouting who'd fall in love as soon as they saw you. Hard little peckers before all the diseases." She looked off and smiled. "I think of them now like a pasture of spring flowers, they'd wilt as soon as you touched them."

She smiled and nodded, "Man, I remember the smell of patchouli and sandalwood and . . . the long silly conversations that were so entertaining. I remember one incredible guy. Shade introduced me to him, I thought they were brothers. He had a golden beard and full lockets of hair, Stew or Moose, some name like that. He cut hammered bronze into these long jagged shapes and . . . I remember kissing him and we wound up making love on a rooftop and later on the Great Lawn in Central Park . . . I guess I was wondering what became of him. What happened to that entire world?" She paused and looked at me.

"I'm sure he's out there somewhere," I assured her. "They all are."

"Maybe, but I have this awful feeling that the best is long behind me and the worst is just ahead."

This sort of despair was a weight I simply couldn't lift.

"You still selling your van?" I finally asked.

"Oh, yeah," she replied. Then she smiled and departed.

This was where the artistic lifestyle failed while the suburban middle class succeeded. The bourgeois could survive on creature comfort, new VCRs and SUVs easily replacing old ones, the latest intrigue at work or school, but for people like Cali, who sacrificed boring, steady jobs and hateful teenage children for *la dolce vita*, there was little else to distract them when friends vanished and the party soured. In this context it was easy to understand June's choice for domesticity.

"Hey, Cézanne." Pablo appeared behind me. He said that he and his Tibetan beauty were hiking up to another poetry reading at KGB, and would I like to join them.

"I don't think so, Cali got me depressed and poetry makes me even more depressed."

"I guarantee that the reading will be over by the time we get there." Then he added in a whisper, "And Blonde Bosoms is behind the counter tonight." I consented and we headed out.

As we walked up A, we crossed paths with Cecil, the over-educated bookseller. He was heading uptown to go on a blind date with a girl he had met on the Internet. He joined us long enough for Pablo to launch into his Nader rant of how corporate America runs this country.

"Look," Cecil replied, tired of the Nuyorican's rhetoric. "I voted for Nader in the last election. I honestly think he's the most intelligent man with the greatest integrity, but even if some miracle occurred and he got elected, do you really think he'd get any legislation through?"

"If people voted for him, maybe they'd get the strength to vote for other Green Party candidates who really want to help this country."

"So if American voters—most of whom are so apathetic they don't even vote—elected a completely new political system, then we'd see real change, is that what you're saying?" Cecil reiterated to highlight the unlikeliness of it all.

"Yep," Pablo replied.

Cecil abruptly parted company with us.

On Fourth Street, we turned west, walked a block and a half, and squeezed inside the tiny hot pub. Crazy Ike, the book pusher, came over, said hi, and asked if I had heard about Mike throwing his books in a mud puddle last week.

"I heard." Even though I'd heard it was Ike who did the throwing.

We all had a couple of drinks. Things got loud and loose. After some people came in and others left, Pablo leaned over to me and said, "You probably don't need to know this, but I just heard something nasty."

"What?"

"It's regarding June, so if you don't want to hear it . . ."

"I know. She's getting married."

"I heard that she and that collector dude threw a wild party."

"What do you mean wild?" I sighed.

"Ecstasy, coke, speed. By the end of the evening clothes started coming off."

"Was she happy?" I asked, staring into my empty glass.

"By the end of the evening," he replied. "I'm told she was ecstatic."

"Then I'm happy for her." I replied trying to sound and be sincere. Soon Pablo left with his exotic girlfriend. I had another drink with Ike, then he left too. The big blond bartender was kissing some guy. Horny and lonely, I headed home alone.

As I was walked down Forsythe along the eastern edge of Sara Roosevelt Park (named for FDR's mother) nearing Stanton, I passed two black, nearly naked hookers. The extra-large one, who wore a big blond wig, was harnessed into a tight, long camisole and wore bright red lace panties below. The other, rounder one wore a tight yellow pair of hot pants way up her crack as though it were a thong. As she walked, her white-gloved fists quickly spun around her equatorial waist like a pair of small moons.

"Should'a slapped her 'cross her bald fuckin' head. Little white bitch stealin' my fuckin' money!" She spoke in a rapid fire to the other, "You see that skank!"

"Should'a shanked the skank. She don't even got no mac," the other replied, glaring in the opposite direction. "Lookin' right at the bitch."

Through a thinned-out line of anemic bushes roughly twenty feet into the park, about five feet off the ground, I spotted a chubby olive-skinned man sitting on a bench with his back to me. On her knees before him, I saw her and felt my stomach, heart, and throat clench up. It couldn't be, but it looked just like Rita of the Allen Street Mall, the shorn-haired beauty who passed out hope to the accursed and damned. Her long white arms were akimbo at her side, palms outspread and fingers scraping along the ground. Her head and neck were gently undulating back and forth like a human jellyfish. Her beautiful mouth, her wide and gentle lips, was obscured by his fat thigh and wide ass.

They were each in their own world as I softly crossed over so that I was only about ten feet away.

"That's it, that's it, bitch," I heard him grunt over and over. Reaching around he grabbed her bristled scalp and rocked it hard back and forth. "That's it, that's it!"

He tugged her close so I could hear her choking, fighting, trying to yank her cranium out of his grip. But not until he let out his final moan did he release her. She fell backward, coughing, spitting, and gasping for air. He chuckled a bit.

"All right!" she said, trying to catch her breath. "Now where's my money?"

He calmly pulled his penis back into his pants, zipped up, and rose.

"Where's my fucking money?" she repeated. Even I knew that prostitutes got paid up front. Poor Rita was a tragic novice. I watched the guy fix his flannel pants and large gray jacket. Then he took out a napkin and dabbed his large shiny brow.

"Give me the fucking cash!" she screamed again.

"First show me your titties," he finally said in a raspy high-pitched voice.

"Fuck you, I gave you what you wanted!"

"Okay, bye-bye," he started walking away. She didn't have a chance without a pimp.

"Goddamn it," she yelled and grabbed the lapel of his jacket. "Give me my fucking money, you fucking pig."

"Show me your tits and you get your money," he calmly instructed, brushing her hand away.

In a flash, she pulled her shirt up revealing a duet of tight breasts, tipped by pointy nipples. He quickly reached up and gave her right nipple a sharp, blinding pinch, causing her to shriek as she pulled away. She was bent over in pain, cupping her right breast as though he had shot an arrow into her. He turned and started exiting as she cursed at him.

As he approached, I grabbed an empty forty-ounce from a trash can and stepped into the street light.

"Give her her fucking money," I said softly. I had just enough liquor in my system to be stupid, but had no idea what I was going to do.

He stopped, calmly took out his worn leather wallet, pulled out a couple of bills and let them sail to the ground. She quickly snatched the bills off the pavement and dashed west.

He turned slowly and walked right in front of me, showing no fear. I crossed the street, never seeing where she went.

By the time I arrived home, I felt woozy and bleak, yet stimulated. My head throbbed with the sacred and unholy image of that fat satyr, half-man, half-goat, seated on a bench. Supplicating before him was the most beautiful of all creatures, engorged on his groin. I found a used canvas with hellish orange streaks and tossed it on the easel. I usually didn't care for orange—the pumpkin color reminded me too much of New York parking tickets—but now it was unavoidable. With a severe erection, I started sketching, wooing, torturing the burning picture from my gray matter, painting at a furious pace and finally collapsing into bed. Numbly, in exhaustion, I could only wonder why, if that was her, would she do such a hideous, odious thing.

As is always the case when falling asleep drunk, I awoke early to a long pee. The morning sky was gray, the window pane, chilled. It was about six A.M. and there would still be good selling spots available on Fourth Street. Then I realized that due to Lynn's infusion of sublet money, I didn't have to rush off to work and could stay home and paint. Looking at last night's canvas, the sadness of that blasphemous memory came flooding back. The work was sloppy and unsellable; but the tortured half-image was breaking out—a virginal princess enthralled and on her knees before an ogre king. I resqueezed my palette with paints. I was careful to crop any actual junction between groin and orifice, only because I thought the viewer's imagination could probably do a better job of filling it in.

On the back pocket of the john, I had accidently splashed a stroke of green and I started rubbing it out. Then I realized that this discoloration was actually a dollar bill peaking out of his pocket. I still didn't draw the troll's upper torso or head, but it was better that way. Making him anonymous heightened the grotesque, even if it meant having to cut the top of the frame down. Initially I wanted to draw him leaning backward, screaming ecstatically skyward, but then I decided that this perverse violation would be his shameful victory. I painted him hunching over his undeserved find, the little pearl. His abnormally large hands forcing her nimble head amid his fat thighs. Hoarding her, not sharing her with anyone. It looked like a Lucian Freud. I should have stopped there; instead I filled her body with arrows shaped as pricks and hypodermics, a female Saint Sebastian. With these heavy-handed strokes, I ruined the painting.

It was around noon and I knew the needle exchange workers would soon make their miraculous appearance at the benches. I washed off my brushes, grabbed one of my sketch pads just in case she showed up, and I headed out. I stumbled over to East Broadway, the hub of business for the area, and bought a cup of coffee at the Happy Lucky Pastry Shop. Then I sailed over to the cheap dim sum joint where I ordered two shrimp in rice noodles. In a cardboard container, they resembled two tiny fetuses encased in embryonic sacs. When I got to the benches and sat with the woebegone, I baptized the dumplings with black soy sauce and gobbled them down.

I sipped my coffee and waited. Nervously I flipped open my sketch pad and drew some of the addicts. I wondered what I was going to say if Rita arrived. It was definitely her I saw last night. Could I ask her why she did such a degrading act?

When the squad of well-meaning youngsters with their tattoos and hairdos and clipboards finally arrived, their wards loosely lined up. I rose and walked about, but there was no sign of her. Without waiting for a turn, I cut to the front and went up to a nose-pierced waif with a peroxide job and asked, "Where's Rita?"

"I don't know, but if you see that bitch, please tell her to return the fucking needles."

"Shut the hell up!" someone yelled at the youth. It was a curly blond geek with glasses. He had just finished allocating syringes to someone. Standing up, he took me aside and said, "Rita isn't working with us anymore."

"What happened?"

"Hold on a sec," he said, looking nervously around him. "José, can you spell me a moment?"

"Sure, Lou," a Latin guy replied. He put away some prep baggies he was distributing and took Lou's seat.

"She has some serious medical problems . . . I can't say anything other than that." He turned to go.

"Hold it." I grabbed him by the arm and gently led him toward the cast-iron gate running along the mall. "Do you know her?"

"'Course, she's a dear friend."

"Last night I saw Rita giving some scumbag a blow job in the park."

"Oh fuck!" he whispered loudly, nervous that others might hear. I silently waited. Finally he said, "A lot of people working here use drugs. She's no different."

"I didn't know."

"She had a bit of a relapse."

"Can't you do something?"

"We tried. You can't help someone who doesn't want help."

"Can't you call her parents?"

"We did everything we could!" he said, and then checking his volume, he concluded, "Please keep this to yourself."

I nodded, numb. I've always been broke, and though it inconvenienced me, it never bothered me that much. The idea of doing something so degrading just for money completely boggled my mind. Lou resumed his exchange of needles as I walked away.

Eleven

Back home, I selected one of Shade's large reclaimed canvases. Then I reviewed the quick sketches I had drawn of addicts who Shade wanted me to paint. As I began sketching the outlines of their ravaged faces I realized that their contours and shades came too easily to me. I knew them from long ago.

Seven hundred thousand people poured into New York just over the past ten years. Most of those living here nowadays don't seem to have a clue what this city was like in the late '70s, early '80s. The prevalent tone back then was that this place was falling apart. Everyone I knew had gotten burgled, mugged, or worse. No one wanted to middle age here, let alone grow old and vulnerable. Almost everyone I knew had an escape plan. Back then pushy dealers, persistent beggars, and slowly slipping addicts were ubiquitous. That was when I first started sketching them. Addicts made good models. They just stood still, or rather, they slowly sunk downward. I remembered doing one incisive piece, as a kid, lost somewhere, called *Stop-Action Addict*. It was a series of overlaid sketches of an IV user slowly sinking in place.

They were a key reason I never did drugs. I knew I was an addict just waiting to happen. I also knew that I was an alcoholic and would develop cancer from smoking, therefore I never took up steady drinking or cigarettes. I only wish I knew that one day apartments would be costly and scarce.

After about two hours, I had to quickly get a second one to put alongside it to complete the mural.

As I filled in more details, I realized that sobriety, something most of us took for granted, was a state of grace for these bench people. They had been singed by the flames and lived to tell. Suddenly I decided to expand the concept. I sketched Rita's lower torso into the upper half of the painting with the bench angels trying to hold her down at their level, while her upper half was being pulled into another world. I was borrowing slightly from Michelangelo's *Last Judgment*, but I needed another group of figures to do justice to my hell. I grabbed a canvas of equal size to the first and fit it on the top frame. Then I got some long, narrow wood screws and attached them to the first painting. Using wallpaper tape, I covered the interstice and began painting on the upper panel, creating a gang of demons who clenched at her upper half, pulling her up, snatching her from salvation.

Although I hadn't squeezed out the paints, I envisioned the colors clearly: A tangle of dark red muscular arms and knobby purple fingers grasped her alabaster skin. One grimy hand bulging with veins clenched at her bristly golden skull. Another filthy hand had his long knuckle-swollen fingers locked into her soft, moist mouth and delicate nose. The third and fourth pairs, powerfully large, tugged at her angular shoulders. A fifth and sixth pair of hands plunged chubby silver hypodermic needles into the soft pearl slenderness of her forearms. Others degraded her beautiful body, broken yellow fingernails scratching into her flesh. Of course I had one hand reaching down, twisting her cold, erect nipple. More rough hands reached farther, scratching through her scant pubic hair. Then it occurred to me to give these monstrous claws identities and *lo!* they became art dealers. The two most fiendish ones, injecting her with heroin, were Barclay Hammel and Victor Oakridge. Swarming behind them, cheering them on, I greenishly painted the spider-like Klein Ritter, as well as a couple of his canine-faced compatriots. For a moment I considered painting June as one of their murdered victims, but then I decided this would be too bitter.

There was no clear heaven or hell in Rita's world. She had only two choices: the purgatory of an impoverished bench redemption, taking drugs prudently and sanitarily, or the narcotic excesses of the privileged classes.

It was ten P.M. For the first time in a while I had worked all day. The painting had taken on a life of its own, subduing me as its maker while transforming into a twelve-foot-long living mural.

Exhausted and famished, I suddenly realized that I was late. I was supposed to meet Lynn at the Mekong Delta hours ago. I dashed down the stairs, around the corner and inside.

"Shit!" she yelled. I thought she was angry about my tardiness. Instead she said, "Do you ever wash off after you paint? I thought you were bleeding." Holding up my hand, I realized the blood red paint I had used as hellfire was streaked along my arms and face. Accented by the actual scabs still on my face, it looked real. I apologized about being late. She said not to worry about it. Hungry, I asked if she would mind if I ordered a Buddha Delight. She took the order, handed me a moist paper towel and put a can of Coke on the counter without even asking if I wanted it. I downed it in a single gulp.

"Do you have the keys?" she asked.

"Oh, yeah." I gave her an extra set of copies that Shade had given me. In return she gave me the rent.

"It's okay for me to move in tomorrow, right?"

"Yeah," I replied and accidentally released a foghorn of a belch.

"Gross!" she shot back.

"Sorry." Sharing space with a woman again was going to require a little getting used to.

She asked me if I was still working on portraits of my former girlfriend, and I told her my ex was getting married. I mentioned that my latest project was of two purgatories. In a moment an old guy came busting in, ordering a big wonton soup. She handed me my Buddha Delight. I wished her good night and left.

Before heading back upstairs for another ten hours of work and a bit of sleep, I dipped into the bar. In the darkness, I scanned the talking figures and spotted Pablo with an exotic new girl, a Euro-blonde.

"Hey Nader raider."

"Hey yourself," he said, interrupting himself. "You know that girl is looking for you."

"What girl?"

"You know, the Australian girl. What's her name?"

"Who?"

"That painter."

"Bethsheba?" I asked. She was the only Australian painter I could think of, but I didn't know that he knew her too.

"I saw her at Barnes and Noble the other day and she asked if I could tell you to call her."

"About what?"

"She said you're supposed to go with her to the Dumbo art festival this weekend."

"Oh that, right." I hadn't spoken to her since we steamed up the van in Brooklyn. Although women usually hated you if you didn't call and reassure them up and down afterward, I knew Bethsheba wasn't that insecure. After all, she had a solo show, reviews in the *New York Times*, and her own group of collectors.

I thanked Pablo and was about to head back upstairs, but something was nagging. I grabbed my bicycle and pedaled around Sara Roosevelt Park. After a quick recon of the area, during which I spotted several tired hookers and their disgusting clientele, I returned to Chinatown.

Back upstairs, I looked at the mural and realized that I had viciously abused the red and orange. Lighter paintings, I always thought, sold better than darker ones, but this mural looked like it had been painted with a cherry lollipop. My color field always got away from me and took on a tawdry life of its own.

I broke out the paints and gingerly fixed and refocused the faces. I had to resist the constant temptation to add yet another canvas to the already ill-planned and overwhelmed work. Finally, when my eyes began to lose focus and I could no longer stand, I laid down and drifted off to sleep.

THE NEXT MORNING, I was awakened by the loud and creaky front door opening. I peeped out and saw Lynn wheeling in a small aluminum luggage toter.

"Christ," I said, behind swollen eyes under a swollen brain. "Is it already noon?"

"Yep," she said. "And I have to move in and do a bunch of chores before work, so—hey, these are nice." I peeked over and saw she was looking at some preliminary sketches I had done of my swimmer.

"I'm doing a series on swimming the East River," I replied tiredly, not thinking anything about it. A moment later I had drifted back into full sleep. When I opened my eyes, a short time later, she was still standing there, fixed before my purgatorial mishmash near the corner.

"What do you think?" I asked, somewhat proudly, hoping to collect my two minutes of false flattery.

She didn't say a word, she just stood there. I gave up on the idea of more sleep and rose to my feet. As I tiredly approached her I realized that tears were trickling down those frozen and unexpressive cheeks—Lynn was crying.

"It's not that good, is it?" I asked her, looking at the piece with her.

She didn't respond.

"Is it that bad?" I asked fearfully.

Still no response.

Finally she said, "It's fine. It just . . . reminds me of someone."

"Who?" I asked, curious that she might know Rita of Allen Street.

"No one," she said. "Someone from the West Coast."

"Her name wasn't Rita, was it?"

"Nope," she replied, and wiped her eyes. She busily wheeled in her little hand cart filled with art supplies.

"Do you need any help?" I asked.

"I'm fine," she said softly and inspected the cleared-out corner that was her official space.

I splashed some water on my face, washing off the remains of last night's paints, then I gargled, dressed, grabbed my keys, and headed down the stairs, followed by Hong Kong Don Juan with his latest young concubine on his arm.

I walked to the Happy Lucky Pastry Shop and got a cup of awful java. But it all turned out to attract happy luck, as I found a quarter and called Bethsheba on a pay phone.

"I didn't know you knew Pablo," I said, instead of hello.

"Who the hell is Pablo and who the bleeding hell is this?" asked Bethsheba.

"It's Or."

"Oh! You don't call or anything?"

"I'm sorry."

"Are we on for this weekend or do I—"

"No, I'm definitely on. Just tell me where to collect you."

"I'm not going back in that death mobile again," she countered. "We'll meet at Dumbo."

"Fine," I replied, and before I could forget, I asked, "So how do you know Pablo?"

"I haven't a clue who you're talking about," she replied.

"You bumped into Pablo, the Nader-supporting poet at the bookstore on Astor Place . . ."

"Oh, the tree planter. I bumped into him at Bruised and Hobbled." I understood her phrase for Barnes and Noble, but I wasn't sure why she called Pablo a tree planter. "He tried to pick me up while I was waiting at your book table, when you were fetching your van."

We agreed to meet just outside the F train exit on York Street, the first stop in Brooklyn, at noon tomorrow.

"Listen," she said, before I hung up. "There's a bit of unfortunate news."

"What?"

"You should call the Pomegranate in Williamsburg."

"Why? What happened?"

"Speak to Persephone. She tried getting ahold of you, but she didn't have your number and because we were there together she called me . . ."

"What the fuck happened!"

"Someone damaged your work."

"What?"

"Someone stabbed your painting."

"My *Latin Fishermen*! Who?"

"Persephone didn't see who did it," Bethsheba explained. "Call her." June must have done it, but she had just gotten engaged. Who the hell else would do such a thing?

"Do you want to skip Dumbo?" she asked.

"Absolutely not." I assured her that I'd see her the next day. Life goes on. Then I called the Pomegranate Gallery. Persephone answered.

"I just spoke to Beth. She said someone stabbed my work."

"I'm so sorry."

"What happened exactly?"

"I'm not sure, I have an electronic bell on my front door, I heard it ring that afternoon while I was in the office, but I didn't see who came in. Then later that day when someone stopped by, they brought it to my attention."

"Exactly what happened?"

"Someone poked a hole in the middle of the piece."

"A small hole?" I could feel a small hole form in my heart.

"Yeah. We found a screwdriver on the street outside."

I let out an involuntary wince that I wished she didn't hear. "So someone must have stood there and cut into it. Yet you didn't hear a thing?" It seemed fishy.

"Or, I'm a curator. This is my life. I would have thrown myself between the point and the work if I knew it was happening. And I mean that."

"Can the piece be repaired?"

"Of course, and I'm intent on selling it if you'll still let me."

"Did you call the police?"

"Absolutely. I insisted that they take fingerprints off the screwdriver."

"What's your insurance situation?"

"Well, you might remember my asking you if *you* were insured, because I said I was not."

"Oh." I did remember.

"I don't want to sound insensitive by bringing this up right now, but you signed a nonliability agreement when you gave us the work. We have coverage for solo shows but not group shows." I knew I'd signed something, but I wasn't sure what.

113

"Or, I want you to know how sorry I am."

"I don't have wives or children or a family or money. I just have my goddamned paintings."

"I understand." She paused. "I've never had anything like this happen before. I don't know if it's of any use, but I can give you a hundred dollars out of my pocket."

"That's okay," I replied. It wasn't her fault. It was mine. I never should have cut up June's work and when she approached me, I should have apologized profusely. She obviously wanted to teach me a lesson and it worked.

"If there's anything I can do," she replied.

"You don't know anyone that wants to buy any art, do you?" I kidded.

"You don't sculpt, do you?"

"Not really, why?"

"I got a call this morning asking if I knew of any bargain-basement sculptors."

"Sculptors?"

"Yeah, for a headstone."

Although I had sculpted a few small things out of stone back when I was at the Art Students League, I never really made a habit of it. I thanked her anyway as the recording came on asking for another quarter.

When a painter looks at his art, aside from seeing what he painted, he sees a reference to a time in his life. For me those fishermen will forever be a monument to the sweltering June of 2000, when I was poor and deeply in love with June. Now here it was a few months later, I was broke, alone, and still struggling with the image of a swimmer unable to cross the East River.

I wandered aimlessly as I thought of the damaged piece, the last of the group of watercolors I had done of Latin fishermen along the East River. They held those old poles with such pride.

◆ ◆ ◆

PERHAPS BECAUSE IT WAS A FRIDAY, it was a slow book day. Since I couldn't do the mural, I used the time to study pictures I had collected of swimmers. I had some ideas, but I really needed a model.

"Hey, Jerry," I asked the comic-book peddler, who was just staring off. "Do me a favor and start swimming." I held up my sketch pad.

"Well if it's for art," he replied tiredly, and then raised his flabby arms. For a while he let me position his head and arms as he stayed in a swimming pose.

"You don't mind if I pull up your shirt, do you?" I asked as I pulled his shirt out of his underpants.

"I guess not," he replied slowly as I studied the sinews in his back.

"You should do some exercises," I commented, trying to strain the muscle out of the fat.

"Maybe I shouldn't let myself be posed," he said slowly.

"You wouldn't mind if I . . ." Without telling him I splashed a little water on his back.

"Hey!" he pushed me off, pulling down his shirt.

"I just wanted to see your skin wet," I explained, "and this light is perfect."

"Yeah, well, it's cold outside and I got to think." He tucked in his shirt and resumed his tired stare. Without intending to, I went too far. I was simply frustrated. None of my images were coming out right. Or maybe they were and I just didn't know. I couldn't understand what the swimmer was feeling. I drew the perspective from nearly every angle, but I wasn't comfortable. Everything from the poor book sales to the stabbed Latin Fishermen in Williamsburg made me depressed.

By five o'clock, I had made only sixty-four bucks. I couldn't leave yet. But tomorrow I was supposed to meet Beth for the Dumbo Art Festival, so I knew I wasn't going to get any painting done. I decided to head home and try to put a little pigment on the canvas.

Twelve

I popped into a Mexican hole in the wall for a burrito before I parked and unloaded my books onto my hand truck. I ate as I wheeled my things homeward, leaving a slight trail of rice and beans.

A zooming piece of flesh darted out of Ludlow Street like a meteor in worn jeans. Looking closely in the dying sunlight, I realized it was Rita, crying and cursing. She was moving with various twitches and strange jerks.

"Are you okay?" I yelled out almost instinctively.

"Fuuck!!! Off!!!" she screamed at me with every red-hot charcoal cell in her perfect and sweaty body. I almost dropped my burrito.

"Oh, you. Sorry." She caught herself. Apparently she had confused me with everyone else. "You're that . . . art boy."

"Are you okay?" I tried again. I leveled off my hand truck of boxed books so that I wouldn't drop them and carefully took out my sketch pad.

"No, I got fucked up badly."

"What happened?" I asked, and nervously took another bite from my Mexican dinner before it got cold.

"Maybe *you* can do me a favor?"

"I was going to ask you the same thing," I said, eager to show her my art.

"I'll help you," she said looking deep into my eyes, "but you got to help me first."

"I don't have any real cash or anything . . ."

"No, nothing like that," she reassured and grabbing my arm, she pulled me eastward.

"Hold up, I got my books."

She let go and raced ahead. I grabbed my hand truck and followed her past the first building of the Seward Park Housing Projects, along the north side of Grand Street.

"Where are we going?"

"I've got to get something from someone."

"What?" I took another bite of my burrito.

"Come on, I'll show you." After weaving a few blocks north, toward Delancey, she came to a halt in front of an apartment and signaled for me to join her.

"What's up?" I said, lowering my hand truck. I was about to take another bite from my burrito when she snatched it from my hands and was about to toss it into the gutter.

"No!" I swiped it back, folded the foil over it, and slipped it into my shirt pocket. Rita wheeled my hand truck against the building so that it was out of the way.

"All you're going to do is pick something up for me, okay? That's all you're going to do."

"What?"

"Just an envelope."

"Should I mention your name or—"

"Hell no, did I say . . ." She took a deep breath to suppress her anger and said, "Don't say a fucking word. They don't fuck around. Just give them the cash. Get the envelope and come back out."

"What is this?" But I knew right then and there she wanted me to buy her drugs. Because I cared for her I didn't just walk away. Instead, I decided to try to make her see reason.

"It's not what you think," she said in a tense whisper looking up and down the street. "It's for my friend."

"Do you know what you're doing to yourself?" I said sternly.

"You want to help me or do I get someone else?"

"I'll help you, but not this way."

"*No!*" she screamed and, grabbing me, spun me up against an old brick wall. Her face was an inch in front of mine. "Listen carefully, you love me and I . . . I love you."

I smiled and unable to contain it, she grinned, "Okay, so that's bull-shit, you'd be amazed how often that line works. But seriously, I'll do *anything* for you. All you have to do is this one little thing. Please! *You have to!*"

"There is *no way* I can do this," I replied earnestly and quietly. "*Because* I care for you."

"Wait a second," she said, "just hold that thought a sec." She turned around and started yanking at the old doorknobs of dilapidated buildings on the block.

"What are you doing?"

"Just one sec," she called. "See, that fucking Luke, he did this to me. Fucker set me up, and then he got them bastards so they won't sell, but he had no fucking right . . ." As she dashed ahead she called out this strange, convoluted explanation as to how she got into this fix. It only underscored that I didn't know this person or her world at all. I had no business getting involved.

As someone was leaving the building two tenements away, Rita hollered, "Hold that door!" The elderly Latin lady who was exiting caught the door with the shopping cart she was toting behind her.

"I left my keys upstairs," Rita said. "Thanks so much, hon." The old lady smiled and headed up the block.

"Hey, Sammy," Rita called to me. "You coming or what?" She glimpsed up the block to make sure no one from the drug house had seen her.

"My name is Or," I corrected.

"And you're just like your fucking name," she fired back angrily, "indecisive. Well I better warn you, Either/Or, the absence of a decision *is a decision.*"

Because it would have taken more of an effort to leave than to be with her, I grabbed my hand truck and wheeled it the twenty feet or so, and then pulled it up the front stoop into the narrow doorway of the dingy tenement. She was already inside.

"I am not buying you drugs," I said emphatically as I rolled my hand truck down the cracked tile hall toward the base of the stairs where she was standing.

I thought she had tripped as she fell forward onto me, kissing my mouth. She slid downward, rubbing her lips over my chest, stomach and finally the crotch of my pants. She went for my zipper.

"What the fuck are you doing?" I pushed her head back.

"Just two fucking minutes, you run over there, get the shit and I'll give you the best fucking blow job you ever had."

"No!"

"You'll come so hard you'll blow a hole through the back of my skull! I swear it!"

"Why don't you go in there?"

"I fucking can't!"

"Why not?"

"Because of that cocksucker Luke they won't sell to me!" she yelled.

"Well I won't do it!"

"*Fuck!*" She screamed and back kicked the flimsy hallway wall.

"You know," I began in a calmer, lower voice, hoping to convey my concern for her, "I painted a mural of you and I think you might really like it. If you want to go for a bite and—"

"How about I let you fuck me up the ass, then will you do it?" she bargained as she turned around and started pulling down the back of her pants.

"Who the hell kicked in my wall!" Some fat, balding troll opened his door, as though he were coming out from behind a boulder. His torn boxers and stained tank top were visible through his parted bathrobe.

"Hey there," she said to the shoulderless ogre.

"Did you kick my fucking wall?" he asked. As she walked down the corridor to his door, his bloodshot eyes looked down her tight shirt and jeans.

"How'd you like your cock sucked so hard you thought you died and went to hell?" I could see the tip of her tongue running along the top of her lip.

"What?" He grinned.

She stepped forward and stroked her fingers over his threadbare shorts.

"She wants you to buy her drugs, sir!" I called out.

"Let me just . . ." she said as she stepped inside and closed the door behind her. At that instant, when anyone else would have made their getaway, I only felt a suffocating sense of panic.

"Get out of there!" I yelled out, banging on his door. After another five seconds I yelled in desperation, "All right, I'll do it!"

Without any connection to the man or the prior moment, she opened his door as she rose to her feet and stepped out into the hall.

I could hear the old guy yelling, "Hey, what was that! One suck and you're done! You can't do that to a war veteran!"

She held open the front door for me as I wheeled my hand truck of boxes out of the building.

While we headed back down the street, she spoke a mile a minute. "Okay, so this is what you're going to do . . . You're going to go into that building—"

"Hold it!" I interrupted, "I want you to do me a favor."

"Fine, whatever you want."

"I want you to look at my sketches," I explained, but it was just a pathetic effort to believe I wasn't a complete slave to her.

"Fine, but after."

She pointed to a building nearly out of sight. "When you see the door guy, just tell him you live upstairs because he doesn't sell to first-timers. You got to be quick. When you get up there, there's usually two guys but sometimes a guy and fat girl sitting on the top floor. Just give them the twenty. They'll give you a packet. Then get the fuck out of there quick, because sometimes they shout down."

She was walking at a frantic clip. I could barely keep up with her. The ends of her blonde hair had grown out and were sticky with sweat. She kept stopping and I could see her trying to hold it together while I attempted to speed ahead with my hand truck.

"Okay, there's the cop spotter." She discreetly pointed to some riffraff with dental jewelry. "Since Operation Pressure Point they stopped doing this shit."

"Can I just ask you one question?"

"Look how many assholes are going in there!" she said seeing two people heading down the block. "Fuck! They're going to be out of shit if they're not already. We'll talk after you got it."

She painfully squeezed something into the palm of my hand. It felt like a pebble. Inspecting it, I realized it was a twenty dollar bill, folded so tightly it was nearly a cube.

"Go!" She shoved me forward. Behind a rusted-out fire escape that would undoubtedly collapse if anyone dared to step on it was a motley, dingy building. As I approached I saw two people crowded into a shallow doorway and realized there were another half a dozen or so in the smelly foyer. I shoved right passed them and heard, "Wait your fucking turn!"

"I fucking live here," I cursed back on cue.

"Next coming up!" I heard. A moment later I saw a large Latin man in a brown fedora turning toward me. A black line of facial hair served as the only division between his massive jowls and fat, bullish neck. He stepped before me.

"I live upstairs!" I repeated my message indignantly. Like Ali Baba, the human mountain moved aside.

I calmly walked up to the first floor, until the line of buyers couldn't see me, then I dashed. Three steps at a time I moved noiselessly. Flight upon filthy flight, I sprinted up the worn-down stone stairs. I grazed my fingers against the metal banisters covered under endless glossy coats of paint. Each floor was tightly bordered by four old apartment doors. As I approached the fifth floor, I felt myself growing increasingly tense and thought how this was absolutely preposterous. In that great road map of profoundly dumb turn-offs and insane flights that charted my meandering existence, this was undoubtedly the Jersey fucking Turnpike of stupid moves.

Rising to the sixth floor just before the roof, I saw two chunky pairs of legs with rolled-up denim hems sitting on the top landing. I could hear them. They were selling to someone so I ducked back down to the fourth floor and waited for the transaction to conclude. The entire time, I felt this petrifying fear. I had to keep breathing so as not to tighten up.

I figured that the fat doorman downstairs would never allow someone to go up while another was buying. It seemed odd that five floors should separate the doorman from the dealers, but I figured the many floors offered a healthy getaway time should the cops try an arrest or rival dealers try to rob them. The dealers could easily grab their stuff and escape over the roof to an adjacent safe house.

In a moment, the sale was complete. A pair of sneakered feet started coming down the stairs and I heard, "Sen' up the nex'!"

As I dashed up the last flight, I could feel my heart fibrillating. All instincts screamed, Move fast. I passed the guy who just bought. A nondescript white guy in tortoiseshell glasses. I feigned being out of breath as I approached the top floor. Two black guys, in their twenties sat there with all the gangsta trappings. Money and packets were spread on the step between them.

"Damn, you was quick," said a black youth in a black fisherman's cap with the rim pulled down.

"Who you?" asked his companion, an ectomorph with a Phat Farm baseball cap. "I don't knows you."

"I knows him," said the fisherman's cap, who I never saw before.

I handed him my square twenty.

"Well I don't knows him."

"Just give him the shit," the first seller spat.

The other kid handed me a packet and I left. As I reached the fifth floor, I heard. "Send da nex'."

"I just sent you one!" bellowed a great voice from below.

"Yeah. Now send the next!"

Two landings down, I saw the other buyer, a slim black dude who was shooting up the stairs like smack in a vein.

"They're still selling to someone. You better wait a moment," I counseled him to give myself a little breathing space so the dealers wouldn't realize what was up. He stopped and I kept heading down the steps.

In another moment, two flights below, I passed another drug shopper, an attractive blonde girl with black frame glasses. "They got a traffic jam up there, you better slow down."

"I knew you cut the line, asshole," she replied under her breath. As I reached the bottom landing, I heard, "What the fuck you doing down there?"

"What you talking about?" echoed up the goon with the massive neck.

"You sending them up two at a time or what?"

In a second I was outside. Dashing down the block, I came to Rita, who was standing behind my hand truck. Through erratic breaths, I could see her wavering between curses and prayers. When I nodded my head, confirming her highest hopes, it all came out—tears fell from her eyes. She was biting her lip. It was as though she had concurrently won an Oscar and given birth to triplets. Although I was seriously pissed, I could only crack a smile. In that single instant I saw the face of pure ecstacy—an expression that I wished I could brush onto the moon so all the world could enjoy it.

"Where is it? Where is it?" she badgered. I held up my fist. "Give it! Give it, fucker!" She snarled territorially when I walked past her.

"They're going to figure out what happened in a minute," I shot back tensely. "Let's put some streets behind us."

She grabbed my hand truck and followed me back down to Grand and then westward.

As we crossed Essex, I said, "You know you really feel close to someone after risking your life for them."

"Yeah, yeah, just give it," she said grabbing at my hand.

"You said you'd look at my sketches."

"Give it first." She let out an exacerbated sigh. I opened my hand and she snatched the tiny glycene envelope out.

I carefully slipped the sketch pad out from between the back of the boxes and the backrest of my hand truck. She yanked it from me and began flipping through the pages quickly. It was the only thing that stood between her arm and her precious heroin. The sketches twirled by speedily at first, and then about midway through she stopped and slowed her pace. Before reaching the final page, she turned back to the front of the pad and studied them carefully. The drawings weren't great, just drafts. The one she took the longest with was a rather surreal up-close expression of the struggling swimmer. I had tried to capture that micro-moment when his head was craned hard to one side. His lips were pushed up along the water's edge, barely able to breathe. His neck muscle strained and his arm was recoiled, just before it knifed back into the cold waves.

"They aren't my best," I sputtered, feeling self-conscious, "I mean, I did most of them today. I just wanted to show you that I . . ."

"The noblest and strangest art . . ." she paused and caught her breath, "is that which can afford to neglect nature—it realizes another nature, analogous to the mind and temperament of the artist."

When I made a surprised expression, she replied, "Baudelaire said that about Delacroix."

So much for the drug-whore stereotype.

"You're a terrific artist." She tossed the pad back to me. Still battling the initial aches of withdrawal, she said, "I'd be honored to sit for you some time."

"What the fuck is an intelligent white girl doing in the Valley of Death?"

"It's the Valley of the Shadow of Death," she corrected. "And believe me, we aren't even close."

"Do you suck old men off just to impress your friends, or is this your way of getting back at Daddy?"

"Fuck you."

I grabbed her arm and asked, "Don't you want to live?"

"More than anything else in this awful fucking world," she concluded, and took off.

Although it felt like a whole lifetime, the entire event had taken no more than thirty minutes. As I pushed my books homeward, I was grateful for all of life's banal pleasures.

Despite the fact that I had enabled a heroin addict while jeopardizing my own safety, I didn't remember the last time I felt a fraction of the thrill, excitement, or terror that I experienced while buying drugs for that Venus de Psycho.

When I finally wheeled my hand truck into the front door of the loft, I saw that Lynn had completely renovated her little corner. She had hung large swaths of rice paper along her walls, and laid down a heavier grade of cotton-white paper on the rough wooden floor. It was perfectly torn, marking her little angle. The fact that it hid all the decomposing paint and filthy, uneven floorboards made the tight space seem new and luminous. Along the two walls she had put up a series of striking works. Five scrolls—five of seven of the city's parades. Chinese New Year, the Saint Patty's Day Parade, the Mermaid Parade in Coney Island, the West Indian Parade, and the Gay Pride. She was still in the process of painting two of them. One scroll was simply painted black, probably a backdrop for her next work. On her collapsible aluminum easel was what appeared to be the Haitian Day Parade, a work in progress. I could see she was painting this one from newspaper photographs. There were a variety of photos from endless other parades taped to her wall: strange floats, baton twirlers, marching bands, crowds, and so forth. Along the bottom of the parade scrolls was a mysterious deviation of roman lettering that must have been Vietnamese calligraphy.

Not even a drop of unmixed paint from her day's labor had made it from the two-by-four-foot scroll to that perfect wedge of rice paper on the floor. I always spilled paint on everything. Moreover, as my painting expanded, I had to take it down from the easel.

After surveying her nearly photo-perfect paintings, geometrically balanced and color controlled, I returned to my sloppy multi-canvas salad of purgatorial earth with Rita the beautiful crack whore getting tugged down the middle. I hadn't moved it at all since I placed it on the floor, yet the fresh line of dribbled colors along the boards that designated where I had initially propped it no longer bordered the work.

For some reason, Lynn had moved my piece. It wasn't just moved a few inches. It had been pushed a foot back and about two feet over. For a second I thought about mentioning it, but I didn't want to sound petty on her first subletted day.

Inside my shirt pocket, I came across the remainder of my half-eaten burrito. Finishing it, I thought of Rita and how terrifying and tingly it was being with her, even when we weren't being chased by drug dealers. I wondered if at that very moment she was shooting up.

For a while I sketched a new Swimmer portrait onto a canvas. I thought I was on to something, but then I realized the portrait was too tightly framed. It was too cautious and controlled. It lost all its urgency. I found myself possessed by thoughts of Rita and was unable to continue.

I broke out the fine brushes and bright paints. From being with her for a half an hour, I had made some new observations of despair and was eager to incorporate them into the mural. I also filled in further hideous aspects of the art dealers and addicts. At midnight I went downstairs to toss out a bag of garbage. When I opened the back door, a pack of rats shot out of the cans so quickly they knocked the half-covered, mismatched lids to the pavement. I heard them squeaking as I tossed the bag in. Retreating up the outdoor stairwell, I brushed passed that big chunk of gray stone that I saw on the day I first moved in.

Upstairs, I painted for a few more hours until I couldn't keep my eyes open. Like a sleepwalker, I washed my brushes, scraped off my palette, brushed my teeth, splashed some water around my tired face, and turned in for the night.

Early the next morning, because of the unchecked gang of pigeons cooing and copulating on my windowsill, I finally gave up on sleep around eight. In my underwear, I stared at the mural. Before even peeing, I picked up a brush and was back in Rita's world.

When I started the work, I didn't have a clear plan. All I intended to paint was Rita in my idea of hell. As it took possession of me, I thought that the piece was going to be important. It might even be great. Now, as I was growing increasingly exhausted by it, I started having my doubts. It had grown too ostentatious, losing all the suggestiveness that initially made it alluring. Around eleven, I decided that I had better cocoon it for a while.

I was supposed to spend the day at the Dumbo fair with Beth and realized that things might get amorous, so I showered, shaved, and tried combing my hair. After years of being victimized at various barber schools around Bowery, I had a difficult time finding a part. I put on some clothes that weren't frayed or filthy. I was about to board the F train when I realized that the new walkway of the Manhattan Bridge had just opened. I could probably walk it and still be at Bethsheba's rendezvous spot in about forty minutes. I always loved crossing the river.

Thirteen

Down Under the Manhattan Bridge Overpass, DUMBO, the gray wedge of blocks around the Manhattan and Brooklyn Bridges, is a natural community for artists. Aside from the striking long views of Man Hurtin' Island, this area's massive highway-supporting columns, ramps, two colossal bridges and their enormous stones are distant, lesser cousins to the pyramids.

I turned onto Sands Street, and circled eastward under Dumbo, arriving a few minutes late. Bethsheba was leaning against a car waiting for me. Wearing some weird kind of lederhosen, she looked like a butch hobbit. We kissed; then, grabbing my hand, she led me down-hill toward the art enclave. The neighborhood, which is usually empty, was now stuffed with art barbarians and bargain hunters.

The drafty buildings were once factories and warehouses erected during the late nineteenth century. Goods were made here and rail-roaded blocks away to various Brooklyn ports where they were shipped around the world. As America became unable to compete with third-world slave labor, the plants and warehouses in this area hollowed out, only to be rediscovered by artists who are customarily forced to rent the neglected and overlooked parts of the city until their very identity gives it a renewed value that causes them to be pushed out.

The Dumbo Art Festival, which started about ten years ago, was a cleverly devised scheme in which all these poor artists got to throw open their musty studios for three days and try to find dealers and collectors for their works. Over the past five years or so, other creative commu-nities started jumping on the bandwagon. The artists in Red Hook, Williamsburg, and around Gowanus Canal all started open-studio weekends. Visiting there, I always found the art uneven, but the living and work spaces consistently intrigued me.

Some of the cheaply reconfigured studios in Dumbo reminded me of modern tree houses carved out of huge brick walls and rickety wooden joists. Many were tight and geometric, with drywall boards that divided and subdivided the originally spacious studios. These boxes were where lessors were forced to sub-sublet their precious space in order to defray the rising costs of the rent. Yet there were always a few studios that were spacious and extravagant affairs. Almost all of them had either a great view of the river, the bridges, or at the very least, the BQE.

We walked past a regiment of kids in black canvas pajamas. They were the cream of the Leon Finklestein Karate School crop, and in near synchronicity they demonstrated the latest "defensive" chops and sweeping Ninja kicks. Bethsheba pulled me around a large circle of spectators staring at a giant Howdy Doody boy in farmer's overalls who was driving a huge motorized tricycle made from spare parts.

"I want to get into this castle," Bethsheba announced, pointing to a soot-layered factory looming about a block and a half in front of us. In we went, and along with an accumulation of uptown monocled types, we waited for a freight elevator. When it finally opened its large, rattly door, about twenty-five people pushed out. Then we all angled in. The door slammed and we silently waited as the elevator creaked upward. Taped along the walls of the rising room were an overlap of flyers advertising specific art spaces, "Studio 912—For the wow! most-kickass art in the city."

We stopped on each landing: people exited. Bethsheba held my wrist tightly as though I'd bolt out like an Afghan on amphetamines. She wanted us to exit at the top floor and work our way down through each story and studio of the converted warehouse.

Finally at the last stop, we exited and began twisting and winding around the concrete entrails of the rotting building, entering into the various cul de sacs, catacombing into studios where the artists were usually chatting with friends as they waited to be discovered. The most hospitable aesthetes would offer small plastic cups of cheap wine and maybe a cubic inch of cheese. Some of the more defensive ones would be sitting there, suppressing a smirk at the petit bourgeois philistines. Occasionally, a few artists, intent on not completely wasting their nervous time, would try to paint as meanderers passed through. They looked like constructive animals in their natural habitats.

Looking at the various works, I began upsetting Bethsheba by asking some artists "intrusive" questions, as she called them. I was curious as to why a husky, squat black guy painted a series of nude middle-aged female Asian amputees, or how long an attractive young blond girl spent sculpting a lengthy succession of look-alike Giacomettiesque German Shepherd skeletons. Obscure visions were executed in found materials. Like Picasso, I was always happy to see a good idea that I might "unconsciously" borrow and get rich from. One young lad offered a stack of riveted boxes made from public street signs.

We slowly wound our way down the labyrinths. Each floor seemed to have a different configuration of passageways and studio spaces. Bethsheba inspected the artwork like a jaded critic. She alotted each studio about ten seconds—one 360-degree spin of her periscope before losing patience, grabbing me, and heading out the door. I always feared that my paintings, upon which I was spending my life sentence laboring, would get the same criminal perusal from others that Beth and I were committing.

We resumed our marathon through the exercise course of modern art. Yet art itself moved slowly. The subtle advances of the impressionists—Manet influencing Monet, Van Gogh affecting Gauguin, and so forth, shaping the expressionists in increments with Munch's despair, Kandinsky's surrealism, sluggishly splattering and dripping like a colorful monster of sludge to the post-expressionists—all were evidence that genius does not gallop. Only Beth did, which probably accounted for her own brusque, imitative style.

"Don't you think we owe it to our fellow artists to give them just a bit more time," I burst out, after our umpteenth getaway viewing.

"My dashing out isn't a critical dismissal," she corrected, pulling me out of an animal woodcarver on the fourth floor and into an abstract Japanese watercolorist next door. "We have over a dozen buildings and each of them have between twenty-five and a hundred artists. And I want to see them all."

"But what's the point of plowing through all these studios when you can't even appreciate one work?" I asked as she started dragging me next to a splashy watercolorist.

"I'll make you a deal." She suddenly halted in the dank and ill-lit hallway. "You get ten free minutes. That means if you see some art you like, pull the emergency cord, and I'll count down the minutes you want to stand awestruck before the work."

"Fine."

Racing through those ever-unfolding spaces, peaking into each little loft, I was very cautious about using up my precious minutes of emergency art appreciation. Back outside, we skipped several blocks, passing the smaller, more idiosyncratic buildings for the bigger, older warehouses paralleling the river where, Bethsheba explained, "We could inhale the most art per breath."

We dashed down those Dumbo streets barreling past sidewalk performance artists, and hurtling through bands of meandering poseurs, until boom—Beth broadsided a banker. A dapper, older gent was on the ground squirming. His too-young, stylish girlfriend stood over aghast. Bethsheba stopped fully and apologized.

"The art will be here for two more days," gasped none other than Victor Oakridge, wealthy art collector and asshole extraordinaire, who sat up and caught his breath.

"It's too bad you weren't holding a pot of boiling water," I said to Beth.

"'Course it would be you, Orloff. Who's your little torpedo?" he asked.

"Bethsheba, this is Victor Oakridge," I said, introducing her to the victim and patron of the arts. "He makes his fortune snapping up unknown works like ours for peanuts and selling them at shameless markups as we freeze and starve to death."

"Oh my gosh," she said, instantly transforming from a Sherman tank into a shrinking violet. "I've heard so much about you. You came to a show of mine a year or so ago at the Hanging Gardens."

"He was also at your Entrance Art show," I pointed out. Both were group shows in which she was one of fifty artists, but who was counting.

"I resold one of Or's pieces at a bit of a markup, and has he ever forgiven me?" he relayed. "I'm glad to see that *you* don't share his hatred of people who'll someday make you rich."

They shook hands, and while protectively guarding his bruised ribs, he inquired about her work. She tried describing it. Even though he politely nodded his head in vague recollection, he obviously had no clue what she was saying.

"You guys should come by later," he wrapped up, "I'm entertaining some people tonight . . . but . . . oh . . .You and June broke up, didn't you?"

"I've got a new lady friend." I pointed to Bethsheba.

"Yes, but June is going to be in attendance, and I don't want to create a scene."

"What you mean," I filled in, with a pleasant smile, "is that Barclay's going to be there and you don't want to make his money feel uncomfortable."

"Well, I'm sure Barclay won't mind me," Bethsheba perked up. Victor bade farewell, and with his silent female accompaniment, he strolled off.

Bethsheba resumed her march to the big buildings on the river's edge. I followed tiredly.

"I'm sorry," she uttered. Passing one building, we saw a large, professionally printed sign that read:

HERE IT IS! The Reason you've come! The most SEN-SATIONAL exhibit since Giuliani tried to close down the Brooklyn Museum! Right upstairs!

Bethsheba silently entered the building and started up the metal and concrete steps.

"I know I was rude to you," she elaborated on what she said to Victor.

"He doesn't buy paintings to enjoy them, let alone to help the artists," I said as we hiked up the long flights. "He only buys and sells art to make money. They're a commodity and he does it well."

"I heard he was a real prick . . . I wasn't trying to . . . hustle my paintings . . ." she talked while hyperventilating. "At least that wasn't . . . my first intention . . ."

"All right, what was your first intention?" I asked. We both finally reached the summit and caught our breath.

"Haven't you heard that rumor about him?" she asked.

"Tell me."

"He supposedly has a room he doesn't let anyone else in."

"Oh, he's into bondage?" That didn't surprise me. He had *sick fuck* written all over him.

"No, he has a private viewing parlor."

"For what?"

She sighed at my opacity. "The rumor is that he bought one of those works that was stolen from the Boston break-in."

About ten years ago, a group of look-alike assailants all wearing police uniforms invaded the Isabella Stewart Gardner Museum and snatched a variety of rare art, including a Rembrandt. The pieces were too hot to move in this lifetime, so everyone believed they had been taken by a rich collector who alone would selfishly gaze upon them forever.

"Studio at the End of the Hall for the BEST ART IN DUMBO!" bragged a modestly printed sign in the hall. Underneath it in a ball-point pen someone scribbled, "And he ain't lying!"

We walked down a series of ever narrowing corridors. None of them had open studios, so we kept marching. Finally we saw a sign taped to a door, ajar. It read, "You're almost there (Damn, I envy you!)" The door opened into midair. The next step was a hundred-foot fall. A narrow courtyard separated our building from a neighboring one.

"Look," said Beth, pointing to a ten-foot plank that bridged the two buildings. It was about two inches thick and a foot wide.

Before I could blurt, *No way!* Beth trotted out over the bouncy ten-foot board and into the doorway of the adjacent warehouse.

"Are you nuts!" I screamed over at her.

"Don't be such a coward!" she called back. "Come on."

"Do you see any art?" I inquired.

135

"It's down here," she pointed into her new building. I hated when my masculinity was called into question. Taking a deep breath, I tiptoed the elastic, splintery plank. About midway across, the board started wobbling, paralyzing me with great fear.

"Come on, move it!" my drill-sergeant date ordered.

I resumed my slow shuffle across the distance.

"Take my hand," she said and extended her arm. I grabbed it and jumped inside. Then putting my hand on my ribs, I could feel my heart thumping to get out of my chest. I remained calm until I caught my breath.

"Goddamn you," I finally cursed at Bethsheba.

"Just relax!"

I reached down and grabbed the board.

"What are you doing?" she asked. I yanked it toward me until it dislodged from its teetering resting place, and dropped a hundred feet down into the narrow airshaft.

"Now no one will ever do that again."

"Suppose that's the only way out!" she replied.

"Then we'll live in this building, which would be a great improvement over our present lifestyle."

"Come on, let's see this great fucking art," she said, and raced ahead down the corridor of the latest dilapidated building. Another sign led us to the farthest end of the floor. There, we came to a big wooden open window that was about fifteen feet tall. A note taped to the right of the frame promised, "Great Fucking Art—Just Swing on Over."

Looking out the window, a long thick rope, like a strong vine, drooped down. It was fastened to some invisible point overhead. The next building that we were supposed to swing to was roughly fifteen feet away. Without a fear in the world, Bethsheba jumped up on the window casement and took the rope firmly in both hands. Just before she could sail, I grabbed her by the leather straps of her lederhosen.

"Are you fucking crazy!"

"It's just across there."

"No! You're not killing yourself on my watch."

She paused a moment, finally grasping the big picture and nodded in embarrassed agreement. She climbed back down into the corridor. The lure of great art had gotten the best of her.

"We've been had," Bethsheba agreed.

"I kind of figured that back at the plank," I invoked my rare patronizing tone.

Downstairs, more studios opened into art galleries. We wound our way around as though it were a funhouse, peeking at the various freak shows along the way. Finally, we came to it, or rather she came to him. We landed smack in the studio of Gunter, the bloodless German landscapist whose zero-gravity work Bethsheba had a serious crush on.

His space was arid and barren, like the surface of the moon. His eyes were neither abstract nor expressive even though his art leaned that way. His large cheeks, flat lips, and wavy, salt-and-pepper hair had a bland integrity.

"I saw your show at the Data Bank," Bethsheba rushed right in.

"Oh, yeah. That was a good one."

"You really should be at the MOMA," Bethsheba cooed, and went on and on about how important he was and all the wonderful things he deserved.

"I hate to be a wet towel," I interrupted rudely, pointing to the back of my naked wrist, "but it's been ten minutes."

"Excuse us one second," Bethsheba said and walked over to me so that she was within whispershot. "I've been saving this for you as a gift, but here." She handed me a scrap of paper. On it was written an address and studio number next to the name Adele O.

"Who's this?"

"It's about two blocks away, I was going to take you there later."

"What the hell is it?" I asked again.

"It's that girl you have the crush on."

137

"Who?"

"You know the lost-girl-in-the-crowd painting." She paused. "The one you thought I did."

"*What!*" I felt my bowels tense up just at the thought of her.

"That's her studio. Go on, I'll meet you there, loverboy."

I graciously thanked her and took off. I dashed through the rotting hallway and down rusting stairs as though the building were crumbling down around me. I fled across the old, half-paved, half-cobblestoned streets and into the warehouse listed on the card a few blocks away. Then up into the building, back through another old stairwell and up to the fourth floor—Studio 401. There, inside of a tiny, dark doorway, I saw a teeny-tiny studio space. A definitive middle-aged woman had a half-burnt cigarette squeezed between two wrinkly knuckles of her right hand. In her left she was holding a chipped and stained coffee mug. She had a huge mop of unkempt black-and-gray hair. A black phone with a long curly wire was pressed to her ear. If I had to use any single word to describe her, I'd choose "lumpy."

As I discreetly inspected her latest offerings displayed on the walls, I listened as she intermittently made "hmmm" sounds into the phone. Of the three hanging canvases, nothing else even remotely resembled her little-girl-in-the-crowd piece.

Her first painting appeared to be two big orange balls of flame. The second was two columns of curling smoke. The last one was of two mountains of rubble. Since they were all abstractions, they could have been anything and were probably nothing. She had to be the wrong person.

"Excuse me," I interrupted.

"One sec," she said into the phone and then looked up at me with raised, bushy eyebrows.

"Did you do a painting of a little girl who was lost in a crowd?"

"Girl lost in the crowd?" she repeated.

"Yeah, a little girl, lost in a crowd, perhaps looking for her mother or something. At Entrance Art."

"Oh, yeah."

"It was a wonderful painting," I began, hoping to deliver some of the awe and amazement I had for her work.

"Thank you." When she approached me, I could see her shiny face was made up of large, sweaty pores.

"I don't mean to go on," I went on, "but you really have something."

"Thank you so much," she said with a wide smile revealing yellow teeth and receding gums. She still didn't put the phone down.

"How'd you choose your subjects?"

"They just came to me, like in a vision."

"I hope you got a good price for that work of art."

"I got a fair price for it," she replied, without revealing the tag. She added, "No one was interested until the last day of the show. Then one guy made an offer and suddenly three other people each raised their offers. But it didn't really go into any extended bidding."

"Too bad. That painting really deserved a lot of money. I mean the work really taught me something about art."

She looked at me searchingly as if she were trying to determine whether I were mocking her with my excessive flattery. But I wasn't, I was earnest.

"As an artist I see a lot of stuff, and your one work moved me so much more than the vast majority."

"It really means a lot to hear you say that," she replied through a twisted, shy smile. But she still didn't hang up the phone. It appeared connected to her like some kind of life-support apparatus.

I took a step closer and though I didn't find her attractive, I tried to balance the brutal reality which was *her*, with her, the maker of sublime art. After all, a person can be born beautiful through no fault of their own. But to use a superior intelligence and great perseverance in the face of constant rejection and material sacrifice, and to finally emerge as a gifted artist—now that was an achievement. Inasmuch as she merited praise and even imitators, ridiculous as it sounded, she deserved to be attractive.

139

I nobly tried to explain to this not-pretty woman why she was great. "The obvious expression in the little girl's eyes was of panic, but you went beyond that. Every detail of your painting was two moves ahead of anyone else."

"Gee, thanks." She scratched her runny, red nostrils thoughtlessly.

"Of course you must have known what you did."

"Well, I . . ." She tugged at a lock of her uneven two-tone hair.

"The expression so totally embodied the modern paradox of realizing we're cursed with just enough awareness to know that we're lost, while being provided with too little intuition to find our way." I paused and took a deep breath. "And you conveyed that brilliant idea in just an *expression*. A few strokes and hues, do you see what I'm saying?"

"Ahhh," she gaped, looking down, and giving me the opportunity to notice the fine morning crust of yellow pus still wedged in the corners of her eyelids.

"To be absolutely honest, that wasn't the idea of the painting," she finally spoke. "It was supposed to be a girl getting excited at coming to the big city."

Huh?

"Are we talking about the same painting?" I moved to confirm. "You did the one on display at the group show in Soho?"

"Yeah," she verified. "Over at Entrance Art."

"Right. How can that be anything other than a girl lost in a crowd?" I asked.

"Well, if that works for you, fine but . . . well," she smiled.

"*Not* fine if that's not what it is."

"That just wasn't what I intended. I wanted it to be the excitement of the big city. I mean, I thought that was what I saw, and what I was doing." She paused and added, "Maybe I was wrong."

"If she's just a little girl in the big city, why is she alone? Where's the girl's mother?" I asked, smiling politely.

"If you remember, there's a hand open near her head. That's her mother's hand."

"I remember hands casually opened around her, strongly suggesting they belonged to people in the anonymous crowd."

"Well one of those hands belonged to her mother," she replied, slightly miffed. "I didn't want to overemphasize it because that's not what the painting is about either."

"Look," I argued, civilly, "I don't mean to be rude, but a painting about excitement in a big city is . . . well, for Norman Rockwell, maybe. Otherwise it's just silly. And this piece was so much more important than that."

"I appreciate how much you like the work, but that's what I intended."

"No it's not." I dropped the smile. "You can't just paint one thing and say it's something else. I mean, are you blind? The painting's of a girl alone in a crowd."

"You know what," she said, still balancing the coffee, the burning cigarette, and the fucking phone, which, I now suspected, was where she was getting her stupid ideas from. "The painting is sold anyway, so I'm glad you like it, but the subject is closed." She returned to her phone call.

A growing intestinal discomfort suddenly bordered on excruciating, clearly the price of my dishonesty. I respected her work, but her description was false, and in trying to spare her feelings, I was being deceitful. Looking at her recent offering of paintings, I felt I owed it to her to be straightforward. "You should stick with realism because then you might accidentally stumble over greatness, whereas these abstractions were boring fifty years ago when they were first done."

"Screw you!" she shot back, instead of thanking me.

I left her smelly grotto and headed down the urine-stenched hallway and out of the old building. I didn't like people closing subjects on me, especially when the subjects were still wide open.

As I waited on the corner for Bethsheba, I knew I had been a major pomo snob. But I was sick of painting art for a class of people I despised; fed up with musty lofts that I'd never be able to afford; burnt out with being a deluded, lonely artist; and pissed that I was sentenced to an impoverished career choice that I made as a traumatized thirteen-year-old.

Just as I decided to tell Bethsheba that I was depressed, she turned the corner and who did she have in tow but Gunter the professionally despondent German, who on this sunniest of autumn days was wearing a black rain coat.

"Look who decided to give the studio a break and join us," Bethsheba said delightedly.

I responded with a sarcastic expression of joy.

"So how did things go with lady love?" she asked.

"The lady didn't know what she was talking about," I explained. "She thought her piece was about excitement in the big city."

"What's wrong with that?"

"There is nothing exciting about living in the big fucking city. And the emotion she was going for was so obvious."

"Are you kidding?"

"No," I replied with righteous indignation, "and I know that I sound ridiculous, but the only thing I'm serious about is art."

"Thank you, Sister Wendy," she concluded, and turned happily toward Germany. "So, Gunter, you've been indoors all day, what do you want to see, hon?"

"It's all the same stuff, isn't it?" he uttered. Hearing modern art was boring was becoming boring.

Without saying another word, Bethsheba slowly headed off. Her iron will and boundless drive to visually conquer all things suddenly snapped. Germany and I followed. Tiredly the three of us dragged ourselves down the street and up into the first distressed warehouse. This time, instead of merrily dashing through, we simply rooted around the ground floor for whatever unfinished plastic cups of wine remained on the courtesy tables. Like an itinerant group of alcoholics we swilled as much down as possible. Then, without even pretending to look at the walls, we'd go to the next space with an uncapped liquor bottle.

"You know, something else," I said to Bethsheba, when my silent train of bitter thought finally emerged from the tunnel of my angry brain, "She really was wasting her time doing those large rhombus ex-splactions."

"What's a large rhombus ex-splaction?" Gunter asked.

"I said, large canvas abstractions," I corrected him.

"Who was what now?" Beth asked, looking at a monstrous photo of a chicken salad sandwich.

"That Adele creature."

In a few minutes, the three of us walked out of the studio and into a large gallery space in the lobby that was covered with amusing needlepoint art of bloody and tragic crime scenes.

"How ironic," Beth said facetiously. "I always feel that that's all the artist wants me to say. So I'll say it—How ironic!"

"I don't give a shit what you say," a gruff guy in his fifties spoke up behind us—the artist. He stormed out of the gallery.

"Oops," she replied. A few minutes of contrite silence passed.

"Beth!" A voice suddenly fell like an arrow from the blue skies. Bear Smegka, a potentially handsome Pakistani video artist, was suddenly hugging little Beth.

As Beth and Bear wrestled, I perused some of the violent needle-point. Gunter stood next to Beth like an obedient attack dog as she talked to Bear.

"So what have you been up to lately?" I heard Bethsheba ask.

"One of my videos is on display next door," he replied. "Oh! We've got to see it!" Bethsheba said, instantly recharged with enthusiasm. She clicked her fingers at me, grabbed Gunter by his blackness, and the three of us hustled a few doors down into another alcohol-free gallery space. Bright letters announced, "A Reptilian's Political Response in a Human Construct."

We all squeezed side by side into a bright red, beanbag sofa in the dark claustrophobic room watching a video projector showing a film of ping-pong balls being shot at an unimpressed boa constrictor—Smegka's latest offering. Although I thought of the piece as an interesting statement of how so many contemporary artists assault the public with their annoying work, I really just felt bad for the snake.

We slowly sunk into the beanbag, and I got the sensation that we were castaways on a tight red life raft meant for two. Another smaller beanbag chair suddenly became available, so I hopped our boat and sunk comfortably into the single seat. The cheap wine had given me a frontal-lobe headache. I closed my eyes, tried to visualize warmer parts of the world, and drifted through the pain.

"Did you actually tell Adele that?" Beth shocked me back into the moment.

"What?"

"Did you really tell her that?" she repeated from between Gunter, who was at her left, and Bear, who was entranced by his own work, seated at her right.

It took me a moment to realize that Beth was referring to my comment about Adele wasting her time with abstractions. "Actually I probably didn't frame it constructively."

"How'd you frame it?" she asked, while Smegka squeezed Beth as though the monotonous video were coming to some exciting climax. Gunter, not to be knocked out of competition, took Beth's hand in his own bony one.

"First, we argued about the nature of the little girl's expression in her painting," I said in a hushed tone.

"Wasn't this about finding love?" she asked quite simply.

"I'm here on a date with you," I said to champion my point. "This is about art."

"Oh, you sweet dear," Beth said, bouncing up to her feet. Smegka and Gunter inadvertently bumped together in her sudden void. Beth plunked down in my lap, hugged me, and gave me a big warm kiss on the mouth. I kissed her back, and looking at the two artists who I now thought of as rival suitors, I saw a montage of veiled Indo-European contempt. Bethsheba decided it was time to go.

She talked at me as all walked out the door and up the big hill. It was at that moment that I faced the fact that I was locked in a strange contest of Sex Survivor. In a little while, we were down the subway steps. Without missing a beat, all three of us guys took out our Metro-cards and swiped our way in. Then we walked four abreast, down the long slow incline toward the F train. As we reached the platform, though, while Bethsheba still chided me about something, I realized that my impulse to beat out the other two guys was stronger than any desire to really have sex with Beth. As I considered this, I remembered that since leaving Adele's studio, what I really wanted was to be alone.

We were going to Jay Street to transfer to the C train to Beth's place in Fort Greene, but when I felt a wind rising and turned around, I saw a slanting ray of light reflecting off the curving rail. The Manhattan-bound train was on its way.

"I hope you guys won't be offended if I just head home."

"It's okay with me," Bear replied eagerly. Gunter shrugged his sheer shoulders.

"No!" Beth exclaimed in genuine sorrow. I gave her a peck on the cheek and promised I'd give her a call.

"You sure you don't want to come over?" she whispered nervously.

"Thanks, but I'm really pooped," I replied honestly and in a moment I stepped aboard my clunky chariot to Chinatown. The sub-way doors slid shut and I was heading home, one stop away. I really did feel rundown and had my fill of Beth for the week. Let some other artists have their shot at her sweaty lederhosen. I wasn't sure if she was using me to make them jealous, or vice versa. I just didn't care.

Fourteen

By the time I got home, I felt gaseous and nauseous from all the cheap wine and finger food. Lynn was there working on one of her parades. I knew better than to interrupt her. I froze upon my hard bed like a rat in a glue trap and squirmed into sleep.

A couple of hours later, when I awoke, Lynn was washing her brushes and cleaning up. It was night but it didn't seem late.

"So how was Dumbo?" She remembered my plans that day.

"Man, I'd die for a space there," I commented, splashing water onto my face.

"Me too," she replied, still whipping the water out of her brushes. "We were just born too late, about twenty years after they gave away all the apartments in this city." She paused a moment and asked, "What's with that guy who lives down the hall?"

"Who?"

"That Mandarin turkey, I think I saw him with some Chinese immigrant girls."

"Oh, Don Juan from Hong Kong. What about him?"

"He was yelling at some poor girl in the hall. She looked bruised and when I asked if everything was all right, he just gave me this sleazy look."

"Lovers' spats are the worst. Want to join me for dinner?"

"I got to work tonight," she said as she put on her coat. I walked her out and stopped in the bar just as Pablo was leaving with his new blond soul mate.

"Hey, Or, what are you doing Halloween night?" he asked.

"No plans, whatd'ya got?"

"Reverend Billy's walking up Sixth Avenue protesting NYU's destruction of Edgar Allan Poe's house, which they're making into a bullshit classroom or something. Want to march?"

"Let me think about it," I replied tiredly.

I went around the corner to Mekong Delta, where Lynn was bagging cartons, and I ordered my Buddha Delight.

"So how's the weather upstairs?" she kidded. A couple of patrons ordered some food before I could think of a witty rejoinder. I sat at the window and looked at cars passing in the night and found myself worrying about Rita.

"Hey, cowboy," Lynn replied after a lull in the ordering. "You eating here, or back at the Ponderosa?"

"Here, I guess."

Instead of putting the food on a Styrofoam dish like they usually did, she placed the rice and steamy vegetation on a porcelain plate. Somehow I sensed that it was her own.

She brought it over to me along with a glass of chilled water. It had been so long since I had experienced an abrupt act of kindness even from someone I knew that it left me feeling embarrassed.

She served more people as I chewed down my chow. When I was nearing the bottom of the dish, she asked if I wanted more. I thanked her and told her I was fine.

"So you're going home to paint now?"

"I suppose," I replied, and perhaps due to my constant compulsion to subvert everything good, I said, "You don't like my big mural, do you?"

"Why do you say that?"

"You turned the piece around."

"I didn't . . . I mean . . ."

"It's okay if you don't like my painting. I just never hated a painting so much that I had to turn it around."

"It's not what you think. It's a powerful work," she replied, but said nothing else.

I really wanted to know why she had flipped it about-face, but it wasn't fair to pester her at work. I thanked her for everything and hoping to part on a positive note, I asked, "Are you planning on painting the Halloween Parade?"

"Absolutely."

"A friend of mine just asked if I wanted to join a group that's marching. Would you like to see a parade from the inside?"

"That'd be interesting," she replied. "I actually get really nervous in crowds so it'd be great to go with someone and—"

A young couple interrupted her, ordering a General Tso's Chicken to go. I quietly slipped out and went back upstairs. As I reached my landing, I saw Don Juan back in the hall with his latest conquest, just as Lynn had described. He yelled something angrily in Chinese to the poor girl. She was weeping furiously. When I approached, he sighed in disgust and looked away. She muttered something in Chinese to me as I passed. When I closed the door to the loft, I heard him screaming at her again.

I had once made the mistake of getting involved in a domestic squabble. I ended up being attacked by both the guy and girl.

As soon as I flipped on the light, the portrait of Rita was there for me, awaiting completion. To look at the same work day in, day out, to be God of the Piece and try to constantly find something new and exciting, was unbelievably exhausting. Though I felt energetic, I was creatively fatigued regarding the Rita mural tonight.

I spent my nervous energy rooting around in the rear of Shade's studio, through forty years of detritus: art magazines; old, hardened brushes; half-coiled, dried-out tubes of paints. Eventually I came across an old canvas tool bag. Inside were stonecutting tools, specifically calipers, chisels, a mallet, some rusty files and wedges. It was there I also located a thought—a remote possibility.

I grabbed a flashlight, a piece of yellow chalk, and a measuring tape, and went out the door and down the steps to the dark, outdoor stairwell. The small stone monolith sat on the bottom landing. For a gleaming, shining instant I had a brilliant idea. It was a scheme that could pay off my parking-ticket debt and finally get me Cali's Ram van 2900. I had only sculpted two small items in my life: a cat that my mother used as a door stop and a train spike that I sold at my second solo exhibit. I wasn't sure what Persephone's client wanted, but I felt pretty confident that I could sculpt something the size of a headstone.

It was late, yet I felt too restless to go to sleep and too fed up with painting to paint. I went downstairs and peeked into the bar. Cali was alone at a table. I didn't have the energy to give an uplifting talk, so I went on a walk instead. Slowly I realized I was looking for the dirty-winged angel, Rita. I ended up twisting east to Avenue C and past the Harm Reduction Center on Avenue C and Third. I dipped into a nearby bodega and got a cup of sugary Lipton's tea. Leaning against a car, I posted myself outside the closed outreach clinic just in case she might pass by. After midnight I started getting chilly, so I headed home.

The next day, Lynn woke me by coming in early. She was eager to finish her latest scroll. It was rainy and gray outside. I took a cold shower, dressed, and before heading out for breakfast, I called Persephone at her Williamsburg gallery.

"You didn't commission someone to sculpt the headstone, did you?"

"I contacted two sculptors I knew, but neither seemed to think the project paid enough."

"That doesn't sound good."

"Why are you asking?"

"I was thinking of doing it."

"Well, frankly, one of the guys said that the amount of money Moe was offering was too little to cover the price of the stone, not to mention the cost of transportation."

"Does the stone have to be marble?" The rock I had looked like white granite or alabaster.

"I don't know," Persephone replied.

"You don't know how much he is offering, do you?"

"No, but I'll give you Moe's number. My . . ." She caught herself.

"Your what?"

"I was going to tell you my commission, but since your work was damaged here and he doesn't sound like he's paying much I'll waive it." She gave me his name—Morton Hammerman, and his 212 number.

I went out and fortified myself with dim sum and coffee, then came home and made the call. I got his answering machine. "Persephone told me that you were interested in having a small statue cut for a headstone."

Someone picked up and a low baritone voice asked, "Who is this?"

"My name is Orloff Trenchant. My friends call me Or."

"What the hell kind of name is that?" he asked just above a hush.

"Or's Russian, but my last name is actually Trencharian, I'm Armenian."

"A very sad yet enterprising people." Spare me the sympathy, I thought. He went on softly, "So tell me a bit about yourself, Or."

I reviewed my artistic training, my shows, my reviews, and my various art projects. His rugged tone made him sound powerful. The fact that he talked in a whisper made me picture him in a boardroom, where he didn't want to disturb the sacred process of making money.

When I began asking my list of questions, he said, "Look, I'm having a Halloween get-together tonight. Why don't you come by around eight? We'll talk." He sounded affable enough. He gave me an address up on Eighty-first and East End. He added, "Dress casually," as if I had a choice.

Despite an early morning rain that sent a lot of booksellers scurrying up to a big book sale in Yonkers, I set up in front of Shimkin Hall. The sky was the same color as the pavement. Maybe because I didn't try to do any sketching and painting, I was rewarded by selling a lot of crappy books. By five, I topped two hundred dollars and completely exhausted the best of my selection.

On my way home, I headed up to Sculptor Garden, a sculpture supply store, on 12th between First and Avenue A, and asked the proprietor what kind of stones he carried.

"Marble and alabaster, both from Italy."

"How much are they per pound?"

"Buck fifty."

"What sizes do you carry?"

"We have pieces that go up to about seventy to eighty pounds here. After that we have stones in excess of a thousand pounds in our Jersey warehouse." I thanked him and was back home in twenty minutes.

Taking a mallet and chisel, I went downstairs and whacked off a slight chip from the corner of the monolith. The rock was actually a lot more malleable than I had anticipated.

Back upstairs, I showered and put on my gallery-opening outfit. Then I headed to a basement barbershop on East Broadway whose patrons consisted entirely of Chinese illegals. For five bucks the barber sculpted the zillion kinky strands of my black mop into a tight little crown with a slight china-bowl roundness to it.

Then I made the mistake of catching the First Avenue bus, the slowest boat out of Chinatown. An elevated train used to shoot up the Avenue but to our great loss, the city tore it down. The West Side still has trains up Sixth, Seventh, and Eighth Avenues, while the East Side only has the trusty Lexington Avenue line. For years the city had been threatening to finish the Second Avenue train. Until that line was complete, I advocated to my fellow Lower East Siders to withhold taxes for lack of equal services.

Fifteen

When I finally arrived at 81st Street and East End it was late. After being announced by the doorman, I found myself in the elevator with a group of well-dressed strangers all going to the same party. As soon as we got to the 25th floor, we were greeted by a coat-check chick who had an aluminum rack set up in the hallway. I surrendered my jacket and went inside. It was a palatial penthouse. For the first time, as I stepped into this glamorous apartment, it fearfully occurred to me that I might meet Barclay and June. Once inside, though, among the cellularized and Palm Piloted, I realized I was safe. A few decorative pumpkins, strange squash, and other inedible vegetables signified both the autumnal holiday and the crowd.

One or two people wore Halloween masks, but they were all well dressed. Solids mingled with striped suits. Armanis with Diors. An integrated jazz quartet played unobtrusively in a corner. The average man was in his mid-fifties and paunchy; the typical woman was in her late twenties and slim.

There's nothing wrong with people having money. What bothered me were those who believed that capricious upsurges of the market made them more valuable as human beings. This was at the core of my disdain for dealers, collectors, and the rich in general.

Slowly, among drinks and chatter, I located my would-be savior and probable adversary. Morton was a small, middle-aged man with tinted glasses, coarse dermabraded facial skin, and a big alligator jaw. As I stepped closer, I could hear a deep, cigarette-graveled voice. He popped down unsalted almonds like Vicodin and took gigantic gulps of unmixed alcohol as he laughed deep from his belly. I sidled up closer to study my opponent. He didn't so much as notice me—but no one could miss his lewd language, vulgar mannerisms, and self-assured tone. He was a serious drinker, and I figured that if I waited until he was a bit drunk I could squeeze the best deal out of him.

His stunning wife appeared wearing a gauzy white shirt without a bra. Her pendulous breasts and brown nipples were just visible. All such a cliché, but what else should I have expected?

A long, narrow balcony wrapped outside of the suite, and I realized that the building was directly above the FDR Drive. He could actually drop a fishing line out his bedroom window into the East River and compete for the same toxic fish as the Latin fishermen from the Lower East Side. From that majestic height, which no one making less than a million a year could even hope to see, the city looked wonderful, as if it was strung in colorless Christmas lights all year round. I filled a glass with the most expensive single malt whiskey that had the most unpronounceable, porridge-eating, kilt-wearing Scottish name, and gazed out over Brooklyn and Queens.

Cars were lined up in slow, bumper-to-bumper ascent over the 59th Street Bridge while planes were cued up in slow descent over the eastern sky. They were probably no higher than four thousand feet as they approached Bensonhurst, two thousand feet by Park Slope, until they roared within meatball-flinging distance over the deafened immigrants of Jackson Heights and Flushing, Queens, to land at LaGuardia. Although I was never a very good vista painter, I would have loved to have had a wide canvas on hand. When a crew of moneymakers saw me enjoying the view all alone on the balcony, they had to steal away my tranquility. High and giggly, they all poured out in the same way they had rushed into the East Village after people like me proved it liveable. I retreated back inside.

Finally, when I had gobbled down as much free sushi and chocolate-covered almonds as I could handle, I decided to meet the master. He too had ingested as much alcohol as his engine room could hold, and was listing slightly to the right.

"Morton." I finally stepped forward. "I'm Or Trenchant." I offered a handshake.

"Crazy-ass name." He shook my hand and smiled. "Grab to meetcha."

"I'm the sculptor that Persephone Miller recommended."

"Right, call me Moe." He was more sober than I thought.

"Let's go somewhere we can talk." He led me into his large kitchen, where tuxedoed caterers were transferring precooked food onto metal steamer trays.

"Here's the deal," he began. "One of my partners died of leukemia about five months ago. I loved the guy. He owned three glatt kosher Chinese restaurants. Two on the North Shore, one on the Upper West Side. After all the food he made, I want to give him a monument that immortalizes his work."

155

"Did you have some kind of shape in mind?"

"I was considering a large fortune cookie."

"It's an interesting shape, but people will laugh when they see it."

"Yeah, see I don't want that." He scratched his head uncertainly.

Looking around the room at the white formica counter, I watched as a caterer popped open a large carton and placed a pile of vegetable dumplings into a steamer tray.

"What about chopsticks?" he asked.

"You need a subtler shape," I replied, and held up the empty Chinese takeout carton by its little wire handle. It looked to be about five inches tall.

"How about something maybe five times this size?"

"How about ten times that?" he countered.

"I can't," I replied. "Five times is the best I can do, about two by two cubic feet." I didn't want to tell him, but the real limit to the sculpture wasn't the piece or the time it took. The reason I decided on two cubic feet was because the weight of alabaster is 145 pounds per cubic foot. Three cubic feet—which was what he wanted—would come out weighing more than I could ever haul.

Even at one ton, this was incredibly heavy, but I figured I actually had a chance of fitting this into my van and slowly driving it out to Long Island.

"Five times, huh?" He seemed amused by the arbitrary choice of five.

"It really is the biggest I can make it."

Looking at the carton, he decided, "This is actually perfect. When you think of Chinese takeout, you don't think of a real meal, you think of food on the run. Just something to kill the hunger. And you probably heard the expression about Chinese food, you're hungry twenty minutes later. But this guy took this throwaway item, this low-expectation fast food crap, and elevated it to something subliminal."

The word he meant was sublime but I didn't correct him.

"I mean, kosher Chinese food is usually an insult to both Chinese and Jewish cooking, but he did amazing, inventive things with it, shaping tofu into pork and so on. He always ranked top scores with Zagat's. And that's what I want to honor, not just the man, but the idea of what he did, taking the unexpected—the disposable—and turning it into high art."

"I'd be honored to sculpt his headstone," I replied earnestly, "but I don't know about the lettering and dates."

"Fuck lettering and dates. He had a Star of David in his heart. Anyone who visited him knew that. He didn't like strangers. He had no illusions about immortality. He was the guy who made Chinese food."

"You should check with the cemetery about restrictions on unconventional headstones."

"I already talked with them. They know I'm giving them something out of left field, but I'll make sure they're fine with it. My friend died before his time and I need to commemorate him."

"How do you feel about leaving the piece rough-hewn instead of smooth?" I asked, knowing how time-consuming the polishing process was. To lubricate my suggestion, I added, "In his sculptures in the Medici Chapel, Michelangelo used rough-hewn to illustrate lives unfinished."

"I like that. But five times seems a little small," he said with sudden second thoughts. "He was such a great guy."

"Then if I built a Chinese carton the size of the pyramids it'd probably be too small."

"That's true."

"And take a look at that carton." I held it up for him. "It's huge."

"Let's do it."

"How much are we doing it for?"

"The money is simple, four grand. Not a cent more."

My parking-ticket debt alone was at least a grand. Cali's Ram van was another three grand. I needed at least six thousand to turn my life around.

"Persephone said she referred you to several sculptors already and they all turned you down."

"Right, and they didn't even have a shape."

"Look, marble costs about a buck fifty a pound. You can call a couple of headstone showrooms and you'll see that this would run you at least three times what you're offering."

He put on a wide, soft smile to show that I was no match for his negotiating flair. Despite all his glaring wealth, he couldn't repress his sporting urge to lowball me on his important tombstone. But I kind of liked him anyway. Once a businessman, always a businessman.

"Here," I continued, and held out the sample chunk of stone for him. He looked at it as though it were a diamond. "This is my offer. Instead of marble, I'll cut the piece in that stone. It's alabaster. I'll even drop it off at the cemetery but I can't do it for a cent less than seven thousand dollars. When you realize you can't get it for less than that, give me a call."

He let out a long sigh and said, "I'll give you six grand if you can have it ready in about three weeks. That's the date of the unveiling."

"About three weeks," I repeated.

In the contractual grasp of his solid handshake, the notion that I was going to have a new van with no ticket debt felt like a new lease on life. But if I had only about three weeks I had to start tonight.

We agreed to talk more during the week, but right now he had to entertain the wealthy and I had to go. As he moved in one direction I slinked back through the crowd, hitting the food trays one last time. Under the indignant eyes of some pompous bastards, I carefully rolled up one pocketful of shrimp, another pocketful of chocolate nuts, and my last blazing glass of single malt. Then out the door. Waiting for the bus, I thought about the vast job that lay ahead and wondered if I could really pull it off.

◆ ◆ ◆

DAYS LATER, OR SO IT SEEMED, when the bus eventually screeched up against the filthy shores of Canal Street, I had gobbled down the pocketful of shrimp and most of the nuts. As I passed by the bar, I spotted Pablo and went in.

"Hey! You still marching in the Halloween Parade?" he shouted out.

"Oh yeah. Protesting NYU tearing down the Poe house."

"Actually, if you want to do that I'll put you in touch with Reverend Billy, but the fact is I'm marching with the Nader people."

"If Bush wins the presidency because of the difference in votes that went to Nader, won't you feel like an idiot?" I asked as I took a seat.

"Reverend Billy is meeting with his group on Spring and Church around seven," Pablo replied, ignoring my comment.

I told him about the sculpture commission and bought him a drink. He talked a bit about his latest girlfriend, who was apparently Croatian.

"What do you do, hang out at rallies for women from beleaguered countries?" His last girlfriend, Twit or Tirt, was from Tibet.

"Actually that's not far from the truth." He said he snagged his last two girlfriends at WBAI parties. WBAI was an infamous radio station that constantly supported left and lost causes. Lately they themselves had turned into a lost cause. Their parent network, which was only moderately leftist, was about to purge them. Without intending to, I started giggling drunkenly.

I thought he was going to get angry, but he started laughing as well. In addition to all the scotch at Moe Hammerman's party, I gulped down four more whiskeys.

Up the stairs, key in lock, turn, and inside. I sat on the edge of my bed and thought about taking off my shoes. Then I contemplated taking a pee, but I lay down a second and fell asleep. The next morning, I should have woken up early, but I slept until early afternoon, when Lynn opened the door. I got up slowly with a hint of a hangover as she banged around.

"Tonight's Halloween," I mentioned.

"Oh, right," she replied, brushes in hand in the middle of one of her fabulous scrolls.

"We're going, right?" I confirmed.

"Going where?"

"We're marching in protest to NYU's tearing down Edgar Allan Poe's haunted house."

"Would you mind if I passed?" she asked without even looking at me, or for that matter putting down her brush.

"Don't you want to see it?"

"I'm working tonight," she said with her back toward me. "I can catch some of it on TV."

"Do what you want," I said, not hiding my disappointment. I didn't like being shrugged off. "It's your art that will suffer."

"Do you experience every action your subjects do?" She asked defensively.

"If I can—sure."

"How righteous!"

"I just thought you could have an interesting view of this parade, so your paintings don't look like they've all been lifted from newspaper photos, and frankly, we had a date," I replied. Finding my toothbrush, I started brushing the post-alcoholic taste out of my mouth.

"I'm not trying to duck out of a date. I just have some difficulty with going to parades."

"Haven't you been going to parades all year?" I replied, with toothpaste foaming from my lips.

"Not since the summer."

"Well that's pathetic. If this city has nothing else, it has parades."

She quietly rummaged through a variety of smaller scrolls I hadn't seen before. One of them was of the thankless army of sanitation workers who wait at the end of every parade to sweep the streets afterward. Another parade, in blue and white, was Greek Independence Day. The green one was of course, Saint Patty's Day, but instead of showing the marchers there were a bunch of drunken spectators. Finally she held up a black scroll. "Do you know what this is?"

I remembered this one when I first saw the others. It was a perfect square of black paint.

"I give up."

"This was the last parade I went to, I covered it over—it's Puerto Rican Day." I stopped brushing and saw her looking out the window. "It wasn't that bad. Fifty-three women were attacked that day and hearing their stories . . . I actually got off pretty easy. I've had problems with parades and crowds ever since."

"And I guess my painting didn't help." She was right in front of my portrait of Rita, the mural of the girl being besieged by hands.

"It's a good painting," she replied, smiling. "It might even be great, but it's a little more than I can handle right now."

"I'm sorry."

"No, you're right. This is a classic case of the cocksuckers winning if I have to change my life even one little iota."

"I'll be there with you," I told her. "And I swear I'd kill anyone if they try anything."

"All right."

I saw her tighten her jaw. A slight gloss came to her eye, then she nodded and said, "What time are we doing this?"

"We can meet here at six thirty and walk over by seven."

She went back to her painting. I collected Shade's canvas bag of stonecutting tools. In it was an old Bosch cut-off saw with a fourteen-inch abrasive blade. It weighed about thirty pounds and picking it up required both hands. It was not going to be easy to operate. I also found goggles and a torn pair of canvas gloves.

I connected every extension cord I could find. The nearest outlet to the stone was next to Don Juan's apartment. I snaked the wires down the hall and out the door and plugged the saw in. When I turned it on, I heard painful grinding and a red dust plumed out of the side. The cogs and gears sounded completely dry and rusted—it needed lubricant. I also lacked a face mask, so I dashed around the corner and bought a box of masks, a can of oil, and a tiny screwdriver at the lumberyard on Division.

Using calipers, I was able to quickly estimate the proportions of the statue, marking the cuts right onto the rock, minus a quarter-inch margin to file down.

I carefully opened the taped-up plastic covering of the saw. Cleaning out the dirt and cobwebs, I then oiled every cog and gear that I could. I pulled the saw's trigger; it buzzed and the lubrication spread throughout. Then I slipped on the gloves, pulled the goggles down, and tucked my face mask over my mouth and nose. I lined up the blade and pulled the trigger. The blade slowly cut into the rock, sending up a steady cloud of thick, white dust.

Toward three o'clock, pausing to wipe my brow, I looked up and noticed some immigrants perched in the courtyard windows, taking mini-breaks from their garment machines, smoking cigarettes, and watching the sculptor in the outer stairwell.

Gradually the length of time between my own rests became shorter and the breaks stretched longer. By six P.M. the sun had set and I realized that if I was going to the Halloween Parade with Lynn, I had to get ready. I was too exhausted to do any more. This was the first day of work and I hadn't even succeeded in cutting down one side.

Sixteen

I tiredly dragged my ass upstairs and collapsed on the bed for about ten minutes. Lynn was painting energetically, bantering on about the history of scrolls. Before I drifted off I heard her saying that the earliest written works were in scroll form.

"We're going to be late!" she yelled, waking me. I jumped to my feet and tossed my sweat-dried carcass into the shower, washing the alabaster dust out of my hair and ears.

As I toweled off and dressed, Lynn was still working on her Mermaid Parade scroll. Voluptuous Brooklyn girls were riding on the hoods of muscle cars surrounded by burly Bensonhurst boys in greasy pompadours. She was doing final touch up, and though we had to get going, I couldn't take my eyes off her paintings. They were done in watercolor but they looked like acrylic.

"Are you hungry?" I asked, starved myself.

"Not really, but let's get something because I know that I will be."

She grabbed a flash camera and we headed downstairs. I thoughtlessly herded her toward the takeout joint.

"There is no way I'm going to eat there on my day off," she said, stopping me.

We ended up going to a deli on Grand and Mulberry called the Italian Food Center where we waited on a long line with yuppies before we each finally ordered Italian cold-cut sandwiches with snazzy names. I got the "Mona Lisa," prosciutto on a semolina roll with red peppers, and a bottle of Orangina. We walked up the block around the corner to Cleveland and Kenmore, where we came to Lieutenant Petrosino Park. This strange gated triangle had neither benches, trees, nor a statue. We sat on the filthy white stone surrounding the square and ate our sandwiches under the faint orange glow of streetlights. We were both pretty zonked from our day of work, so other than intermittent grunts, there wasn't a lot of deep conversation. I gobbled my sandwich down in five monster bites. She opened up her roll and nibbled on a few select slices of roasted red peppers, but she didn't care for the rest. She was about to toss it when I asked if she'd mind. She surrendered it. Three bites later the sandwich was no more.

As we headed west, the crowd thickened, mostly with out-of-towners. Though I hated falling back on New York memories, it was difficult not to be nostalgic. Back in the late '70s and early '80s, the Halloween Parade, like so many little local events, was both quaint and more interesting. Like the Wigstock festival, it had started out as a drag event, an opportunity for queens to strut and promenade.

That seemed like a lifetime ago. Two guys were dressed in baseball outfits. One wore a Bronx Bomber jersey, the other a Mets shirt. A girl dressed as "The Flushing Line" was in a rectangular box painted like a train. She hugged the Yankee ballplayer—a statement on the Yankees winning the subway series less than a week earlier. That was typical: young lookalike whites cleverly worked in packs developing some topical, droll theme. There were also a lot of tacky advertisements. A variety of floats publicized pop radio stations and hyped, failing dot-com companies. Amid this ruckus of crass commercialism, Lynn and I spotted Reverend Billy and his slim gathering of antiestablishmentarians.

Reverend Billy was a recent local celebrity who as best I could tell took up preservationist causes. His biggest crusade to date had been against the corporate evils of Starbucks. Although I was pretty certain he wasn't a real minister, he had adopted a mock-evangelical style. Along with a flock of followers he would go into one of the hundred-plus coffee franchises in the city, pull out a megaphone, and do a stand-up rift against the corporate coffee octopus.

Lynn and I introduced ourselves to his group, and we were graciously accepted into the fold—the last members of a dying breed of hippie activists. Someone passed us plastic masks with long beaks. Everyone except us was dressed in raven black.

"Nevermore," muttered Lynn.

"Raven copyright 1840," I joked, guessing at the date of the poem. We strapped the black beaks over our faces and were handed signs. Mine said, "NYU Sucks!" Hers read, "Save the Poe House."

More people packed into the parade's staging area south of Houston on Sixth Avenue. Various flatbed trucks filled with dancers, musicians, and performers were idling, waiting for the parade to commence. Finally it started. As we marched up the Avenue of the Americas, I was surprised to see how many people lined the streets. Lynn periodically handed me her sign and snapped photos when she'd spot an interesting clump of spectators. Together we kept up with Reverend Billy and his group who would periodically shout out, "Save the Poe House!"

In this illiterate age, I doubted whether most people knew who Poe was, but even if they did know, they probably thought we were saying, "Save the Poor House!" So I tried spelling it out a bit by clearly stating our case, "NYU is turning Edgar Allan Poe's home into a date-raping frathouse!"

Hopefully, I was wrong, but I suspected that no one really cared. Together, as we marched, I'd notice publicity giveaways littering the parade route: plastic kazoos, small bags of M&Ms. I'd periodically scoop the crap up and toss them into the bordering crowds. Spectators always competed in catching them.

"Are you enjoying yourself?" I asked Lynn as we passed Twelfth Street.

"I'm just so glad that there's a big police presence," she replied. Several times we slowed down as the parade would bottleneck or we'd have to stop for traffic.

Finally, ten minutes later, as we approached Twentieth Street, we sensed that the parade was coming to an end.

"You know," she said to me softly, "my only regret is that I really didn't get to see more costumes."

"No problem," I replied, and grabbing her elbow, we broke off from our little political cell and turned around.

"What are we doing?" she asked nervously.

We were walking down the parade route. "We'll be able to see the parade behind us and still wind up downtown."

"God, I never thought of it this way," she said. All eyes were turned southward looking at the marchers coming up Sixth Avenue. "A parade is one-sided."

As if we were invisible, we walked against the floats, past the same huge crowds and details of cops at every corner. With camera held high, Lynn snapped away. Among the many costumes of the day were death row inmates about to be executed by presidential candidate George W. Bush, and a bevy of butchy Hillary Clintons who were running for senate. In one case a guy dressed and masked as her presidential husband was contritely behind her, on a leash.

The best of all, though, was the running vagina. Someone was elaborately costumed as a six-foot-tall female genitalia. He or she had a thick tuft of pubic hair triangled on their head, wide labia wings for arms, and several other anatomical details that were a complete mystery to me. The vagina raced past us uptown. Not far behind, it was being chased by a terrifying taller penis. It would have been a painful union if the monstrous gonads ever crossed.

"Do you think that vagina is a man or a woman?" I asked.

"A man," she imparted. "I saw a female in the penis."

As we pressed on, we also passed an unthematically costumed marching band complete with a group of camp followers wearing ghostly white paint on their faces who were passing out Nader flyers and Green Party stickers. Among these political zealots, I spotted Pablo with his blond Balkan bombshell.

Amid the screams and hollers and noise and people, we could only wave in passing. Pablo and his politicos pressed northward, and Lynn and I continued against the grain. When we reached Fourth Street, a vigilant cop finally stopped us and asked what we thought we were doing.

"Heading down to Spring," I explained, still wearing my Raven's beak mask.

The cop pulled us off of Sixth Avenue and shoved us behind the barricades. We were sucked up into a slow-moving crowd, which was making its way east. Lynn was clearly growing nervous. We broke out of the crush at MacDougal and Waverly, and she dashed off, running along the outer margin of the street between the parked and slowly moving cars into the relative emptiness of Washington Square Park. There I could see her taking deep controlled breaths. Exhausted, she came to a bench and took a seat. The panic slowly diminished from her eyes as she looked nervously at all things around her. I sat and let her just have some space.

Out of the darkness, an old black guy appeared. He seemed to be talking to himself. The park was still the last free zone in the Village where the cops let dealers deal, so I thought this clown was going to try to sell grass. I shook my head no, we didn't want any, but with smaller and smaller steps he timidly came closer.

Before I could say fuck off, he started singing. One of the many forms of homeless extortion was having to suffer through a pathetic Broadway show tune. I reached into my pocket to just give him the buck and be free of him, but it was too late. He was well into *Moon River*.

His voice was delicately ridged and softly textured. The more of it he sang the better he got and the more we liked it. Soon, no amount of sedatives or couch time could have soothed Lynn as he did. All I could afford to part with was four bucks, which I slipped into his hand.

He thanked us and left.

Lynn turned to me and asked, "Weren't you working on a painting of someone swimming Moon River?"

"Swimming the *East* River," I corrected.

"Did you give up on it?"

"I don't give up on anything, or few things anyway." It would be a lot safer to give up at times, like if you're dating a heroin addict, I thought.

"Obsessive-compulsive," she diagnosed.

Looking up Fifth Avenue from under the Washington Square Arch as we passed through the park, I added, "I am, about art anyway. I'd love to swim that river. If it doesn't kill me it'll make the art stronger."

"Last year, I was stronger . . ." she said in a remote voice. "It's the things we're not afraid of that wind up killing us."

"I can swim the river. I know I can," I replied.

"I was in the center of Central Park heading east at the time. It was a great day. There were all these people. I never felt safer. I didn't want to see the whole parade, just a glimpse of it. I had my camera. Even though it was a hot day, I had an overshirt and a T-shirt." She paused a minute and added, "And my bra."

"You don't have to go into this," I said, because I really didn't want to hear it.

"I reached that area just beyond the Rowboat Lake, where the café is?"

"I know it."

"Some young guy, a Latino, was walking past me, and he fucking warned me, he said, 'Lady you better not go down there. The guys are crazy down there.' He tried to tell me and I just ignored him. I couldn't imagine. Then the next thing I know, I'm walking past a group of guys and one is pouring water on my head and someone else is yelling, 'Chinese chick, Chinese chick.' I turned and started running away and I hear them chasing me, and suddenly this hand shoves me forward, knocking me down and another guy starts grabbing me, and then more water is pouring on me and some asshole is pulling at my shirt. I smacked him and another hand grabbed my shirt and yanked it right off. Then someone else grabbed my T-shirt." She pointed to her back collar.

"I was knocked to the ground and these two fucking animals are dragging me along the ground by my shirt." She paused. "I recently saw this show on the Nature Channel. A bunch of hyenas were fighting over a baby gazelle. And you could see they weren't fighting with the gazelle, they were fighting with *each other* over it. They fought over me like that. Like I wasn't even alive. There was some point when they weren't even ripping at my shirt, just tearing at it like a skin, trying to pull me from each other."

When she paused a moment, I could feel my consciousness retreating into the back of my skull and my heart beating in my ear.

". . . I started screaming for help and crying, trying to cover myself . . ." She suddenly shut down as if she blew a fuse.

About ten minutes of silence passed before she said, "I feel guilty

169

even mentioning it. I heard women describing so much worse that happened. The whole thing lasted just a few minutes. They didn't shove their fingers up into me. But the feeling of being fought over like that . . ." She shut down again. ". . . And all these people were around, men and women. . . . I feel so unsafe in crowds and . . . I fucking hate Latin men! I think Puerto Ricans are pigs who should all be killed."

As we headed down LaGuardia Place, I could have said how it was unfair to judge an entire people just because of a contemptible few, and that they might not have even been Puerto Rican, but I'm sure she knew all that. As an Armenian I wanted all Turks to die for brutally annihilating my people, stealing our ancient homeland, and just getting away with it. But this was really about inconsolable pain.

I gently put my arm around her as we reached Houston Street. We silently headed southeast, walking off the painful recollection.

Once we arrived at the loft, we sat on the bed and talked about the difficulties of the art world. She went on about her fear of missing the deadline for her show, which was only a few weeks away. Afterward, she had to leave for her trip to Vietnam.

"Why did you choose to go there?" I asked as I turned on a lamp.

"I don't even know how to explain it."

"Try."

"Isn't there some place in your life that you find mysterious, romantic, maybe even painful, an area where you sense a great and important truth is waiting for you?"

"Other than in my paintings, not really."

"It's getting late," she said after several minutes of silence. "I ought to be heading back to Flushing."

"Why don't you sleep here? You can take the bed, I'll sleep on the floor."

"No, I can't," she replied. "I actually have some family business early tomorrow. I'm not even sure I'll make it back here."

"Well," I replied tiredly, "I've got a van, I'll drive you."

"That's silly. I take the train every night. Besides, it's Friday. There are still a lot of people riding the subways."

"Look, if I don't take you home, I'll spend the entire night worrying that you didn't get there safely."

"I just hate for you to have to drive all the way across town for nothing."

"It's for my peace of mind."

"Suit yourself," she said, and together we headed out through the empty Chinatown streets.

I didn't tell her that I had to move the van anyway and once I was driving, it really didn't matter to me if I drove a block or a hundred miles.

As usual the bridge was always a concern, but once we were across we seemed to be going well. Soon we passed Shea Stadium and drove along the LIRR train trestle. Eventually, we arrived on Main Street, Flushing, Queens—the new Chinatown. With its abutting Indian and Korean communities it was actually more of an Asiatown. She pointed her way through the streets of the neighborhood until we finally pulled into a spot half a block down from her two-story stucco house.

"I really enjoyed marching in the parade tonight," she said with a wide smile.

"I'm glad."

"It gave me a great opportunity to do a scroll from the participant's point of view."

"Great."

"And I feel really safe with you, Or."

"Me too," I replied on autopilot. I was tired and just wanted to unload her and get to bed. She sat silently next to me.

"Well, have a good night," I said to cue her out of the van. But she didn't go and I couldn't throw her out so I sat and waited. After a few minutes, I gently leaned over toward her and gave her a peck on the cheek.

"Well, I better be going." She clicked into the moment with a completely flustered look on her face.

When I yawned to imply that I too was tired, I accidentally knocked her handbag over. Her keys, cash, lip gloss and a million other pieces of purse paraphernalia fell to the floor of the van. We fumbled through the darkness to retrieve everything. Afterward, she gave me a quick kiss on the cheek and with a click of the door and a few steps up the walkway, she was gone.

Starting my little rig, I looked down, and saw her lip gloss near the brake pedal. I picked it up, slipped it into my pocket, and began the long drive back.

After about a half an hour, the van seemed awake to the fact that I had taken it far outside its tight little circumference of comfort. Like an irascible old mule, it started going slow on the inclines, and by the time I hit the bridge we were going at a crawl. When we finally reached that dilapidated Queensborough Bridge, the engine started revving, and it dropped down to a solid fifteen miles an hour. Although there wasn't a lot of traffic, crazy cabbies and large private sedans with big red call numbers blasted their horns as they swerved around me.

The van seemed to sniff its own trail when we were back on the FDR. It actually picked up speed as we headed up the Houston Street ramp. I zoomed across Houston and down Essex, past Stanton and Rivington, hitting the greens all the way, while keeping an eye out for a parking space.

Seventeen

Just before I could beat the yellow across Delancey,
I saw her turn a corner. I swerved to a halt and backed up to a spot in
the middle of the block, in front of a hydrant. I pulled the key out and
dashed around the corner.

She was moving east on Delancey like a heat-seeking missile. A
young beauty all alone on an empty street with only intermittent cars
sliding down from the Williamsburg Bridge. Her hair was shaved back
to a quarter-inch bristle, like an angry halo. As I walked up loudly
behind her, she didn't so much as turn around. I could have been Jack
the Ripper. She just didn't care.

"Looking for drugs or someone to buy them for you?" I asked. No response. I dashed up so I was walking alongside of her, and there I noticed big dark bruises on her right cheek. "Oh shit!"

"Oh shit yourself. It's And/Or—Indecision man," she returned to her riff on my name.

"What the fuck happened to you?"

"I was going to ask you." She kept walking in a rush.

"Where the hell are you going?" I asked. It was three in the morning. A gypsy cab slowed to see if we needed a ride. The only thing open was a corner bodega a few blocks away.

"To die to sleep."

"Don't you live the other way?"

"Not tonight. My boyfriend and I got into a bit of a tussle."

"He hit you?"

"No."

"So where are you going?" I asked nervously.

"Relax, I got my medicine. In about an hour, I'm shooting half a bag," she said quietly, still huffing.

"So exactly how much do you shoot anyway?"

She pulled out two small plastic bags. "I'm down to about four bags a day, which is nothing."

"What does nothing cost?"

"Each one is about ten bucks."

"So you have a forty-dollar-a-day habit," I clarified.

"Let's see, ten dollars a bag, times four is forty, and I suppose what I have is popularly known as a habit, so, oh my God!" She feigned a shocked Valley Girl. "I *totally* have a forty-dollar-a-day drug habit!"

"Can you handle that?"

"You know, it's actually perfect," she said. "I used to be up to a hundred and twenty. If I can stay at forty dollars, I can probably even hold a job at Starfucks."

"Aren't you high all the time?"

"Not anymore."

"So then why do you do it?"

"Just to keep from being sick. If I want to get high I'll do an occasional speedball. Whatever."

"Where are you going now?" I asked, as I was having trouble keeping up with her.

"Meeting a friend."

"Maybe the friend is me."

"Maybe," she said with a smile.

We walked for about a minute in silence before I asked, "So you said you used to be a writer?"

"I never said that but coincidentally I am an important young poet."

"So let's hear some," I asked, uncertain if she was kidding.

"Sure, let's see." She looked up. "'To be or not to be.'" She paused a moment, looking at me. "'Not to be.'"

"Anything else?"

"Tomorrow and tomorrow and tomorrow / I shoot in this tired arm from day to day / till the last hypodermic full of recorded time." She smiled and added, "See, you have to understand that Tomorrow was the name of a popular brand of heroin many moons ago." She paused. "And actually I can't find a vein in my arm anymore."

"Anything else?"

"What a piece of shit is a man / How horny with reasons / How infinite in big-ass cars / In form and movement the cocksuckers haggle for twenty-dollar blow jobs."

"Isn't that Shakespeare?" I finally asked.

"It's crack-whore Shakespeare, but I don't smoke crack, and I'm not a whore so . . ."

"Can we sit down?" I asked as we crossed Allen. I was breaking into a sweat.

We took refuge on the traffic island on Allen. She sat on a broken concrete bench. I sat next to her.

175

"Got a cigarette?" she asked.

"Don't smoke."

She looked along the ground, found a butt that looked like it was burned to the stub, and slipped it between her lips, then lit it.

"So what poets do you like anyway?" I asked, trying to ignite a conversation.

"Elise Cowen," she shot back.

"Who's that?"

"She was Allen Ginsberg's girlfriend back in the early '50s when he was still screwing whatever he could find. She wrote some wild poetry: 'I wanted a cunt of golden pleasure / purer than heroin / To honor you in . . .'"

"Does she have a book out?"

"She jumped out of a window back in '62. She was twenty-nine. Her parents burned most of her stuff."

Suddenly, as though stung by a bee, she jumped to her feet and took off running north. I thought she was having some kind of weird, hallucinogenic freak-out until I saw the red lights dappling the surrounding buildings. A cop car sped ahead, cutting her off at the west corner of Rivington. She smiled as though she was just playing with them. A handsome young cop, not much older than her, got out.

"You know better than to run, Rita," the boyish peace officer said to her.

"Is everything okay?" I approached timidly.

"Turn around, with your hands against the vehicle," the other cop demanded. I did this as he patted me down. I had nothing.

"We saw you shooting up," the lead cop, a tall baby-faced kid said to her.

"Come on, neither of us did anything, Roger." She knew him by name. "And you know it."

"So he's your trick then."

"Give me a break. Does he look like a trick? I know him from the exchange."

"Okay, start walking, John," the cop said to me. I started walking south back to Delancey. "I don't want to see you again."

"Fuck!" I suddenly heard her scream. I turned to see Rita crying. The cop who was frisking her had found her two bags of heroin.

"Come on, I'm not some bullshit jungle junkie," she shouted, "I'm trying to clean up . . ."

The other cop turned to me with a look. I knew it was his last warning before arresting me as well. Much as I cared for her, I turned on Delancey and slowly headed east back to my van.

In a moment, I heard yells behind me. I turned to see her walking quickly toward me, waving her arms. I stopped and waited.

"Man, I thought they had you," I replied when she was finally within talking distance.

"They are such shits, you know what they do? We're entitled to have syringes. Hell, the city *gives* them to us. These cocksuckers will take our needles, run them through the lab and if they find some trace of heroin—bang! you're in jail. I mean is that fucking entrapment or what?"

"You had two bags," I corrected.

"Well, this time, yeah."

"So why didn't they arrest you?"

"They never arrest me anymore. Too much paperwork. They just take my stuff. But that thin cock's a real topper. He's a backdoor man. His last cavity search nearly ripped out my kidneys. When I push his play button, he gives me this unbelievable look." Without missing a beat, she asked, "You know Luke?"

"Who?"

"Forget it, let's get down to it." She turned down Orchard, ducked into the doorway of a tenement, and effortlessly hip-shoved open the rattly, old locked door. We walked past the stairway, down a smelly, ill-lit corridor to a doorway leading to a concrete backyard. It was obvious that she had been here before.

"I know I owe you one from last time, but I can't give it to you now," she said inexplicably.

"Give me what now?"

"I'll need twenty bucks," she said. This time, at least, she had the good sense to ask for the cash up front.

Although it never crossed my mind to ever pay for sex, from day one I was on fire for her. I reached into my pocket and counted out twenty bucks—meal money for two days. She handed me a condom— A Taste of Mint. Rolling it on took only a second. My erection was already so intense it felt as if it was going to snap off. She bowed before me in the darkness.

"You don't have to do this. You can keep the twenty," I said feeling a sudden tingle of guilt.

She looked up at me with a sweet smile. Instead of some cold, bobbing-for-apples blow job, she opened her mouth and exhaled on my penis. The condom felt like it wasn't there. She seemed to come as close as she could to it without touching it, as though any contact would destroy her. Finally, slowly, her mouth rubbed along the side of it. She let her dry bottom lip trip and bump along the shaft. Then she looked up with this am-I-pleasing-my-master smirk. In a moment she broke loose, lunging, swallowing, and letting herself go, forgetting the penis was even attached to anything, bathing in the wonderful degradation.

Her engorged mouth was the most splendid and vulnerable thing I had ever seen. Try as I could to delay, to get the most bang for my bucks, I still couldn't but shoot like a thirteen-year-old boy, stumbling forward emptily when I was done. Standing up, staring me in the eyes, she said, "That was a kind thing to say—that I don't have to do it."

"I meant it."

"You might have meant it, but you didn't really want that. You wanted the blow job, didn't you?"

"I want every inch of you. I want to save you from all this. I want—"

"What's your name again?"

"Or Trenchant," I said and added, "I'm Armenian."

"Don't Armenian names end in 'ian'?" she asked as she took out some Chapstick.

"Usually, yeah. The 'i-a-n' translates to 'son of.'"

"So Bitchian means son of a bitch?" she joked as she rolled the ointment over her lips and smacked them together.

"I guess."

She kissed me gently on the cheek. I rolled the used condom off, tossed it into the backyard, and zipped up. She squatted in a corner. I thought she was taking a leak, then realized her pants were still on. I took a step forward and glanced over her shoulder. What looked like a little cosmetics bag slipped out from behind a board where she must have stashed it earlier. From it she located and shook a tiny plastic envelope of heroin, a bent spoon, a little container of bleach, another of water, a thin hypo, and other issued items all neatly placed around. She performed her little ritual at high speed, mixing, cooking, filtering, cleaning, yanking down her pants, searching and finding a vein in her leg, and finally the divine moment of injection: anticipation fell to joy fell to ecstasy, then she just fell over. A few minutes later the big smile, and just as quickly, it was gone. Slowly, unevenly she stood up.

"Fuck!" she uttered, making an expression of great discomfort.

"What?"

"You don't want to know," she said as she quietly staggered out of the building, devolving back to her own subhuman existence. I definitely knew you couldn't rescue someone who didn't want to be saved. As she tiredly limped, I realized she was having some kind of physical problem.

"What's the matter?"

"I'm a mess," she said plainly.

"There are places that help you . . ."

"Nothing like that," she replied. It was clear I didn't understand. She stumbled forward. I grabbed her arm, trying to assist her. She instinctively pulled away.

"Do you live near here?" she asked.

"Yeah, why?"

"Can I use your shower?" she asked.

"Sure," I said, heading toward my van. "I'm parked over here." I turned down a dark, empty street.

"Wait a sec! You're not going to *do me*, are you?" Her face had this stunned, terrified, almost excited expression.

"Do what to you?"

"Rape or kill me?"

"You're doing that all by yourself."

"I'm just saying if you do kill me, just do it quick," she replied, "and don't do any weird *Silence of the Lambs* shit to my corpse, 'cause my parents will want it back. They've been waiting for closure for years now."

Did she really think that if I was a killer, her wit or erudition would rescue her? As I led her down the empty street, she seemed so vulnerable to the world at large—a casualty just waiting to happen. As this beautiful blonde girl tripped and dragged herself slowly before me, I was compelled to wonder how many murderers might have killed their victims if only to end the anticipation of their being murdered, or even further, how many killers had slain their victims if only to protect them from even more monstrous murderers.

My van was parked in the middle of the block. An orange parking ticket was on my windshield.

We got in, she rolled down a window, and I drove down to China-town. After about five minutes I found a parking space and we headed up to my loft. She seemed to slowly be running out of consciousness. In the building, I helped her up each step. When I finally got her into the loft, I became aware of a pungent odor. She tiredly explained she had an accident.

"Heroin does things to . . ." she couldn't finish her sentence. She was nodding out. I helped her onto the toilet. Then I undressed her, made the water temperature just right, and helped shower her.

Her underwear was ruined but I was able to clean her pants and hang them to dry. Then I helped her onto the bed.

"Sleep it off," I counseled.

"What are you—"

"I'm going to take advantage of you artistically."

"Immoralize me," she piped, throwing her arms back glamorously.

"No, I'll just sketch you," I muttered, and located my sketch pad and box of charcoals. After sketching a while, I decided to take full advantage of her presence by pulling my huge twelve-foot-long mural out front and filling in some minor details.

When she finally returned to the land of the conscious, she blinked her droopy eyes a second, then widened them in shock and screamed, "Holy fuck, you just painted that!"

She saw the purgatorial mural I had been working on for limitless hours, and thought I had hastily painted it during her catnap.

"I'm a quick sketch artist." I decided to see how long I could sustain the fallacy.

"There is no fucking way!" She got up, and inspected the piece closely and could see most of it was dry. She smiled and said, "You really got it."

"Thanks."

"That's a good trick. Paint a mural around some nude female, but keep the face blank. Then pick up some drugged-out bimbo and when they've fallen asleep, you fill it in and say you just did the entire thing."

"I did this a while ago," I told her. "I just wanted to fill in some details. It would be easier if you went back over by the bed." She returned to the bed and tiredly flopped back down.

"Listen, I know this sounds a little abrupt, but considering I washed you and all, could I possibly get your phone number?"

"I have a big, mean boyfriend who'll kill and eat us both if he found me with you."

"I guess it's silly to ask if you have a work number or a beeper."

"I'm leaving soon," she said simply.

"How soon? Where?"

"Back home, Vermont. I'm not sure exactly when."

"I'll come up there and visit you."

"You can't." She smiled. "I spend every moment tapping trees, making syrup, and . . ."

"There are safer ways of doing this. You don't have to blow strangers to get drugs. You can work in safely monitored houses where they watch out for you. And dealers have these little things called cell phones—they deliver."

"You just caught me on a bad day. Two bad days. I usually don't do things like that." Then she paused and revised her story. "I do it once in a while with exceptional guys, like yourself."

"And that charming ogre in the park?" I reminded her.

"Oh, the nipple pincher." She sighed. "Well, beauty comes in many ways."

"And apparently at a low price."

"I only serviced him the one time because he offered me a hundred bucks and with you because you bought me shit and I liked your sketches." This was a classic loser dynamic, reducing their self-destructive pattern to isolated episodes of bad luck.

"Give me a break. You're going to be hooking again when you leave here."

"Not if you pay for my medication."

"I'm the poorest artist in New York," I explained. "That's what I'm known for."

She silently took my sketch pad from the bedside table and flipped through some of the newest drafts of the *East River Swimmer* that I had been working on.

"These are powerful. I can see that the mural might be difficult, considering the subject, but you're telling me you can't sell these?" She seemed earnest.

"I haven't tried."

"Why not?"

"I'm just not there yet."

"You're there and back again," she replied.

"They lack something, some kind of authenticity." I revealed my doubts. "I just don't feel the wet, freezing sensation . . ."

"Art is a world of its own. You can't compare it to life."

"You're right, it's beyond life, so I need to feel it that much more acutely."

"So go jump in the East River," she suggested. "You might feel all those things more acutely, but let me know if it makes you paint any better."

"Aren't you afraid of AIDS or hepatitis?" I asked, cutting through the bullshit.

"What do you think?" she shot back angrily. "You think this is a fucking joke?"

"You're the one on heroin."

"I can't explain it," she said, and then tried to: "There comes a point where you just have to find something that pushes death out of your head, and this is the best I could come up with."

I had no idea what she was talking about. I sensed that she was spouting another bizarre rationalization in her vast bulwark of impenetrable psychological defenses. She closed her eyes and started drifting off. Looking at her, even though I honestly didn't want to feel it, I found her irresistible. More attractive than she ever deserved to be.

She simply didn't earn herself. I had an incredible urge to hold her against her will and protect her from herself forever.

183

As she slept, I painstakingly drew a series of sketches, just of her face, from various angles, one after another. I highlighted her different aspects, harsh distance, warm tenderness, flippant self-amusement. Despite my deep fatigue, drawing her seemed to be an energy source all its own. The last sketch I did was just of her lips. Finally I curled up next to her and fell asleep.

Eighteen

"Priin-cesss," I heard softly sung. "Or, get up."

I opened my eyes to see the giant Scot and rightful lord of the loft. Standing over Rita and me, Shade was wearing a sheepskin vest, resembling a nineteenth-century dairy farmer.

"What the hell are you doing back early?" I asked with a start and a yawn.

"Can I have a word with you alone a moment?" he asked, apparently not wanting to wake Rita. Her mouth was open and she looked as though she were in a coma.

"You don't mind me occasionally bringing home a date, do you?" I asked as we headed off to the farthest corner of the loft.

"A date, no, I don't mind. But an obvious IV user in *my* bed—yes," he replied, incensed. "What the hell are you thinking?"

"I met her downstairs," I explained. "She was with the clean needle exchange people and last night she was desperate."

"You're a handsome, talented artist, you can have your pick of twat. You can't get drawn into shit like this."

"Shit like what?"

"You've never been close to an addict or an alcoholic, have you, man? They pull you down like bricks. Well, you're already down. If you date this girl I want you out of here."

"Okay," I said to push him off.

"Or!" I suddenly heard behind me. Rita was up. She had found her pants drying in the bathroom and had slipped them on.

"One sec," I called to her. I assured Shade that I wouldn't bring her to his almighty place again.

"I don't want *you* seeing *her* again. It's for your own good, boy."

"We didn't have sex or anything." I replied. I didn't regard a blow job as sex.

"Thank God for that," he replied.

When I returned to Rita I found her dressed, standing by the door.

"Why don't we go to breakfast?" I suggested, feeling bad that she had to leave so suddenly.

"I ought to scoot anyway," she replied sluggishly. "I was just wondering if you could do me a small favor and lend me some cash."

"How much?" I asked, instead of explaining that I was broke and didn't want my hard-earned money going to drugs. I knew a sermon was pointless. My only choice was to keep her on her terms or cut her loose.

"Twenty." I gave it to her. She smiled and left.

"Cali tried to kill herself," Shade said as he heard Rita close the door behind her.

"No!"

"Yes." He took a seat on the edge of the trundle bed, took a deep breath and added, "She's gone."

"Gone? Where!"

"She went back to Greece, the land of the ancients."

"When? How?" I asked, amazed by it all.

"It happened very quickly and quietly and I'd appreciate it if it didn't get out," he said softly.

"Is she okay? Is there anything I can do?" I asked bewildered and saddened.

"She fine. She's staying at her sister's villa on the biblical island of Patmos."

"So she's okay?"

"She's healing."

"What about all her things? She had a huge art collection and—"

"What she didn't sell, she gave away."

"You're kidding."

"No, but don't worry, she got well compensated."

"How about the van?"

"She gave it to me to sell to you . . . I know I can get a sizeable amount for it, but if you still want it . . ."

"Shit, I was hoping she might give it to me."

"She left you something much more valuable," he replied, and before I could ask what, he smiled and stated, "She left you her love."

"I would have preferred the van," I muttered. Then, remembering that she had at least five of my paintings in her collection, I asked him if she sold them.

"She sold three pieces and gave away two."

"Gave them to who?"

"Klein Ritter."

"You're kidding! He's such a worm! Why?"

"Nothing is free," Shade said inexplicably.

Suddenly the door opened and the beautiful Asian scrollist entered.

"Morning gentlemen," she addressed Shade and me.

"Morning to yourself," Shade replied, immediately attracted. "My my, you *have* been busy, Or."

She looked over to the side of the bed. I realized that she was checking out the final sketch I did last night—Rita's beautiful lips.

"I didn't think I moisturized my lips that much last night," she commented.

"They're . . . They're . . ."

"They're what?"

"They're beautiful," I said, a bit flustered. I didn't want to reveal they were someone else's lips. Nor did I want her to know *I* was longing after a heroin addict, particularly after all the candor the night before.

"My name is Shade," the Scot said, not waiting to be introduced. "I'm sort of lord of this castle. And who might you be?"

"Just a damsel here." She extended her hand. "Name's Lynn."

"Lynn, are you familiar with the age-old privilege of *primo noche*?"

"What's that?"

"In feudal Europe," he said with a smile, "in each lord's domain he had the duty to deviginate any lass prone to be married."

"Well I'm not getting married, just subletting the tip of your turf." She gave out the one piece of information I was praying she would withhold.

"Sublet, huh? Naughty boy," Shade said to me. "I distinctly told you subletting was a no-no."

"I'm sorry. She's just here part-time," I clarified.

"Well at least she's clean and sober."

I quickly pulled on some clothes.

"Say, this is impressive," Shade said, eyeing my mural of Rita being yanked between dealer devils and addict angels.

"That's for you, but I'm actually taking a break from painting for a while," I explained as I pulled together the canvas bag of his stone-cutting tools that I had been using.

"So what are you working on?"

"That meteor in the stairwell."

"My rock?"

"You said I could use it."

"You're actually cutting the stone?"

"Slowly."

"Into what?"

"A Chinese carton."

"A Chinese cartoon?"

"No, carton, you know, a white Chinese takeout carton."

"Why?" He had a disgusted look of befuddlement.

"I got a commission."

"How about a freakin' egg roll? That'd be a more interesting shape."

"We agreed on a Chinese takeout carton."

He issued a disappointed expression. "Over the years I envisioned so many noble heads and profound forms in that stone. It for me was the living embodiment of great possibilities, but I never made time to sculpt any of them. I suppose something kitschy and campy is better than nothing at all. How far have you gotten?"

"Not far, just one side."

"One side? I never heard anyone cutting only one side of a rock."

"Come downstairs and take a peek," I suggested and hoisted up the canvas bag with his tools onto my back.

"You got an aspirator and goggles?" he asked.

I pulled out a dust mask for him.

"Better wear two if you're going to use that," he said and warned, "the dust is really bad for your lungs, it can collapse them. And the shards can get in your eyes."

As we headed down the stairs together, he recounted his trip to Scotland, the greenery, the single malts, the struggle of a peaceful country folk trying to compete and survive in a cyber-competitive, increasingly urbanizing world.

189

"Did you meet up with your ex-wife Sheila?"

"Yes and no. I'm convinced that she summoned me there."

"What do you mean?"

"It turns out she died of breast cancer two days before I arrived. After waiting forty years I show up two days late. What's the odds of that happening?"

"My God."

"Her husband, along with two of her other ex-husbands who married her after me, were all pallbearers. I came late that day, but completed the group."

"At least her husbands didn't drive her to an early grave," I joked, as we came to the final landing of the back stairs.

When Shade spotted the stone, he gasped, "My God, what'd you do to her?"

"What are you talking about?"

He ran his fingers over its rough surface and looked at it closely. Some rainwater had collected in a discarded coffee cup that happened to be squeezed into the metal piping banister. Shade took it and carefully poured the water over the top of the rock.

"What are you doing?"

"Looking for cracks," he said, inspecting as the water trickled over the piece. "I don't think you ruined it but . . ." He ran his fingers through his beard. "Why are you sawing it?"

"What am I supposed to do?"

"Alabaster is a soft stone. I never understood how someone could sculpt with a saw." He looked at the rock as if it were a baby. "Give me a hammer."

I plunked down the canvas tool bag and took out a mallet.

Going through the bag, he located a hammer with a long wooden handle. "You start with the heavy tools and you work your way to the finer ones."

I explained that my plan was to slice into the sculpture with the saw, knocking off all the outward rungs. When that was done I had intended to smooth it all down.

"Let's try it," he said.

As Shade lifted the long sledge-like hammer, I flinched, expecting the stone slot to crack off and shatter. When he whacked it, though, nothing happened. He hit again, this time with all his might. The stone chipped, but the prescored slice didn't crack off.

"As I suspected," he declared. "You spaced the cuts too wide apart and made them too shallow."

"Shit!"

"How long did it take you to zigzag this?"

"All yesterday," I said discouraged. He pulled the electric saw from the canvas bag.

"Amazing you were able to do this much," he observed. "This blade couldn't cut butter." He held the blade of the saw toward me and I could see that the teeth were so worn down, I had been cutting with what resembled a vertical strip of metal. "Maybe luck was on your side," he went on. "You would have ruined the stone for sure."

"Look, this is a straightforward geometric piece," I explained. "It doesn't require a lot of fancy curves and twists."

"You're always looking to cut corners, aren't you?" he commented, while rooting through his tool bag. "This is art. It takes time." He pulled out another hammer with a rough end.

"I took a class on sculpting some years ago," I filled him in, "so if I'm a bit rusty . . ."

"Well let's give you a bit of a flash course, shall we? What are you trying to do?"

I explained my calculations. He made some chalk marks. He pulled out an old hand drill and slipped a bit into it. Then, turning the little crank, he slowly drilled a hole through it. "See how easily it breaks away? It's a particle stone, not like marble. Easier than wood. Grab the other drill and help me."

"What the hell am I doing, exactly?" I asked, following his instructions on faith.

"First we make a series of perforations." He did this as he said it. "Make the holes shallow up at the top, say around an inch in depth. As you work your way down, drill it about a half an inch deeper with each downward hole." He then held up another item. "Do you know what these are?"

"I forgot."

"Shims, and these?" He picked up another metal piece. "These are . . . ?"

"Wedges?"

"Very good," he replied. "Once we finish drilling you're going to slip in the shim and then tap in the wedge until the surface stone splits, like thus." He demonstrated for me, cutting a flat ten-pound slab of stone from the bottom end.

He then plucked a hammer out of his canvas bag of tricks.

"This is a bush hammer, it's probably the best tool for creating a plane." He plucked out a round-edged chisel. "This can be useful for chiseling it down, but I prefer using points." He picked out a long pointy tool—a point. "You should run this along the piece, working it down slowly. Don't just do one side or you'll lose proportions. Keep walking around the piece working all sides. Try to think of yourself as a farmer plowing a field. Then when you're done you can grind it down. How polished do you need it?"

"I knew that was going to take the most work so I got him to agree to a rough finish." Shade nodded; apparently I had done one thing right.

Together we worked the drills, each of us doing one side at a time. Then slowly we wedged out slices of stone.

"What's our delivery date?" Shade asked.

"Mid-November."

"Mid . . . ! That's in two weeks!" he exclaimed. "What is this, fast food?"

"It's a headstone for a guy who ran a Chinese takeout restaurant, so it does commemorate fast food."

"Are you supposed to carve anything on it?" he asked.

"He didn't want religious symbols or dates."

"Well, at least it'll have integrity. Michelangelo once said that a good sculpture should be so solid that it should be able to roll down a hill without any parts breaking off."

"How about if it rolls off the back of my van?" I kidded.

"What does that mean?" He smiled.

"Nothing, I'm always worried about rolling out."

"Wait a second! You can't just toss this into the back of your bloody van." He seemed angry.

"Why not!"

"It's too heavy and I've seen your van. It's a piece of shit packed with shit."

"It'll hold," I assured him.

He let out an exhaustive sigh. "About twenty years ago this one fellow I knew, an American Indian, got a hold of an incredible piece of stone. He was just like you. I remember he had an old pickup truck. He bought the piece from a stonemason. I happened to be visiting. I watched as they lowered the object onto the back of his flatbed. Wham! All four tires went flat, the shocks collapsed. The engine died right there. He ended up losing his truck and the stone."

"That's not going to happen here," I rebutted.

"See, this! This is what I'm talking about!" He suddenly became inflamed. "You think you're special but you're not. You have this half-assed way of doing things and after all the work you put into it . . . This is not how you move a piece of art!"

I assured him everything would be okay.

He looked at me with slight disappointment and said, "Or, I don't have children. As an artist all I really have are protégés, and I regard you as one, perhaps the most talented young artist I've met in years. I know you think you've had the worst luck in the world, but that's not true. You are just so intent on always sabotaging yourself. You make your bad luck and you don't even see that!"

"What choice do I have?" I asked. "I'm broke!"

He didn't say a word. We returned to work. After the better part of an hour, nearly finishing all the bores on the final side, I interrupted our silent collaboration. "I'm sorry about going against your instructions and inviting Lynn to move in."

"She's pretty and nice and doesn't appear out of her mind. I'm just nervous about getting evicted. I've lived there all these years by not calling up a lot of attention. The landlord lobby in Albany is always growing stronger. They're always making new laws and cracking down," For a long time we didn't say a word. We switched tools and slowly drilled and wedged the four sides down.

By sunset, tired and sweaty, we headed back upstairs. Shade said that he was going to stay at Cali's. I thanked him and pressed on. Except for the intaking and expelling of solids and liquids, I kept working.

Around midnight, too exhausted to continue, I went upstairs and lay down. In a minute I was fast asleep. The buzzer woke me up. I tried to sleep through it, but it kept buzzing. I pushed the intercom half expecting to hear Shade's voice.

"Ring me in goddamn it!" It was Rita.

I buzzed open the door and waited in the hallway as she slunk up the stairs. She passed me without a hello and pushed into the bathroom. Without closing the door, she bent forward and vomited into the toilet. I went over to see if I could be of assistance. She numbly grabbed the end of the toilet paper and without tearing it off the spool she wiped her nose. The paper was covered in blood.

"What happened?"

"Nothing, I just need a moment," she said, pushing me out and pulling the door closed. But the lock didn't catch and it slowly swung open a bit. I watched as she carefully took out a hypodermic. With trembling hands, she cleaned it out with the tiny bottle of bleach. Out came the clear, tiny plastic Ziploc bag of powder. She mixed it with water, cooked it to a bubble, filtered it into her needle, and pulled down her pants. I watched sadly as she searched for a vein in her legs, lifting her knees and ankles. Finally, using her belt as a tourniquet, she shot herself up. Her hands clung along the walls as she slowly slid down to the floor. When she came to, she took a deep breath, and seeing me watching her, she pushed open the door with a ready-made smile and said, "Did I mention I was a diabetic?"

"And I'm tubercular," I said tiredly.

"No kidding," she said merrily. "Let's grab some air."

"It's late, I was sleeping."

"I thought I had a temp job here."

"What are you talking about?"

"Twenty bucks? Andrew Jackson for some johnson action."

"I'm a little low," I replied, unamused.

"Sorry, thanks for the john, good night." She was about to leave.

"Hold on," I replied, looking through my wallet. I realized I had only thirty-two dollars, but didn't want her to leave. "Twenty bucks for the night?"

"You know, you're in luck," she replied. "My one-time bargain-basement offer, a champagne and caviar evening for twenty bucks."

"This might sound like a strange request," I replied, "but I want you to get back on the toilet."

"You into water sports?"

"I just want to do a couple of caricatures of you on a surfboard or in a go-cart."

I located the Strathmore sketch pad in which I had her earlier images.

"Oh, you want the Angelina Jolie tough girl." She took a seat on the toilet, put her belt around her forearm, holding the end in her teeth. Then taking the needle out, she aimed it dramatically at her arm, and made a severe face.

195

"Actually can you put it where you had it before," I requested. She pulled down her pants and pointed the needle into her right thigh.

"Can you put the tourniquet on your thigh?"

As she did so, she asked, "Did you find a buyer for your mural?"

"Not yet," I said as I sketched.

"You should send it to my mother. She buys art. Usually the clown and puppy variety, but considering her daughter is the subject . . . You know you should actually send her your swimmers. She likes Thomas Eakins's athletes."

"Can I say you recommended me?"

"Sure, she'd definitely buy it then." I sensed she was being sarcastic. When I was done I did another sketch of just her hand, then just the needle, and finally just her thigh.

After about a half an hour, she inspected the work. "Smack Madonna—perfect." Tiredly, she sat on the bed.

THE NEXT MORNING, I was awakened by Shade making a racket as he collected a change of clothes from the far reaches of his closet.

"Are you up, boy?" he shouted.

"Now I am," I said with my eyes still shut. Then nervously I sat up and looked around. Rita was nowhere to be seen.

"You left the front door open," Shade commented as if reading my fears.

"Did I?"

Shade tossed an envelope onto the bed next to me.

Inside I counted ten crisp hundred dollar bills. "Oh my God!"

"That's more than enough money to hire shippers to move your paperweight to Long Island."

"Oh god, Shade, I can't take this."

"Spare me the bullshit," he replied. "You're getting ten grand for this piece, aren't you?"

"Not quite that much but—"

"Just pay me the first grand off the top. No interest, all I ask is one thing."

"What?"

"I want you to raise your standards. All the amateur stunts you've done before—that's behind you. No dating addicts. No loading valuable artworks into your broken-down heap. I want you to move forward. That was all in the past. Promise me you'll leave it there and you won't look back."

"No looking back," I vowed.

He nodded and left. As I worked through the day, I obsessed about the mystery that was Rita. Normally I'd either fear or be repelled by a heroin addict. They had always seemed so doomed from the start. Yet her existence was like some incredible, violent, icon-smashing work of art. I associated her sharp angular features and slightly Waspy, New England accent with money. She looked groomed to marry a banker or politician. Yet with the needle drugs and street whoring, she blew her own stereotype to smithereens.

When I was so hungry that I couldn't think of anything else, I finally took a break and went and out for my first meal of the day. Afterward it was back to stonecutting. And back to my Rita thoughts: the fact that she was young and intelligent, yet intent to die, was unspeakably tragic. I constantly had to fend off the hope that I could reach or rescue her. Ironically the sadness that emanated from her had somehow enwrapped itself into her eroticism.

Later, I realized that it was dark. I flipped on a flashlight and kept working. Eventually it became difficult to stay awake, but I kept my chisel moving.

Ultimately when I pushed aside that bizarre blend of horny sadness that I felt when thinking about Rita, I realized that there was something about her I actually envied. She had absolutely no fear of death, but dreading death was important. I had almost died under that fucking train, and knew that there were just so many hours and days before I too would be dead. I was intent to fill the empty vessel of those days with my work. Since I met Rita I couldn't help but wonder if that same mortal fear forbade me from going to certain places with my art. More and more I began to wonder if those risky extremes weren't where greatness resided.

Looking up, totally exhausted, I saw that Rita was suddenly standing before me.

"How'd you get in?" I asked in disbelief.

"I rang every bell in the goddamned building until some one-armed paper hanger let me in. When I found your door locked, I just followed the sound of the scraping."

"Want to help?" I asked, eager to press on.

"Not really," she replied, "I was hoping to grab some cash and shoot up."

"I'm usually amused by your hard-as-nails brand of humor, but if you don't even crack a smile, I'm not sure if you're joking or not."

"You sound like Lucas."

"Who?"

"The father of the children I'll never want—the monster boyfriend."

"Maybe you should go back to him," I said testily.

"Now you're the one not smiling."

"Do heroin addicts fall in love?"

"Isn't that a Philip K. Dick novel?" She leaned against me. When she saw I wasn't kidding, she sat on the stoop above me. "The awful truth is I know you're broke and I'd have a better chance squeezing a zit out of a fruit fly's ass, but I miss you."

"What a way with words."

"Hey, my parents won't speak to me, my johns don't pay, my dealers don't sell, and my boyfriend either cries or hits me—you're all I got left."

"If you break your habit all that will miraculously change," I suggested.

"Actually, you're wrong," she said, and laughed. "They all regarded me that way before." I smiled and she added, "I'm not even kidding."

I bolted up suddenly and grabbed her. She shrieked and laughed and looked me right in the eyes with a tiny, irrepressible smile. I could tell at that moment she wanted me to kiss her. I hungered to, but I was genuinely afraid of catching something. She looked down nervously and said, "Well, I don't want to be a pill, but this is john rush hour, right after all the wives drop off to sleep. If I don't get out of here and make some *dinero* in the next few hours, I'm going to be seriously fucked all tomorrow."

"How much do you need?"

"Fifty bucks," she replied immediately.

"Fifty! What happened to twenty?"

"Five bags."

"I'll give you thirty."

"Then I got to find a dick that'll pay twenty."

"Spend the evening with me and I'll give you fifty bucks." Money was more than love to a drug addict, because it bought drugs.

I pulled a small rough-edged chisel out of Shade's canvas bag and demonstrated how to go over the surfaces of the sculpture very delicately. She tried doing it for a while, but I could see that her hands were trembling and she found it frustrating.

"Are you in pain?" I asked.

"No, I just did some about two hours ago, I'm okay until around four. Then I have to do another half bag. How are you holding up?" she asked.

"I could use a cup of coffee."

"What the hell is this anyhow?" She stepped back and looked at the rock.

"It's going to be a headstone for a guy who had a chain of kosher Chinese joints."

"Are you kidding?" she asked, sweating. I tiredly shook my head no.

She sat with me and watched me work for a while until she passed out. Soon after, so did I.

"Police officer!" I suddenly heard. Four large plainclothes cops were suddenly shaking Rita and I awake. She shrieked and I bolted to my feet.

"Shut up," one of them said to her.

"Sit back down," another said to me.

She did; so did I.

"What's the matter, officer?"

Rita sat on her hands nervously. We both knew she was carrying.

"The guy on this floor, you know him?" the oldest cop asked. He pointed up to the second floor of the bank building.

"This building is all businesses," I replied.

"Don't shit me," he shot back, and I realized he was talking about Hong Kong Don Juan, the only other person who lived in the building.

"Oh, yeah. He's a big man with the ladies. What about him?" A couple of the cops laughed.

"Ever talk to his ladies?" one of the cops asked.

"I never heard them speak English," I replied.

"Did he kill one?" Rita anticipated.

"He was slave trading," the cop explained.

"What?" Rita spoke up.

"He was a part of a slave-trading ring," he replied. "He brought in girls from the southern provinces of China and sold them to whorehouses."

"That is so eighteenth century," Rita replied, no longer fearing the group.

"I guess this means . . . his apartment will be available," I said timidly. One of the cops chuckled and they all marched out of the building. I went back to work.

At three in the morning we helped each other up to the apartment. She spent the night sleeping on the edge of the bed, next to me.

Lynn woke me early the next morning.

"Oh shit." I jumped up. The bed was empty. "Did you see her?"

"Who?"

"Um . . . I thought someone else was here," I said.

"Who?"

"I must have been dreaming." She nodded sadly.

In the bathroom I found some of Rita's prep items. I was glad that she had vanished. She was so obviously heroinated that it would have been difficult to explain her. I mentioned the arrest of the smooth operator downstairs to Lynn.

"He wasn't a Don Juan at all. Those poor girls were trapped here in his slave-trade ring."

"Shit!" she replied angrily. "That's what she must have been saying and I didn't understand her!"

"I think she's okay now," I responded. Lynn just stared off sadly.

I DRESSED, HEADED DOWNSTAIRS, and began a new day. Shade's sculpting instructions were invaluable. For the first time I felt a genuine optimism that the piece would be done on time. I drilled, shimmied, wedged, and hammered, working down all four sides together. Time began to speed up.

Through dirty goggles and a crud-caked face mask, I experienced a dusty new world. At first, I felt like an outdoor miner, but gradually over the grind of days, my metaphoric fantasy shifted. I daydreamed I was trying to break out of a prison. Each chisel thrust was a stroke closer to freedom. When the monotony became too much, I fantasized I was crossing a stone desert, slowly sinking deeper into it, one chisel stroke at a time.

As the daily sounds of the outside world died down, I kept working until I felt as though everyone had forgotten about me. When the hours grew bleak and empty, the only relief came from looking forward to

Rita. She would show up around midnight, bringing me a cup of coffee. From her hands it tasted like the nectar of the gods.

There was something wonderful about the fact that no one else knew about her. The privacy of her outlaw existence made her seem all the more mysterious and exciting. She'd keep me company as I worked.

She would never ask, but each night I'd "pay" her fifty bucks. Unfortunately we'd never get around to the prostitution part. She'd just perch quietly on the steps above me, watching me work until she'd eventually nod out. After an hour or so, I'd awaken her and we'd go up to my place. When she saw me taking a shower, she climbed in and we washed together. I rubbed her back, soaping up her stubbly hair, down her arms and legs, spotting her newest yellowish puncture marks.

"I'm amazed by all the places you inject yourself," I commented one night.

"Truth is I'm a voodoo lady," she joked. "It works in reverse. There's a little Barbie doll with my likeness up in Great Neck going through sheer hell."

Afterward she'd usually lay nude on one end of the bed and I'd sit up naked on the other. Even though I'd doubtlessly be exhausted, I'd sketch her.

"Of all the sick shit I've done for money, this is the sickest," she said as she awakened during one session.

"Years ago," I said to her, while sketching, "I lived in a run-down tenement on Twelfth Street between First and Second. Do you know Twelfth Street?"

"I did it once with that creep. Just once." She immediately knew where I was heading. Twelfth Street was a well-known prostitution strip. "I don't whore!"

"Well, that's good, because I never pimped, johned, or bought drugs for anyone before. I'm just saying that I lived there and every so often, a beautiful girl like yourself would show up. They'd have some pimp who'd kiss them and smack them. I'd see the same older ugly hookers all the time. Some of them are still there, but the pretty young ones would just vanish."

"Maybe they'd enroll in veterinary college," she suggested. "Ever think of that?"

"Do you know Joel Rifkin?"

"Sure. My old dentist?"

"He was a serial killer they caught about ten years ago. After they arrested him, the newspapers ran the mugshots of all the hookers he killed, around twenty girls I think. I recognized two of them from the street."

"I won't get killed," she assured me.

"You probably won't. Most of them didn't. They just wound up used and ugly and crushed. Their tricks got uglier and cheaper until they couldn't even pick up a caveman."

She lapsed back into silence as I drew her. Eventually I fell asleep. Early the next morning, before Lynn arrived, she gently shook me awake. Rita had dressed and was antsy for a fix. I handed her the cash and, remembering our conversation from the night before, I said something like, "I know you don't want me to talk about it, but I care about you and . . ."

"Look," she interrupted me. "I know it's not fair to put you through this." She handed the cash back to me. "It's best for both of us if I don't see you again. For both our sake."

I didn't respond and she left.

I didn't see her the next night or the next.

Finally starved for human contact, I quit working early, and without changing my clothes, headed downstairs. Once inside the bar I discovered that I had missed the last presidential debate, but was in the center of a lively argument.

"The only question you should consider"—Cecil stabbed the air toward Pablo—"is which man will do the least harm to our great country."

"The slight difference between the two . . ." Pablo began.

"How'd the debate go?" I interrupted.

"Which man will do the least harm?" Cecil bulldozed.

"Nominally, Gore," Pablo finally conceded.

"Then with polls showing them neck in neck, that's who you Nader nuts should vote for," he resolved.

"How's Gore in the polls?" I asked.

"Whichever candidate wins," Pablo ignored me, "it isn't going to be by five measly percent."

"And suppose it is?" Cecil asked. "You're gambling the American presidency on naïve idealism."

"Look, if Nader gets his five percent, he gets matching funds. That means in the next election he will be able to capture even more votes and slowly his popularity will build and eventually snowball."

"A snowball's chance in hell," Cecil summed up. Both were too snippy to chat. I was exhausted anyway.

Though I had the urge to go out and search for Rita, I headed back upstairs and collapsed into bed. I was overwhelmed by the amount of work still ahead of me to finish the sculpture. I always hated schedules, but now I was locked in one: wake up early, move the van, grab a light breakfast, back upstairs, refill last night's one-gallon jug of tap water. Sometimes I'd bring a radio and then I'd begin chiseling.

The absence of Rita's beautiful face and barbed wit robbed me of my late-night energy. The loneliness left me feeling unanchored, yet I was able to sleep more and get considerable work done during the daytime hours.

Nineteen

While chiseling in the stairwell four days later, a shadow fell across me. I looked up and there was Rita.

"I must be dreaming."

"I never left," she replied. She didn't look good. Her clothes were filthy. Her skin looked jaundiced. In addition to various scratches and scabs, a long bruise ran down her arm.

"Who did that?" I pointed to it.

"The wind. I bruise easily."

"Need money? It's over there in my shirt pocket. Take it and go,"

I said, too tired to be enchanted by her bullshit. My shirt was entangled around the piping banister.

"What's the matter, one bruise and I'm no longer pretty?" she asked. She handed me a cup of coffee that she had brought with her.

"I just have to keep working," I said, and drank down half the cup in a single gulp. "If I miss the deadline I lose the commission."

"I'll help you." She picked up a huge mallet, but before she could destroy my piece, I pulled it from her.

"You've done this before," I replied, giving her a smaller chisel. "Just gently run it along the surface of the stone. Do you see this little ridge?" I pointed to a strip that looked like a row of baby teeth breaking out of one side. "Just wear down that ridge until it's flat."

Gently, she worked a small chisel along the rock. Even after I began seeing double, she stayed with it. Diligently, tenderly, and tenaciously she worked the little knots out of one side.

"Maybe you need the hard edges worked out of you," she kidded. Her eyes were moist and red. It was clear she had only just shot up.

She put the chisel down and started rubbing my lower back. I was impressed by the strength of her grip. I found myself turning to dough and drifting to sleep.

"Come on," she said, nudging me. "Let's get you out of here."

"Before the police arrest us for slave trading."

Together we went upstairs. Both of us stripped down. We skipped our joint shower, but as usual we slept heads and tails on the bed. After a few hours I awoke to find that in my sleep I had flipped over, and was holding her in my arms, sleeping like spoons. I had an erection and could feel the moisture through the front of her undies. I pulled her panties to one side and gently fondled her.

"It feels great, but you shouldn't."

"Why not?" I asked, still quite exhausted.

"I might be HIV positive."

"I have condoms." I said, sitting up. A sudden shooting pain went up my back.

"It's not just that," she replied as I ran my fingers through her pubic hair. "I also have a boyfriend."

"Doesn't he wonder where you vanish off to at night?" I felt spasms in my legs and arms.

"Why don't you let me . . ." She started stroking my hard-on.

"It's okay." I turned away. "I should get some sleep."

I closed my eyes and tried to slip under. But there was nothing worse than being both aroused and exhausted—unable to either fuck or sleep.

After a minute, she asked, "You're not angry at me, are you?"

"I'm just not feeling well."

"What's the matter?"

I considered the agony of all the hard labor. "Every bone and muscle in my body is in pain. I'm constantly tired yet I can't sleep and my head's a blur. I've never worked so hard for so little and I can't believe I put myself in this fucking situation."

She chuckled and replied, "You loosely described what it feels like to go cold turkey and you don't even get the benefits of the high."

She sat up and pulled on her pants.

"What are you doing?" I asked.

"It's a nice night." She nodded her head toward the window. "Let's go out."

"Where?"

"I don't know, just outside. I love being out at night when there's no one around. I feel like . . . like I'm in the spirit world."

"What the hell," I muttered, unable to sleep. "I have to move my van in a couple hours anyway."

"He has to move his van," she repeated. "What a wealthy man, to have so much."

"I have nothing," I corrected as we dressed. "This apartment is a

207

sublet that I have to vacate in a short time. Hell, I usually live in the van."

"You live in it?" She sounded aghast. When she saw that I was not amused by my meager existence, she shut up.

Soon we were silently strolling down Canal and along Essex. The city was like an emptied ocean where great energy had once been expended. Now it seemed all burnt out. Not a soul was in sight. We found the remains of an old bench on Essex facing west and from there we were able to get a vantage of the bottom-lit skyline before us.

"So, you're moving your van?" she finally interrupted the silence.

"Yeah."

"You mind if I take my insulin there?" She was politely referring to her next fix.

"Didn't you just do one?"

"Hey, life is yin, heroin is yang. Life is emptiness, heroin is fullness," she explained as if she were singing a song. "All it really comes down to is dosage."

"I could use a sleeping pill."

"Life is like that," she went on. "Too much joy too early in life, and you're on antidepressants later."

"Don't you resent being held hostage by heroin?" I refocused.

"Life enthralls us with a million little things every day. Eating, sleeping, shitting . . ."

"Loving . . ."

"So do you resent those needs?" she asked.

"The only thing that bothers me about life is knowing that someday I'm going to die, but at least my terror and anguish is out of my control. But heroin addiction . . ."

"I could stop in a second, if I wanted to."

"Why don't you then?"

"Because I'm not taking it for the same reason as all the other losers, I have no choice. If I stopped doing it . . . I'd die."

"I'm pretty sure that if the medical establishment agrees on nothing else, it's just the opposite, that shooting heroin is actually bad for your health."

"There are always anomalies and I'm one."

"How is it that you and you alone are kept alive by this awful street drug?"

She closed her eyes impatiently. It was evident we were reaching the outer ring of her upside-down galaxy. She spoke as though she were tiredly reciting a prayer, "It's a medication. I'm ill and there are certain properties in the heroin that keep me alive."

"You're joking right?"

"No, ironically, I'm not joking. Heroin goes to the endorphin receptors and blocks all traces of adrenaline and keeps the cancer in remission."

"This sounds harebrained."

"Adrenaline is released during stress, it's highly carcinogenic." When I rolled my eyes, she added, "Look, I don't know all the proper terms, but if I did, I'd write a comprehensive article and send it to the *New England Journal of Medicine*."

"Who told you . . . Where did you get this stuff?"

"Mainly I pieced it together from the Tuesday *New York Times*, the Science Times, but I've tested it!"

I hoped she was joking. Only two other times in my life, while I was in the middle of a conversation, did I suddenly realize that the person I was talking to was nuts. I delicately asked, "What exactly are you diagnosed with?"

"You want my diagnosis?" She suddenly tensed up. "A pathological case of the poor starving artist's syndrome."

"What the fuck are you talking about?"

"You! I'm talking about *you*—living in a van. Dressing like a bum. You're always broke and you think you're doing all this for art."

209

"Maybe so, but I'm not shooting up heroin, calling it medicine, while whoring myself on the street and denying it."

"The difference is, I don't have a choice. I'm fucked by fate, but you, you can get a part-time job and still do your art. You don't have to do this."

"Tell you what, I'll seriously consider what you're saying. But what ailment exactly do *you* have?"

"I don't want to go into it."

"Why?"

"I just don't want you thinking of me as sick."

"I won't, just tell me what you got," I pressed.

"Nothing anyone can catch."

"Look, if you just say you like heroin or are addicted to it, I can accept that . . ."

"But that's not it. If I were healthy I'd kick it right now."

"So what disease can heroin cure?"

"All!" she finally yelled out, holding her head and closing her eyes. Then after a moment, she opened her eyes and said, "Okay, I'm sick of all."

"You're sick of it all?" I clarified.

"Just all," she reiterated.

"All what?"

She closed her eyes again. "All. And I can't say any more than that. If you ask me one more time, you'll never see me again. I swear it." Except for when she was hurting for a fix, I didn't remember her so pissed.

"Let's go," I said, rising to my feet. I was ready to move the van and be done with all this bullshit for the night.

We arrived at the vehicle. As I quickly moved my crap into the back so that we could sit inside, she picked up one rejected painting of my swimmer and studied it. Finally, when I created enough space, she put it down and took out her little shoot-up packet. Leaving the back door of the van open for light, I watched as she robotically laid out all her little paraphernalia in a ceremonial fashion. It was evident that she did this sacred act so frequently, and with such control, that she could do it blindfolded. In a moment everything was cooked, cleaned, and ready to go.

She tugged down her pants and started her search for a great and generous vein, a bloody Nile into which all tiny red rivers flowed. Unfortunately there was none. Digging her thumb into her shapely inner thigh, she tried to worm the vein up to the surface. Unable to see anything in the dark, she hopped out of the van in her panties and shoes. Using the street light she wrestled with parts of her contorted body, looking again. She finally stood up in winded frustration.

"Do me a small favor," she finally asked, "look on my back for a vein. Do you see anything?"

"What does it matter if I do, I'm not shooting you up."

"Shit, at this rate I'm going to be shooting it into my eyes soon," she commented.

Eventually she found the elusive conduit, a small dark line near her groin. With a dab of spit, she "sterilized" the spot, and slowly, carefully, she sank the needle into her skin, steering it through tissue as though it were just fluff that blocked her happiness. The fact that their voracity for drugs superseded the inconceivable pain of stabbing into themselves four, five, six times a day with dull needles was perhaps the greatest testament to an addict's devotion. Just a paper cut and I was queasy.

When she was done, her head drooped back into blissful emptiness.

"Man, if you only knew how I felt right now," she finally cooed. She tiredly stripped down naked and pulled herself back into the van, lying on my mattress. Leaning back, she revealed a flat stomach and newly pierced belly button. Her thighs and long legs were blissfully inviting. She closed her eyes, slowly rolled onto her stomach, and teasingly wagged her cheeks at me.

"Hold that pose," I ordered as I grabbed a sketch pad that I left in the van. "I'll call this one *The Night with Two Moons*."

"I got a better idea," she said as she patted her hand on the mattress next to her, summoning me. The back of the van was still open, facing an empty dark street. I crawled onto the foam rubber next to her. She reached into the back pocket of her removed jeans and took out a sealed condom—Trojans, nonlubricated and ribbed.

"I thought heroin kills the sex drive," I said.

"Speedballs always get me going," she replied.

Apparently her shot was a cocktail. It made her moist and horny, but I was getting butterflies.

"Do you really think you have HIV or hepatitis?" I asked, pulling off my pants and slipping on the condom.

"I am death," she replied and held up her hands like claws.

"You don't have a second condom, do you?" I asked.

She rolled her eyes in amused disbelief and handed it to me. "Just for the record," she said, "I only blow johns with rubbers. No one catches my snatch."

Although the double-treaded vulcanization of my penis completely knocked out any sort of surface sensation, the two rubbers were like a pair of tourniquets holding every drop of burning blood frozen in my pecker. I worried that it would grow gangrenous, but it remained hot as ever. Ultimately, the sensation didn't even matter, just the thought of being in her was enough. Her legs rose high in the air, so that she could have worn her ankles as earrings. I entered slowly, trying to discern at least the heat of her burning body. I wanted to feel her tenderly as our bodies kissed. Most important of all, I wanted her to realize how important she was to me. Immediately she grabbed my ass and bounced me into her groin like a tetherball. Then, instantly, I was too aroused to restrain myself.

As I pounded away, just looking down at this ravishing beauty who was groaning and screaming and howling ecstatically—this girl of my dreams—bypassed the need for any topical sensations.

We fucked and rocked, and eventually changed positions. I peeked out the back door of my van onto the small patch of dry grass in the little park across Essex Street. Three centurgenarian-looking Asians were lined up doing tai chi in the predawn light, sneaking glances at Rita's beautiful ass bouncing up and down on our merry ride to kingdom come. Although she seemed to be having the time of her life, my hermetically condomed dick felt more like a strap-on.

When she ultimately screamed and pulled the plug, she said that she couldn't fuck anymore. After a moment of repose, she realized, "You haven't come, have you?"

"No, but it was fun."

"Christ, look at this thing," she said inspecting me as I began to stiffen up again. "In ten thousand years the *Starship Enterprise* is going to find your erection floating in outer space. You want to last forever, or you want to go out with a bang?"

Without waiting for an answer, she snapped off the outer condom so abruptly I felt recircumcised. In a moment I sprung back to life. Her moist lips parted and she took me all the way in her mouth until she was gagging a bit. Then pulling it out, she twisted around so that I was right between her open legs.

"Get over here!" she ordered brazenly.

I fucked her hard for a few minutes before I yanked off the second condom and reentered her, screwing her bareback. Slamming my hips back and forth so hard, I hammered her body forward, through boxes of used books, old canvases, used sketch pads, jars of brushes, cakes and half-coiled tubes of paint, driving her until the back of her head was forced up against the interior cage of the van. Finally, unable to catch my breath, feeling stitches in my side, I pushed those final strokes until a pyroclastic flow convulsed from my loins and I toppled forward.

When I awoke amid the wreckage and found her lying naked below me, I softly proposed, "Marry me." Heroin, AIDS, and anything else she had picked up—it didn't matter.

She hugged me tighter. Love had an overwhelming center of attraction surrounded by repelling forces that slowly grew more powerful. Eventually you'd be shot away as though from a cannon, but one had to forget that. Just enjoy the fleeting moments.

"I love most of you," I said earnestly.

"Please don't say that." She pulled apart.

As she tugged her pants on, clearly pissed, she said, "I have to run."

"I love you," I said again, gently grabbing her by her elbow. I didn't mean it maliciously.

"Let go." She yanked away, trying to escape—a little vampire trying to race back to her coffin before dawn.

This time I tugged her back on the mattress and pulled the back door closed. "You can come up with all the bullshit excuses and defenses, but I can't stop thinking about you. I love you and I'm not letting you go."

"Get the fuck off!" She tried to bolt out. I grabbed her, shoved her back onto the foam rubber, pinned her shoulders down and just stared into her incredible face as her eyes desperately fluttered around the dark van.

"Just hear me out. When I finish this sculpture, I'm getting a nice pile of cash. I'll be ready to get out of this city. We can leave here. We can go up to Vermont if you like, find some nice little place to live and make a new start. We can get some mindless jobs in some small hippie town somewhere, a health food store and find a place to live and . . ."

She started making this twisted expression.

". . . I'll give up this bullshit art stuff and you can try writing or whatever the fuck it is you do . . ."

Her body was tensing up. When I let her go, she quickly bolted up to a sitting position. Her face lost all its color. I thought she was about to barf all over my van. She suddenly let out this otherworldly yelp and burst into tears. She cried hard and painfully, unable to budge. I grabbed her and held her so tight I felt one with her. She wept and wept and kept mumbling some phrase over and over. Eventually I realized that she was just repeating "I'm sorry" until she was completely out. In the back of my van, on the filthy cushion, she fell deep asleep in my arms. I sat and held her softly, soaked in her tears.

As the minutes turned to hours, I could hear the city outside coming to life. The screeching and honking of cars, the footsteps and chatting of newly awakened people all filled the morning air. Eventually I heard the street sweepers, then the traffic cop who wrote me my morning ticket and slapped it under my windshield wiper.

Still Rita slept, so I didn't budge. I didn't want to stir or ever be apart from her, but eventually when my legs and arms became numb and painful, I shook her and asked if she wanted to come upstairs and sleep in the loft.

"No, I got to get home." She stretched. "Shit! Luke is going to freak."

"You want me to drive you?"

She smiled and shook her head no, not about to be tricked into showing me where she lived.

"Could I borrow this though?" she asked, grabbing my sketch pad with all the drawings I had done of her.

"Are you kidding?" I reminded her, "That's what I paid all my money for."

"I know," she said. "I just think they're wonderful and I want to show them off."

"Will you bring it back tomorrow?"

"You should never take the word of a junkie, but in this instance, I swear." She pulled her shoes on and staggered up Orchard.

Twenty

As I walked home, I passed a line of people outside of a public school. It was the day of the presidential election. When I got home, I elected to take a quick shower and get some sleep, but the phone rang. It was Moe Hammerman.

"So are we on for next Tuesday?" he asked. "'Cause I got notices in the papers and a zillion people coming to this."

"Absolutely."

"Let me just clarify, I don't need the piece late. This is an unveiling. If it's late you can keep it." I answered him that I'd have it at the cemetery the night before. I was so tired I could barely hang up the phone, but I was still racing the clock.

I pulled myself to my feet, put my clothes back on, and dragged my supplies downstairs. I worked until noon. When I could no longer keep my eyes open, I slept with my head on the unfinished takeout statue. When Lynn stirred me awake, it was dark.

"Christ," she said. She had my usual box of Buddha Delight. "Did you even go to sleep last night?"

"On this rock I built my church," I said, quoting Jesus.

"Are you okay?" she asked, looking into my eyes, perhaps assessing my sanity.

"I'm a little rushed, but fine."

"I'm racing my deadline too," she said.

"What's that?"

"My last scroll—the Halloween Parade." She added, though, that because of me it was marvelous.

"That was a great night, wasn't it?" I reflected.

"Did anything unusual happen?"

"You were there."

"I mean after you dropped me off."

"Nothing I can think of," I replied. My mind had blanked out by the long day of work and the night with Rita.

She departed and I worked on my piece. Toward the end of the evening, the only thing that kept me working was the thought of seeing Rita. When midnight came and went, and then one o'clock rolled by, I realized that she was not coming. The caprices of love are only further complicated when dating a drug addict, I thought dismissively. Unable to hold a tool any longer, I remembered that the voting had ended so I went downstairs to check the results.

As I entered the bar, it felt like I was in a dream; everyone was cheering. Everyone who ever sold a used book on the street or did a painting was there, except Shade.

"They just declared Gore the winner," Cecil said with a big shit-eating grin. Pablo was right behind him with his Balkan girlfriend.

"Did Nader get his five percent?" I asked him.

"Almost there," he replied optimistically.

"That's great!" I toasted with two glasses of ice-cold water. It was the best drink I ever had.

I crawled back upstairs and went to bed. I slept till noon the next day then went back to work.

That evening Lynn delivered my food. She set the bag down hastily, then, without saying a word, turned to go.

"What?" I replied, a little hurt, "not even a hello?"

She stopped and stared at me with buttoned lips.

"You know," she began. "I don't think of myself as . . . territorial or jealous, but I thought we were friends."

"What are you talking about?"

"When we went out Halloween night and then afterward you drove me home, I mean, I had no expectations. I liked you. I opened up to you . . ." She fell silent.

"So what are you saying?" I had no clue.

"The next day, when I came in and saw your sketch of the lips, I knew they weren't mine. You saw another girl after you dropped me off at home, didn't you?"

I didn't respond.

"A while ago, when I came in and you asked me if there was a girl here . . ."

I sighed, not quite red-handed, but certainly with scarlet streaks. She got me. This was what she was after yesterday when she asked me about Halloween night.

"I guess I thought we were maybe going somewhere and . . ."

"Look, you're right. I *am* seeing someone, and I didn't tell you 'cause the whole situation is kind of an unresolved mess. I'm sorry." I paused a moment and tried to give her an honest assessment, "I really do like you, I swear it. I just felt that neither of us were really ready . . ."

I stopped. Her lips, which were twisted into a knot, slowly disentangled.

Without looking at me she said, "You're probably right. I guess I felt bad because you lied."

"I'm sorry," I replied. "It was really stupid of me. This person I'm seeing, well, I know this sounds awful, but the real reason I didn't say anything was really 'cause I'm ashamed of being with her."

"Ashamed?"

"It's a long story." That was partly true.

"When you're ready to talk about it," she said. "You don't have to worry about me getting jealous."

I apologized and thanked her. Then back to the sculpture, monotonous work all night. No midnight coffee. No Rita. Achey sleep.

While obsessing about my beloved junkie, I realized that I had made a mammoth error. We had a nice little thing going. She was coming by regularly, letting me love her from afar, with occasional moments of spontaneous intimacy. But I got too greedy. I shouldn't have tried to take so much. I should have been the one to draw back. That was when it first really hit me. I had unprotected sex with an IV-using hooker. It seemed heroic at the time, like I was demonstrating my overwhelming love for this she-pariah. Now that I had risked my life and she wasn't even coming by, I felt like a total fool. How could I get so close to someone who by nature was so cynical and jaded she seemed born to be an addict, a user. What was this awful variety of love that made some people more attractive based on how doomed or disabled they were?

After exhausting myself with blame, I began worrying about her. She had gone through roughly four hundred dollars of the money that Shade had loaned me. Who was paying for her habit now? What disgusting old dick was she sucking? For an instant I feared that she was going to sell my precious sketch pad, but then I realized that art had no real street value.

Instead of staggering upstairs to sleep that night, I unlocked my bike and went into the filthy, diseased night and started cruising the empty streets looking for my addicted muse.

I started up Allen but didn't get very far before I saw her in black jeans and a white-and-gray-speckled T-shirt curled up on a park bench like an old pigeon. She wasn't even wearing shoes or socks. I screeched my bike to a halt and yelled, "You know you suck!"

She peeked up over her bent knees. Any normal person would have been chilled, but she seemed to be sweating.

"I know I don't have the right to expect anything from you but you are the queen of bullshit."

"Leave me alone!" she shouted.

"Where are your fucking shoes?"

She sighed and shrugged.

She sat up and I could see a big bruise on her cheek.

"Who was it this time? The sadistic boyfriend? Some friendly john? A dealer who wouldn't sell?"

"Actually, it was that voluptuous lady of leisure and color up on Houston." I assumed she was referring to the fat black hooker I had seen a while ago. "She took my fucking money and slapped the shit out of me."

"I feel like such an idiot," I said inspecting her swollen lip.

"It was *my* fault," she replied.

"You were pissed because I told you I loved you and stuff."

"You can't say shit like that to me," she replied in a scratchy voice. "You just can't. I'm already practically married and I feel guilty enough."

"I'm sorry. Here you are having an affair," I replied, enjoying the absurdity of it, "while you're supposed to be out blowing strangers." She smiled.

"And I Tiresias have forefucked them all in your filthy van, on your greasy foam-rubber bed / I who have whored by Thebes below the wall / gave blow jobs to the lowest of the dead / bestow one final patronizing kiss," she puckered her lips, "and grope my way finding the street unlit . . ." She grabbed my arm.

"Quit vulgarizing Shakespeare."

"You're such an idiot! That's Eliot." She laughed and when she did, I saw a new gap toward the rear of her mouth where a tooth was missing. By the way she was rocking back and forth, I could see she was hurting. She had gone too long without.

"Come on," I suggested. "You don't look well."

"I have to wait here," she replied.

"Why don't we go back to my place?"

"I'm actually expecting a delivery in the next twenty minutes."

"A Domino's pizza?"

"The last pie in the city. This fucking island is going through one serious drought."

She compared three or four different brands of heroin as though they were varieties of skin-care lotion. Putting her feet to the filthy ground, she leaned forward.

As I listened, I thought I was seeing things, little greasy streaks of night moving around me. I believed they were optical illusions as a result of my own exhaustion. But when one of the streaks froze, I realized that a pack of rats were all around us.

"Rita, let's get the hell out of here." I shook her. "This place is covered with rats."

"Oh relax," she said with droopy eyes. "Rats are people too. Here ratty, ratty, rat, rat . . ." Still seated, she jokingly reached out toward one huge rat that was trying to pass.

I looked down just it jumped off the ground and onto the front of her bare foot.

"Oh shit!" she screamed, kicking it into the air. Then, pulling her legs up, she grabbed her bare foot, and started laughing in disbelief.

"Fuck!" I yelled. A bunch of the rats scattered across the eastern side of Allen Street. I looked at the wound. The nip was just above the ankle. A small pinch of skin was missing and blood was oozing out.

"Look at this shit! Rats spend a lifetime eating garbage and their choppers are as sharp as . . . I don't brush for a couple days and my teeth are . . ." She couldn't complete her sentences.

"Come on," I yelled, hailing an approaching cab. "You got to get to a hospital. Beth Israel is right up the block."

"No fucking way!" she shot back. "Not until I get my shit."

"Sweetheart, you've been bit by a rat. You could get . . . the plague."

"Don't even try," she warned, pressing the oozing little wound to the leg of her filthy pants.

"Look, I've put up with a lot from you, but this is it."

"Leave then!" she seethed.

"Fine." I started walking away. "But don't ask me for any more money." It was a pathetic thing to say, but it was the only card I had.

"Fucking hold it a moment." She leapt in front of me. "He's going to get here any minute. Let me shoot and then we'll go." She looked at me with tears in her eyes and said, "Please, Or, the pain I'm feeling is a million times worse than being bit by some ghetto hamster."

I sighed, without a choice. We took seats on the filthy benches and sat very still.

Slowly, as the cars passed, a scary-looking black guy seemed to congeal from the darkness. As he walked stiffly over to us, I thought we were going to be mugged. He marched right up to Rita's face and asked, "You got any, do you?"

"I wish," she replied tiredly without even looking at him.

When he walked away, I asked, "Who the hell is that?"

"LBJ," she said tiredly. "The Loose Brotherhood of Junkies. He's just looking for somewhere to score."

"Isn't someone coming to sell here?" I asked.

"Yeah, and fuck if I'm giving away my source."

"I'm just glad he didn't attack us."

"They're all a pretty useless bunch." Then thinking about it a moment, she revised her statement. "Actually they're not bad."

As I looked at her wearing her dirty, torn T-shirt spotted with crud and blood, the filthy ripped jeans and blackened bare feet, I wondered if she knew how awful she looked. In the street light, her skin had assumed a reddish tone. For the first time, she actually looked worse than the sickly rendition I initially did of her in my purgatory mural. She must have sensed my dismay, because she abruptly said, "If you knew for an instant how much range I've experienced in this little life."

"What do you mean range?"

"I grew up with money," she said proudly. "I mean you probably think I'm lying, but I had a tennis coach, a horse named Barron. Prep school, Ivy League. I had my fucking coming out at the Waldorf. I met Reagan when I was a teenager . . ."

"Do you have your little jigger of water?" I asked.

"Why?"

"Why don't you wash off your bite," I suggested, seeing how filthy her ankle was.

"My mother was compulsively clean," she said as she sprinkled some drops on the little laceration. I gave her a clean napkin that was in my pocket. She swabbed it gently. "Mom was always washing her hands. No kidding. We weren't permitted to swim in public pools or even beaches. Antibacterial soap—always. 'Wash your hair . . . wash your feet . . .' I went from all that to . . ." Her voice trailed.

She didn't need to finish. At that moment, nursing a rat bite, while waiting for a fix—it had to be "this."

"In ten years I'll be amazed if Allen Street doesn't become a high-rental strip mall—Eastlito," I said, imagining an extension of Nolita. "Or maybe Nochoto—North Chinatown."

"Right now, it's just Shit-o," she replied. "It should be a fucking Disneyland exhibit—Shitland." She came up with a catchy tune: "The people are shit. The air is shit. I eat shit. Hell you're shit too!"

"A shitty place for me and you," I concluded.

"Remember, on our first date, I crapped my pants."

"I didn't know that was a date, but yes, you did soil," I replied.

"See, you even try to extract the shit from the conversation." She looked off. "All of it. All those awful things Mom tried to protect me from, all she tried to wash away. Aging. Disease. Death. All those nasty germs. But you can't keep it away. You know five percent of the tap water down here is raw sewage? You're washing in shit. Bottled water? Forget it! Where does that come from, mountain springs on Mars? No, it's from *here*—Shitsville. And do you know what all that means? Shit means disease and death. It's already in us. And all the chemo and surgery can't get it out. We're born with our death inside of us." She grew silent. I tiredly listened to cars whizzing by.

A Latin kid who looked to be no older than sixteen came out of nowhere, and jumped the curb on a brand-new five-hundred-dollar mountain bike.

She hopped to her feet and dashed over. They talked in quick whispers. When the two seemed to shake hands, I knew there was an exchange. He zoomed off on his bike as though in pursuit. Rita dashed back over, with the little bag she had just purchased. On the bench, she took out her works and proceeded to perform her little ritual. But a tremor kept her hands shaking. I could tell by how she was clenching her body that her stomach was going south on her. Suddenly she leaned forward and dry heaved a couple of times. Nothing came up. The heroin had probably taken her appetite.

"Are you okay?" I asked.

"Keep an eye out for the cocks, cause if that Rogerfucker grabs me now . . . I swear, I'll grab his fucking gun and shove it up his ass! That cocksucker *ever* tries that again, I'll fucking . . ." She slowly caught her breath.

"Relax." Obviously he had done something awful to her. "I'll keep an eye out."

"I'm just a little tense after waiting so fucking long and . . . my nerves are jumpy," she said. Her head and body jerked and shook uncontrollably as she talked. Dipping her finger into the little baggie, she rubbed a dab of the powder along her upper gums. She closed her eyes and just sat calm for a minute as though meditating.

In a moment, she seemed to have conquered her trembling hands. In the next instant, her fix was cooked and injected and she was breathing deeply, just inhaling and focusing on the special events that were occurring somewhere between her heart and brain. A row of minutes later, she underwent her great internal transformation, turning from cold-turkey girl to Super Heroin Woman.

"Come on," I said as I pulled her to her feet. Her rat bite needed attention.

"I'm really okay," she replied, slowly frozen in ecstasy.

"You fucking promised," I said angrily. "And you're not getting anything more out of me unless you do this."

"Okay," she conceded tiredly. I locked up my bike and we walked up to Delancey. There I finally waved at a cab coming down off the Williamsburg Bridge. Rita was still blasé about the entire gash, which was now beginning to scab. We got out of the cab on the corner of Sixteenth Street and First.

Twenty-one

"My friend just got bitten by a rat," I said as I entered Beth Israel. A bored desk nurse told us to go around the corner to the ER. As we walked up to the automatic sliding double doors, Rita paused, took a deep breath and said, "Do me a favor, let me handle this."

"What do you mean?"

"You'll see," she responded.

I figured she was pulling some scam, but gave her the benefit of the doubt. When she kicked open the door, she started screaming at the top of her lungs, "Help me! Oh fucking Christ almighty, help me!"

An orderly and a nurse came running over.

"What happened!" one screamed. Rita bent over and toppled to the polished linoleum floor, grabbing her foot, writhing in pain.

"What's the matter!" the other asked. Two orderlies and I lifted her onto a gurney. They wheeled her past a large, well-lit room full of needy people sitting down the corridor.

"I got bit by a fucking monster!"

"We have a rat bite!" One nurse said to another as if Rita had been attacked by a great white shark.

"Put her in four," said the administrator.

I went into the room with her.

"Oh God! I'm in pain, oh fucking God!" she cried, rocking back and forth, clenching her foot. A nurse came over, pushed Rita's hands away and looked at the wound.

"Where are your shoes?"

"I took them off."

"It doesn't look too bad," she replied.

"The pain is shooting up my fucking leg!" Rita replied. The nurse got a hypodermic and then, looking at her leg, tried to find a vein. Finally she tied on a rubber tourniquet. After a minute, the nurse spotted something that looked like a dark line streaking under her thigh, but she couldn't locate it.

"Who hit you?" the nurse asked Rita, referring to her facial bruise.

"An accident."

"Is your drug problem an accident too?" the nurse tiredly replied. Rita didn't respond. After spearing poor Rita two more times in her leg and reapplying the tourniquet to her arm, she finally hit a vein and injected her with a painkiller called Toradol. Then she left the room.

"How you doing?" I asked after seeing her get jabbed more times than a retired tailor's pincushion.

"It's actually refreshing to feel a new needle," she confided. "My old one cuts like a fucking butter knife."

In a moment, as the painkiller calmed her down, Rita said, "If I knew I was going to get a injection, I would've shot up later."

"So why did you put on that big show of being in pain?" I asked her.

"There is no fucking way I am waiting four hours to have a Band-Aid put on," she explained. "That's all these people are going to do."

She wasn't far from accurate. She was given a registration form, in which she offered no real information: no residence, a false date of birth, no pre-existing health problems, and no next of kin. She was even reluctant to give her name, which she finally listed as "Bridget Jones." After returning the form, two more hours passed. I sat in the chair by her bed and tried to sleep. It wasn't until four in the morning that some foreign teenager who passed for an intern popped in and even looked at her ankle.

"I understand you were bit by a rat," he said.

"It looked more like a Rottweiler with a long tail," she replied, slowly coming down from her own buzz.

"Actually," he replied as he irrigated the little wound, "I think Rottweilers have tails, but they get snipped off." He shot her with some antibiotics, then brought her into another room where he gave her three stitches and bandaged her.

"We should do a blood test to make sure you don't have rabies."

"It's not necessary," she replied. "The rat was wearing a condom." Perhaps because it was evident she had no way of paying for the visit, the doctor didn't push it.

"If I give you an antibiotics prescription, will you take it?"

"'Course, and I also need a painkiller." He scribbled out a prescription and handed it to her. As she read it, he added, "You can get an over-the-counter painkiller."

"You really know how to fuck up someone's high. They teach you that in medical school?"

"Ms. Jones," he added tiredly, "if you're interested, the nurse can give you a brochure listing various drug rehabilitation centers."

She didn't respond. One of the nurses provided her with a green pair of disposable hospital slippers. In a moment we stepped out onto the street, where she squeezed the prescription in a ball and tossed it at a cab. We slowly started our long walk against the traffic, down First Avenue.

"That was really stupid of me, wasn't it?" she asked. "Getting bit by a rat."

"Just another thing in a long line," I replied stoically.

When we finally reached Fourth Street, we rested on the benches near the projects. I was as groggy as hell, approaching total collapse. She was still in her own wacky heroin-Toradol nirvana.

"I'm sorry," she managed to say. "Sorry for meeting you, and fucking with you, and putting you through all this."

"I don't understand you. I really don't understand why someone would want to do . . ." I caught myself, not wanting to make her any more miserable than she already was. "Do you think there's an afterlife?"

"The here and now is my hereafter," she answered. "You can't fully live if you're worrying about death."

"If you really feel that there is nothing afterward, how can you live so cavalierly?"

"Life is esssentially disposable, no matter what we do. Billions have come and gone. Billions more will be born and die. So fucking what? There's a reason nothing lasts. Do you think your art has a chance of withstanding time? If anything, I think what *I'm* doing makes a lot more sense than what *you're* doing."

"Is that how you justify living like this?"

"And I thought this was a theological argument, when actually we're back at square one again." She groaned.

She was right. I had no business being with her in this hell, complaining about the heat. I had to get back to my own purgatory.

"I'm just worried," I explained. "I have a few more days to finish that fucking rock or I'm seriously screwed."

"Well, you should just be working on it until you're done," she replied. She sighed, "In fact . . ."

"In fact, what?"

"I'm leaving tomorrow."

"Leaving?! Where are you going?"

"This city is in one severe dry spell. I'm heading south for a few days to get some good shit, but . . ." There was something she wasn't saying. There was always something.

"What's the problem?"

"Well I know this sounds awful, but do you think you can loan me some money until I get back? I mean, you should be rich in a few days, right?"

"How much do you need?"

"Nothing. Two."

"Two what?"

"Hundred," she said. When she saw my face frozen solid, she explained, "I just got a great tip from an old friend in Jersey. For two hundred bucks, I can take a bus through the tunnel, make a big score, and be back up in a couple hours with enough shit to last me a week."

I felt tremendous guilt having spent most of the thousand dollars Shade had loaned me on Rita's habit instead of hiring moving men to ship the sculpture to Long Island. The only detail that appeased this was the fact that I hadn't spent a cent of his money on myself.

"Two hundred dollars for drugs," I said without disguising my disgust. "Are you increasing your habit?"

"No way. This is quality shit at a great price!" she swore. "And you won't have to pay me for a week, two weeks! Hell, you're getting a bargain on me."

"It sounds like a MacDonald's gift certificate." I replied, tickled pink that she could get high at a discount. We didn't talk for the rest of our long march down to Chinatown. I used the time to try to rally some resistance to her.

Just turn and say, fuck off. Die on your own fucking dime. Leave me alone. But each time I looked at her I gagged. Heroin was her addiction, and she was mine. I knew that eventually my love could weaken and I'd be able to leave her. But the fact that I knew this did not give me any greater power at that moment.

When we finally reached the loft, she came upstairs and I reluctantly counted out ten twenty dollar bills that I couldn't afford to part with. I held the money in the air.

"I want one last thing in return," I said, folding the bills tightly in my fist. "What I'm going to ask you is bogus, okay?"

"What do you mean bogus?"

"I just want you to give me a little phone sex without the phone."

She smiled at the idea of role playing. "You mean like I want to lick your . . ."

"I want you to look me in my eyes. Pretend I'm someone else. In fact, pretend I'm Lucas." I could see the amusement vanish when I said his name, violating her private world. I leaned close to her and softly articulated, "I want you to look me in the eyes and just say, I love you."

Her face grew sour and she looked to the ground conflicted, unable to stand there, unable to leave.

"I know it sounds pathetic, but I'll give you the money if you just say the words."

More minutes passed. She didn't leave, but she wouldn't say anything.

"Can't you just close your eyes and cough it out?" I watched as her beautiful eyes began to tear.

"How about, I like you an awful lot?" I finally offered.

She smiled and, reaching up, she cupped my face softly in her cold, grimy hands and gently stroked my unshaven cheeks. My whole universe became a short tunnel, with her eyes at the other end. Leaning forward, she kissed me gently on the lips.

Finally, she pulled back. I just couldn't punish her for withholding her last shred of dignity. I put the money in her hand and walked her downstairs. When she crossed Canal, I stayed on my corner. Bowery and Chrystie Street were being repaved, so a stream of cars coming off the Manhattan Bridge were being rerouted up Allen.

"See you in three days," I called out above their engines. She waved good-bye from the far side. I turned to go, when I heard my name.

"I just wanted you to know," she yelled between the walls of shooting vehicles, "I studied art in college! I have a graduate degree in art history!"

"You're kidding."

"There's something about great work like da Vinci's or Giacometti's that compels someone to say the piece is fully realized."

"What's realized?" I could barely hear her above a succession of passing trucks.

"Their art is fully finished, that's a sign of greatness," she shouted. "If man survives another thousand years, people will still imitate their style, and use their ideas, but no artist will be able to improve upon them." As an interval of quieter cars passed, I heard her say, "Some of your work has that quality, it really does. It has greatness."

"Thank you," I replied, wishing I felt that way myself.

"It probably comes as no surprise that . . . I only hurt those I come into contact with. The fact that you're a great artist is far more important than anything I can say." She paused and added, "My love would do you no service."

"It's all I want right now," I replied earnestly.

"There's no one else in this world right now who I actually look forward to seeing. No one else who . . ." She stopped herself and then, angrily, she conceded, "Shit! I do love you."

"What's the matter with that!" I wanted to rush across the street back to her, but cars were being waved through the green light.

"I just hate giving away that much power . . ." Her voice trailed off.

"You don't have to worry about me," I assured her.

"Not to you. To life. Believe it or not," she took a deep sigh, "it took a lot of work to get to where I am now."

"What the hell does that mean?"

"It means I fucked up, and I love you. And good-bye." She turned and dashed off. Again, in her topsy-turvy universe where everything meant the inside-out exact opposite, I was not sure what she was talking about. Like most seriously fucked-up people, she seemed to talk through me to a lifetime of traumas and unresolved issues. All I was sure of was that for a single instant I felt wonderful.

I slept late into the next day. Lynn didn't wake me. When I finally got up, had my coffee, and was situated back at my rock, it was five o'clock and the sun had set. There was still a question as to whether I'd make my deadline. I worked as hard as I could at doing the final careful chisels.

When I finally went upstairs, it was eleven. I was beat and the work was nearing completion. Covered with sweat and white dust, I pulled off my mask and goggles and was ready for the shower. Then the phone rang.

I answered to hear Bethsheba's sultry voice: "I tried calling you all evening, where were you?"

"Working."

"Amazing about the election huh?"

"Yeah," I replied tiredly.

"There's a big opening tomorrow at the Luftwaffe Gallery on Twentieth Street. Are you game?"

"Who's showing?"

"Elmer Elder." He was a big, hot sensational downtown something or other.

"What the hell, I can use a laugh." On a Post-it, I absentmindedly scribbled "Tomorrow nite, foto show," and doodled a pair of large breasts next to it.

"Let's meet out front around seven," she suggested.

"See you there." Upon hanging up the phone, I thought I'd drop in to the bar downstairs.

I tried to dress, but my arms were too tired to pull on my pants. My fingers cramped when I tried to button my shirt. I rolled onto the bed and fell asleep.

Twenty-two

Stonecutting late the next morning, I was jarred out of my fried mental state by a heart-stopping boom behind me as the fire exit door swung open.

"Look who's almost done!" It was Shade. "You should've switched tools by now," he instantly snapped. "Remember, I told you to go to smaller, more delicate tools as you get deeper into the piece."

"Yeah, well," I began tiredly, arching my aching back and yawning.

"Be careful how you hold that point," he further cautioned me.

"I've been doing just fine up until now."

"Yeah, I know about doing fine," he replied, holding up his thumb. The top knuckle was flattened and the nail was shaved off. "I've known sculptors whose ligaments realigned freakishly from a lifetime of holding chisels the wrong way."

"Thanks for the tip," I concluded, not feeling receptive to criticism.

"God, look at your hands," he said clutching at my rough palms. "My poor baby is no longer a virgin."

"Girls like a rough-handed man."

"Actually they don't," he shot back. "You better buy some Jurgen's before your callus gets so thick you won't even be able to jerk yourself."

I yawned and commented that I was starving.

"Amazing about the election."

"Everything worked out for the best."

He chuckled, looked at me strangely, and said, "How long have you been out here?"

"Why?"

"I'm going to take you for lunch," he said. "The world has changed, my son."

"Changed how?" I asked as I rose to my feet and straightened out my aching back.

"Don't you listen to the radio or read any headlines?" Shade didn't have a television, and papers always made me depressed. "The nation is in the grips of a constitutional crisis. A major recount is going on, my boy. Thousands of ballots for Gore were thrown out, and now Bush is ahead by less than three hundred votes."

"You're bullshitting me, right?" I stopped walking. "They can't just announce someone is president and then . . ." Everything seemed slightly unreal. "I feel like I awoke in the opposite of *It's a Wonderful Life*."

"Don't give up hope, son. Gore is challenging the count," he repeated. "All we need are two or three busloads of American Jews who are visiting the holy lands. Once they count their mail-in ballots, Gore will prevail."

We walked over to the budget dim sum joint, chatting about the election as we bought some of the local fare. We parked on the benches where we sat and gobbled down our hot, doughy appetizers.

"Hey, Shade," I heard, and looking up I saw him.

"Wayne," Shade said, "it's so good to see you!" Shade jumped up and the two men hugged.

It was the face of evil—the diabolic bald man that Shade had selected as one of his precious portraits worth keeping. Staring at him as he kidded with the older painter, I saw that the hairless visage of spiteful cruelty had aged about twenty years. I continued eating to signal that I was on to this disciple of the devil.

"Wayne here is responsible for my seductive smile," Shade commented.

"What?" I swallowed down my last bite.

"He was my dentist years ago. And when I didn't have a pot to piss in, Wayne would still do my fillings and root canal out of his own pocket."

"Well, Shade gave paintings in return," the older bald man replied. "They still adorn my office today."

"Just drippery," Shade said modestly.

"He did a variety of paintings of me with my two sisters," Wayne explained, grinning. Those must have been the two women who were cropped in the portrait upstairs.

After Shade opened his mouth and the tooth doctor quickly inspected his own gallery of work, Wayne the diabolic D.D.S. was gone. I didn't reveal that I had secretly glimpsed the painting of the man and assumed it to be a portrait of sin incarnate. I did, however, start doubting my artistic interpretations.

Shade noticed some of the addicts, his old acquaintances, were slowly coming up the block. Not wanting to get entangled in any superfluous conversations, he bid me good day and ducked out.

The needle exchangers arrived moments later. The users lined up to swap their old spikes. I stuck around, praying I might see my own little sickness, Rita, hoping she might've returned early from her big Jersey score. Obsession and eternal hopefulness were the withdrawal pains of love. When one of the staffers passed nearby, I discreetly asked, "Seen Rita?"

"Man, you better speak to Lou!" He pointed to a small, skinny kid with pimples, springy blonde hair, and glasses.

"Have you seen Rita?" I repeated the question.

"You're not here for the exchange, are you?" he asked tightening his brow.

"No, just a friend."

"Yeah, I remember you from before."

"I was the one who told you I saw her in the park."

"Right." He stepped very close to me, entering my personal space. "You might remember . . . she had a drug problem."

"Unfortunately I do happen to recall that detail," I replied, and sensed I was about to get a sermon.

"Some people helped her, giving her money and resupplying her." He spoke slowly and looked right in my eye.

"Well, I'm an artist. I don't use drugs," I said softly, feeling a twinge of guilt for funding her habit.

"*You're* the artist?" A light seemed to flash on in his head.

"Has she mentioned me?" I asked, suddenly feeling a surge of joy.

He nodded silently, smiling, and took a step back.

"She took my sketch pad and I was hoping to get it back," I said, instead of explaining my irresistible devotion to her.

"You did those sketches of her?" he asked.

"You saw them?"

"They're amazing," he replied with a big smile. "Did you do anything else of her?"

"Actually I did a mural. But I did it earlier and it's a little more stylish."

"God, I'd love to see it," he said, lifting his brows.

"So have you seen her, or what?" I asked. The hippie kid was beginning to get on my nerves.

He looked at me sharply. I sensed that he had something to say but was trying to determine whether I could be trusted or not. I smiled and tried to look concerned, hiding my own shame. After all, in addition to money, I had bought her drugs *and* fucked her.

"Her parents came and did an intervention, so she's back up in Vermont with them to clean up."

"You're kidding?"

"No. She's an inpatient at a rehab clinic up there."

"I'm amazed that she didn't fight them."

"Yeah well, I'm not sure how much she agreed to it and how much they forced her."

"So she's out of town," I replied. "I wish you just said so in the first place." I was annoyed about all the bullshit I had to put up with just to get a simple answer.

"Do you have a phone number or anything?" I asked.

"I don't."

"Shit." I asked, "How can I get in touch with her?"

"That's what I'm trying to say. I don't think she's coming back."

"Well, what are her parents' names? I'll look her up in the book." Even Vermont must have a phone directory.

"Why don't you give me your number and the next time I see her I'll pass it along."

"Sounds good." I scribbled down Shade's phone number. He looked at the number and suddenly cringed, looking down and away.

"Shit!" he said, clenching up his face like a fist.

"What?"

"Some shit just got in my eye." His hand covered his face.

"Want me to look at it?" The air on Allen Street was thick with soot.

"No thanks," he replied finally. "She had the soul of an artist, you know. I think that's how she initially got into drugs. She felt as though she had to experience everything to understand it."

"Why do people feel compelled to suffer hell in order to render it into art?" I asked rhetorically, addressing my own life as much as hers.

"I think it's like drowning," he replied. "You don't know it's happening until it's too late."

I headed back to work, a latter-day Sisyphus doomed to roll my stone forever. After about an hour, quite unexpectedly, I found myself at the end of my forever. At roughly five o'clock, I realized all four sides were in perfect proportion with the top. And the angles were exact— I was done. I still had two more days of sanding, but one more whack or scratch of a chisel could have damaged the piece.

While I was filing down some large bumps, Lynn visited me.

"I'm almost embarrassed to say this," I announced, "but it's finished."

"Finished?" she said as though the word were foreign.

"Well, I'm done with the chisel anyway."

"Congratulations." She paused a moment stepping back awkwardly. "You sculpted a real statue."

"Yeah, and I'm never doing it again."

"You're telling me you learned an entire skill just to make one piece?"

"I only did it because the stone was here."

"Lucky there wasn't a rifle out here, you might've hired yourself out as a killer," she kidded.

As she was about to leave, she added, "Don't forget about your opening tonight."

"What opening?"

"Weren't you supposed to meet a pair of breasts at some photo show?"

"That's right!" I had completely forgotten about my meeting with Bethsheba.

"I saw some strange Post-it near the phone," she revealed with a smile.

Intense hours of finishing work still lay ahead, before delivery. But after being sentenced to this stairwell hell for what felt like years, I finally was entitled to this breath of freedom. It was six o'clock and I had to shave, shower, eat, and arrive in Chelsea by seven. Tiredly I pulled myself up the stairs and scrubbed in the shower. I dressed while still wet. Before dashing out, something occurred to me. I grabbed one of the early studies I had done of Rita's beautiful face, and carefully rolled it up.

I bought a cold pork bun from an outdoor vendor, and an awful cup of wake-up coffee at a newspaper stand. By six forty-five, I caught the F train at the East Broadway stop. As I rode out there, I kept wondering why I had agreed to go to another bullshit art opening when I had to finish and deliver the sculpture in less than forty hours. I grabbed a bus across Twenty-third to Tenth Avenue.

Bethsheba was already there, wearing a tight, strapless dress that seemed to be sewn around her boobs. She was standing outside the building among a bulge of fashionable types on the otherwise empty street talking to a flamer I called Microsoft. His real name was Microft, but, having a problem remembering names, I simply referred to him as the software giant. He was a tall German queen, complete with a purple buzz cut. Tonight he had tightly strapped himself into a bright orange jumpsuit. If he didn't dress like a Day-Glo, gay disco skater, he could have been the pride of the Rhineland.

"Hey guys." I joined them. Beth gave me a peck on the cheek.

"Or," Micro leapt right in, "let me ask you a very important question. Do you sign your exquisite pieces?"

"Just the backs, sometimes. Why?"

"Do you title your very exquisite pieces?"

"I used to title them, in the old days." I smiled. "But only the very exquisite ones."

"Do you have an exquisite work entitled *The F-Train Blues*? A colorful picture of the F train in the Second Avenue station?"

"About one square foot?" I recalled.

"Yah!" he replied. "That's the one."

I remembered dashing it off one cold afternoon in late winter. The subway station was the only place I could stand for an hour without having the cartilage in my knuckles freeze. On the back, with a black caligraphy pen, I had scribbled *The Fucking Train Blues*—then I whited out the "ucking." I also remembered selling it right off the easel to some rush-hour slave for about fifty bucks. "I did it about ten years ago. What, did you see it in some Goodwill?"

"No, at a big party in the Hamptons this summer," Microsoft said.

"In the Hamptons! Really? Who has it?"

"Leon Noel, the commodities trader. He has it in his bathroom."

"Well, I hope it relaxes him while he craps. Let's get this over with." The building at 531 West 20th Street was devoted to galleries. Eleven floors with as many as five art spaces per landing. We were going to the third floor.

Silk screener Elmer Elder was blasted out of a publicity canon about twenty years ago, along with a group of young downtown artists, all Andy Warhol protégés, who were overhyped and oversold in the early '80s. One by one they vanished by the end of that decade. In the mid-'90s, Elder's reinvention started when his amateur Polaroids of street hustlers and local celebrities began appearing sporadically in the pages of downtown magazines. Below them were shockingly scribbled captions, like "Loves to suck cock."

Although his artistic merits were frequently questioned, his work, whether fatuously pornographic or vapidly violent, was rarely boring. Finally, after five years, enough of his images had broken through the collective consciousness of downtown society, and some dealer conceded him a show. Tonight was his second opening.

The wait for the elevator seemed particularly long as spectators accumulated. Although the gallery was only on the third floor, no one dared the stairs. Several people muttered comments about the election, but Microft and Bethsheba were louder. They were discussing the hot cable TV show *Sex and the City*. Beth was mentioning the latest fetishistic episode: "I tell you, this week Carrie eats crap."

We heard the freight elevator finally stop. From inside, the operator pulled open its doors. Along with the rest of the art community, we packed in. As the car silently lifted upward, they decided to resume their conversation.

"Come on, Carrie didn't do any such thing," Micro said, referring to the principal character in the series.

"It's only acting, I mean, I don't think Sarah Jessica Parker *actually* eats shit," Beth mitigated. "It's probably just chocolate pudding."

"Now I know this has got to be a lie, because if they were using some prop for poop they wouldn't use something soft like pudding."

"Well maybe it was a brownie, I don't know. They showed it quickly."

Even though Beth was keeping a straight face, I knew she was getting a rise out of annoying everyone in our padded cell.

"I don't know if I should believe you." Micro weighed the possibilities. "If this was Germany, maybe, but American TV . . ."

"It's not TV, it's HBO," Beth tagged on.

"Look, I know the producers will degrade those poor girls to no end just to keep the ratings up. On the other hand, I honestly don't think America's ready for coprophagy."

The operator finally yanked open the clanky door and we all tumbled into the art space. It was a lot smaller than I remembered. Even before our crowd unloaded, the gallery was unpleasantly packed. We strained through the existing crowd and slowly mixed in. Unlike the usual mundane turnout, this gang had a few minor celebrities. I spotted Victor Oakridge laughing across the room. Abandoning Beth and Micro, I went over to him.

As usual he was immersed in a conversation with two other wheeler-dealers. Together they seemed to be plotting to rob the up-and-coming artists of the day.

"Excuse me, Vic." I grabbed him by the elbow. "If I could just speak to you alone a minute."

"Or, please don't touch me," he said as we walked.

"This is important." I brought him off to the side and there I uncoiled my sketch of Rita. "Do you recognize this girl?"

"Give me a paternity test. I swear I didn't sleep with her," he kidded. I ignored him.

"She had long hair when I saw her talking to you."

He held the sketch up to the light and I could see a gradual stirring of recognition.

"Or." The nasty critic Klein Ritter crawled down beside me. "I want to tell you that—"

"Later!" I swatted him away while Victor considered the portrait.

"But tomorrow the new issue of—"

"Fuck off!" I yelled at him, and again asked Victor, "Do you know her, yes or no?"

"Is she here?" He looked around.

"No, who is she?"

"This is the youngest of the Wood girls," he introduced. "What's her name again?"

"Rita?"

"No that's not it. It begins with an E, Like Eustace or Eudora, some literary name like that."

"Are you sure we're talking about the same girl?"

"What's the matter, you don't have enough faith in your rendering?"

"No, that's her, but—"

"You don't forget someone like that. The last time I saw her was at least a year ago, probably closer to two. She has graduate degrees in both art history and museum administration." She had only recently revealed as much to me. "She was about to get some big assistant curator job."

"A curator? Like a painting curator?"

"More like Americana stuff. It might have been textile arts, something arcane like that. She really knew her stuff too. I remember reading a scholarly article she wrote, 'Street Culture and Outsider Art.'"

"Are you sure we are talking about the same girl?" I asked.

"With a sexy little laugh and a rather biting sense of profane humor."

"Yeah."

"And as I recall, a great ass," he added. I nodded absently. "I spent about a week trying to get her into bed," he mused. For an instant I felt like a million bucks. I got to sleep with her and he couldn't. "How much is this? You really caught her."

"Sorry, not for sale," I said snatching it out of his hands.

"How the hell did she wind up on your speed dialer?" he asked.

"I just met her on the street." I didn't want to reveal too much.

"Well, I don't mind telling you that if you're looking for a fast track, she's it. She's Ivy League, money, connections up the wazoo. What's she doing now?"

"She's back with her family," I said curtly.

"Well, I'm glad to see you two together again," Victor said to someone behind me. I turned to see June. If I hadn't been swept up in the awful spell of Rita, I probably would've still been hurt. But our relationship now felt like a lifetime ago. She was in an expensive dress, looking puffy with a swollen, unfamiliar bust. I suddenly realized with horror that she must have had a boob job.

"I have to get back to my group," Victor said, meaning his class. Then he was gone.

"I want you to know, Or, despite the fact that you hurt me deeply, I really did love you, and I suppose part of me always will."

"I'm so sorry for destroying your work," I said sincerely. "But most of all, I'm sorry for ruining the best relationship I ever had."

"I forgive you," she said formally. "And I'm sorry for stabbing your Fishermen portrait. And I still have the Swimmer piece I took from the Entrance Art exhibit, if you want it back."

"Consider it a wedding gift. It goes nicely with the one Barclay bought." I paused again and repeated, "I really am sorry about destroying your work."

"Look what it led to. There is no way I could have traded those three pieces into this lifestyle." She chuckled. "It all worked out."

"Please don't say that. I never did anything so awful in all my life," I replied. "And you have such a great gift and—"

"You know being an artist is as much about endurance as it is about talent," she declared, "and I just couldn't take it any more."

I wanted to tell her that she was trading a future of greatness for toys and luxurious distractions, but what good would it do. She was married to the man. They lived together in splendor. Once in heaven, no one willingly goes back to hell.

Beth didn't even notice that I was talking with my ex. She was still fruit-flying around with her German queen.

"This is Barclay!" June pulled the skinny rich kid from the thick, oily crowd, as though he were a rabbit in a magic show. His little hand absently slipped into mine.

"He introduced us," he reminded her quietly.

Surprisingly, I no longer wanted to kill him. Life had brought me to a completely different place. Now, I only wanted to ask if he was the one responsible for surgically ruining the most beautiful set of breasts I had ever seen.

"Bar!" someone behind him called out. He turned, and I could see the rich youth was glad to be pulled away.

"Did you hear about Cali going back to Greece?" I asked, unable to think of anything else.

"Yeah. You know, the last time I saw her, we got into a fight," June explained.

"You're kidding. About what?"

"She came to my wedding reception, got totally shitfaced, and told me that I had dumped the prince for the frog." I chuckled. She continued, "I mean, I'm not deluded, Or. You are better looking, but you know, I never left *you*. I left the lifestyle."

I thought she left me because I destroyed her art, so I felt compelled to ask, "Did you cheat on me, June?"

"No, but if I knew the outcome, I would have."

"What the fuck is that supposed to mean?"

"I just meant . . . Look, I just wanted to say that if you need any help or money—"

"What would I do with it?" I fired back. "Oh, I know, I'll get a bad boob job!"

"Oh, you think . . . ?" she asked, instantly realizing I was talking about her. "I'm pregnant, asshole! And I was just trying to be nice." She turned to find Barclay the bankroll.

No sooner was she gone than I wanted to apologize. She had condemned herself to this polite yet boring millionaire. Maybe her tradeoff wasn't so bad, particularly since she had more than her fill of deprivation. But to me, at that moment, the passion, the reversals, and all the little intrigues and gambles, with no guaranteed outcome, that was the whole point to life.

After looking at the work, I located my campy little duet, who were still amusing their insecure narcissistic selves. I grabbed Bethsheba by her arm and led her into the larger space next door. Micro followed, still talking to her. At every opening I always made a habit of looking for the best piece; then I would try to congratulate the artist for it. To me, money and popularity notwithstanding, a genuine compliment from one's peer was a profound reward.

The entire show by Elmer, though somewhat titillating at first, was simply a pathetic rehashing at still-life *Candid Camera*. One series of large photographs entitled *Do You Know How to Get There?* showed a sequence of a stunning blond woman with exposed breasts, nonchalantly asking directions from average Joes on the street. The first pigeon was a construction worker who seemed to politely try not to notice her beautiful knockers. The second photo was of a young cop who seemed conflicted between enforcing the law and taking the situation in stride. *Condescension to the Working Man*, would have been a better title. Beth and Micro didn't even notice the series, still engulfed in their silly, self-parodying chat.

In the next room the exhibit pressed on. A large banner explained, "The Sacrifices Some Dilettantes Will Make to View 'Great Art.'" The series of photos were located in a familiar setting. Then I realized it was Dumbo, and immediately I recognized the scene. In another moment, when Bethsheba abruptly fell silent, I knew she noticed it too. One picture was of a middle-aged woman dangling from a rope out of a window. Another was of a geek perilously balanced on a plank suspended a hundred feet in the air. In the next two poster-size pictures, there we were: Bethsheba was dashing out of a window with the rope in her hands. I was tiptoeing on a slumping wooden beam across the courtyard. The cocksucker had secretly taken photos of the entire event.

"Son of a bitch!" Bethsheba uttered.

Perhaps a bit too passionately, I tore the massive photo off the wall.

"What the hell do you think you're doing!" someone yelled as I ripped down all the other pictures in the exhibit.

"Elmer! Roy!"

"What the fuck are you doing to my work!" A tuxedoed, bleached head immediately grabbed me from behind, yanking my arms into a full nelson. I felt pretty sore from the past week of chiseling and I braced for more pain. Instantly, though, all that changed. Bethsheba flew across the room like a killer koala bear, right onto Elmer's unsuspecting back, knocking us all face forward across a reception table. Beth was up on her feet first, kicking the sensationalist in his kidneys and the lumbar region of his vertebrae. I turned around and punched him once with all my might across his narrow fish-like face. Then I grabbed Beth just before she could slam a heavy marble vase onto Elmer's nimble skull, which doubtless would have killed him.

Everyone crowded into the tight room.

Victor picked up part of a torn-down photograph and hollered, "I just purchased this piece!"

Since I knew a healthy smattering of the spectators, I took the liberty of trying to acquit myself. "This asshole tricked a bunch of people into risking their lives so he could secretly snap these stupid photos."

Turning to the curator, I added, "And by the way, we are going to sue this fucking gallery, 'cause he never got releases for any of them!"

"I tricked no one," he said, standing up, wiping the blood off his nose job. "I merely put up signs! If you morons risked your lives that was your own stupidity. And I made certain not to take photos of your ugly faces."

"This will play great with the article," squeaked the critic Klein Ritter, softly clapping his spongy little feelers together.

"Next time you do something like this," I shouted into Elmer's bruised face, "realize that you're risking your own life too!"

As Bethsheba and I stormed out, June gave me a sympathetic nod.

"I'm sorry," I said to her regarding my own nastiness earlier. "If you can forgive me twice in one evening . . ."

"Forgiven," she replied, as though she were stamping a form.

Too cowardly to join us, Microft remained as Beth and I raced down the three flights of stairs in an effort to escape before the police arrived. All I could think was that June must think I'm making a personal mission of destroying other people's art. We walked to Eleventh Avenue where we caught a cab down and across town. Maybe, because we both felt like halfwits for getting ourselves into a situation where our sublime idiocy could be immortalized on film, we didn't utter a word. As the cab came to a stop on Delancey and Allen, I took out seven bucks, my share of the fare. Before I could wish her a good night, she looked at me, red with embarrassment, and said, "Why don't you come back with me?"

"I can't," I replied. "I have a big deadline coming up. Maybe after that."

Even though Rita had a boyfriend, I still felt involved with her, and at very least, until I had an AIDS test, I couldn't sleep with another girl.

Twenty-three

As I walked south down Allen that night, though she was supposedly in Vermont, I searched for my drug-addled muse. Of course, there was no sign of her. I pictured her strung out, muttering profane corruptions of classical poetry, curled up in some dark and dirty doorway. So much the better; I was almost out of time on the sculpture, with only tomorrow to sand it down, yet doing it manually was just too exhausting. I was completely beat from the long day and dramatic evening and could only collapse onto the bed. Holding the pillow, I imagined I had Rita in my arms as I went to sleep.

Early the next morning, I went to Pearl Paint and rented an angle grinder. I also bought a variety of different grade sandpaper. On the way home, I spotted a newspaper announcing new figures on the recount. Gore was closing the gap. The Holy Land votes were coming in.

Once upstairs, I took the old heavy-duty extension cords from Shade's closet and plugged them together as I headed downstairs. Since I didn't have the proper aspirator for the grinding, I slipped on two face masks, one over the other, and the old pair of goggles. Through a cloud of white dust, starting at 60-grit sandpaper, I carefully polished the sides of the stone, slowly orbiting around it to keep a sense of proportion. In the course of the day, as the stone grew smoother and the chisel grooves vanished, I worked my way up to the finer, 120-grit paper. This left it rough-edged, but still acceptable.

It was warm without a breeze, and cutting that stone with all the dust shooting up and swirling around, I constantly felt sweaty and itchy. I worked steadily sanding the piece without a break. By sunset, my arms felt like rubber. I had no sensation beyond my wrists and my fingers were beginning to go white. But I pressed on, working down the ruts and scratches.

Finally at seven I could no longer keep my head up. I pulled off the masks and goggles, and rubbing fingers along the surface of the piece, I deemed I was finally, totally, and completely done.

By eight o'clock, having showered, I gulped down about two gallons of ice-cold water, tossed myself across my bed, and dropped into black sleep.

A desperate disturbing dream, someone trapped, struggling to get out, begging for help, a girl, I couldn't make out a face, but I had a tremendous affection for her. It was obviously Rita.

I jumped out of bed to take a desperate piss. Afterward, I opened the faucet to discover that for some goddamned reason the water was shut off. I was still exhausted, but with an incredible case of cotton mouth, I was dying of thirst.

It was only one in the morning. The bar downstairs was still open, and I needed to enlist help to move my sculpture. I grabbed Shade's old terry-cloth bathrobe and slippers and shuffled downstairs.

"The Florida Supreme Court is mainly Democratic," Cecil was saying to someone at the bar. "If it goes to them they'll protect democracy."

Pablo glimpsed at me from a far corner; he was chatting with his girlfriend. Just from his tight body language I sensed his defensiveness. Whether it was Nader's loss or Bush's win was unclear. The presidential election had taken its toll. About six or so others who I knew from bookselling were talking and drinking.

"How many of you guys can help me tomorrow?" I asked aloud.

"Oh sure, we want to help you," some snide voice called out.

"I'll give you twenty bucks for ten minutes of work."

"What time?" Pablo responded.

"One o'clock for ten minutes."

"I'll help you," he replied. After a silence, I looked at some of the others.

"For ten minutes I guess I can too," said Ike. Others also agreed to meet me at Shade's next door early tomorrow afternoon.

"Why do you need everyone for just ten minutes?" Cecil asked.

I explained that I just wanted to load my Chinese takeout piece onto a wagon and then heave it into the back of my van. He said he'd try to join in. Without a word about Gore, Nader, or the election, Pablo nodded that he'd try to help too. I thanked them all and went up to sleep.

Around nine the next morning, I awoke contemplating the monumental task of bringing the mini-colossus out to Long Island, moving the mountain to Moe Hammerman. I first dashed out and returned the angle grinder, getting my rental deposit back. I knew I'd need every cent available.

It was quite warm out. It felt as though an early September day had snuck into the mid-November lineup.

By the time I was home, I was suddenly panic-stricken with the epiphany that once I had gotten to Long Island I was not going to be able to crowbar the sculpture out from my van. I called Moe Hammerman's office and I explained to him my problem.

"Call the Star of David." That was the name of the cemetery. "Ask for Marty, he's my friend's son. Maybe he can help you. And for the record, kid, we agreed that moving this would come out of your pocket."

I told him that was not an issue.

"How's the piece looking?" he asked.

"It's just like we agreed, a rough hewn two-by-two foot Chinese takeout carton."

"With the top flaps open," he completed.

"Flaps open! Hell no—"

He started chuckling. "Relax, relax. I'm just dimpling your chad." I let out a nervous chuckle. "Sounds perfect. The unveiling is set for tomorrow morning. I got the entire North Shore of Long Island coming."

"Great, be sure to tell them who did it," I injected.

"I will," he replied. "Now I'm going to be out there in the early evening, soon as I get out of work. Am I going to see you?"

"No, I'm going to drop it off in the afternoon." With my broken-down van, I needed to beat the rush.

"That's fine, but I don't pay until I see the work, so I'll drop a check in the mail once it passes mustard." I didn't correct him.

"Has the cemetery been warned about the headstone's unusual size and shape?" I confirmed.

"Yeah, they're fine with it. It's lucky we didn't make it any bigger."

I called the administrative offices of the Star of David and asked for Marty. Some reedy, youthful voice answered. I told him that Moe Hammerman suggested I speak to him and carefully explained my problem. I needed something to lift the sculpture from my van and set it onto the grave site.

"How heavy is the headstone?" asked the boyish-sounding administrator.

"About a ton."

"We have an old cherry picker, it's more of a hoist, really. It should work, we've used it for standard-sized stones, but it hasn't been used in a while."

"Sounds good."

"Ever operated a New England 129 Hand-Operated Electrical Hoist?" he asked.

"No."

"If you want I'll rent it to you and help you for a hundred bucks."

"I'm forever grateful." I had roughly a hundred and sixty dollars to my name. At that moment it occurred to me that once I paid five guys twenty bucks a piece to load the stone into the van, I wouldn't have enough to pay him.

"What time will you be here?" he asked.

I figured if I got the van loaded by one, the drive couldn't be any longer than two hours beyond that.

"Three o'clock should be fine," I said confidently.

"I'd appreciate it if you could pay me in cash," young Marty softly requested, giving me the impression that he was doing this behind his boss's back. I told him that'd be fine.

"Whose burial is it?"

I pointed out that it was actually an unveiling, and gave him the name of the deceased.

"Tell you what I'm going to do, I'll get the hoist and meet you at the site at three." When I explained that I was a little fuzzy as to where I was going, he gave me detailed instructions on how to get from Manhattan to the cemetery and then to the grave plot. I thanked him for all his help.

It was a little after eleven and I was starving. I dashed downstairs to the dim sum dive and got several shrimp pieces. Feeling thoroughly satisfied with all my sculpture-moving plans, I brought the food to a bench on Allen Street.

"How you doing, darling?" An older transvestite addict rested her weary bones on a splintered bench across from me. Her body seemed to be rejecting the lumps of silicone unprofessionally injected in her lips and cheeks. That, along with the tawdry makeup, wig, and clothes, created a sad portrait of a man driven to the gates of womanhood, yet unable to enter.

"I saw you with Shady the other day," she went on.

"Yep," I said curtly. This section of town always reminded me of New York in the '70s, a time I both missed and hated. The city was affordable, but I feared it.

"I didn't see you at the memorial," she kept talking.

"What memorial?"

"Rita."

"What about Rita?" I stopped eating.

"Her boyfriend had the memorial the other day. I saw you guys talking afterwards."

"What the fuck are you talking about?" I felt a sudden and tremendous collapse.

"That girl that used to work here, Rita. Don't think I didn't see you hitting on her." She grinned.

"What happened to her?" I hunched forward and felt myself tense up.

"She got a hot shot. Found her dead."

"When?"

"A few days ago," she said tiredly. "A whole batch of bad shit went out. Like six people in Jersey City died. She was the only one from around here."

"Who found her?"

"Her boyfriend Louie."

"Lou?" The name clicked. It was the name of that skinny, pimply kid who was asking me all those dumb questions the last time I was out here. I remembered that Rita's lip was swollen, and her left eye was blackened. She said a hooker hit her, but she gave me the impression that her boyfriend was some violent inner city–gangsta type. She always sounded afraid of him.

"Rita and him were together like since high school." I remembered she referred to her boyfriend as Lucas.

"When did she . . . die?" I asked, having difficulty saying the word while resisting the thought.

"Like two or three days ago. When you and Shade was here."

It must have been the day after I last saw her.

"You was that painter," the old tranny recalled. "I remembered when you drew me."

"Yeah," I replied numbly. No wonder Lou said she was in Vermont. I would have taken him out right there.

"Hey," the addict suddenly had an idea. "Maybe you can paint a memorial wall for her."

"Doesn't Lou work for the needle exchange?" I asked, discarding the uneaten dim sum.

"He works at the Harm Reduction Center," she said, and quaintly added, "He reduces harm."

"On Avenue C and Third Street?" I asked eagerly.

"Yeah, that's it. You got a cigarette, hon?"

I didn't but I thanked her, got my bike, and cycled up there. The money I gave Rita, she would've gotten anyway. If anyone was responsible for Rita's death, it had to be this punk. As I angrily pedaled my bike past the Tenement Museum, tears started coming to my eyes. I decided at that moment that I was going to kill him. Speeding through red lights and across busy streets, working myself into a frenzy, I started looking for a brick or something to crush his skull with.

Death was the most amazing magic trick of all. How could people go from something—to me she was nearly everything—to absolutely nothing in the blink of an eye?

In about fifteen minutes I was at the Harm Reduction Center, where I was planning on doing some serious harm. I walked inside and saw a nicely framed photo of Rita that must have been taken a few years ago. Under it a caption said, Rita Wood 1975–2000. She looked young and beautiful, and just looking at it, I knew that when the picture was taken she hadn't even considered heroin.

"Can I help you?" asked an older Latin man who looked like a serious ex-con.

"I'm looking for Lou," I asked.

"He's not working right now," the ex-con type began.

"Oh yes he is," piped up a middle-aged woman. "He's in the back."

"Can I speak to him for a moment?" I tried to hold it in.

"Sure," she replied, and jokingly hollered out, "Louie!"

I flashed a smile. In a moment, out popped Lou, the skinny kid who couldn't have weighed more than a hundred and fifty pounds. He was about five foot nine, with wire-frame glasses and a slim gold earring in his right ear.

"You're the artist," he recognized. "We were just watching CNN. Can you believe this fucking election?" He shook my hand. I couldn't attack him there because the others would help him.

"You didn't tell me Rita died." I came right to the point.

"Oh, I . . ." he sputtered. "Let's go for a walk."

He stepped outside and I followed him.

After we were about a block away, he began, "I know this sounds awful. I saw your work but I knew that she couldn't have any lasting relationships. I just figured that if you had no other connection to her I'd be doing you a favor by not telling you."

"Bullshit," I replied, setting a clear tone. "You were just throwing me off."

"She died. I was just trying to spare your feelings."

"Where is she?" I wanted to see her body.

"She was cremated yesterday," he replied. "Her ashes were scattered in the ocean." I couldn't hold the idea that such a lively, original, and conflicted person no longer existed.

"She told me that there was a painter who she was falling in love with," he said gently. "Well, I loved her too."

"So you beat her up?" I said fiercely.

"Don't be silly."

"She fucking told me that you hit her!" I yelled, grabbing him and shoving him into a doorway.

"It's not what you think!" he replied, trembling.

I punched him in the jaw, knocking his glasses off. He tried to grab my arms, but I started walloping him and crying.

"I was trying to keep her from buying drugs!" he screamed covering his head. "I've never hit her! The only time I ever got into a fight with her was when I tried to keep her from getting high. You bought her drugs! *You* bought them!"

"She told you that?" I stopped. Tears were blinding me.

"Yeah," he said, looking up. "She said you bought her drugs when no one else would." He paused, trembling, and got to his feet. "I've known her since she was a kid, we went to college together and came down here together."

"She said *you* got her *into* drugs," I retorted.

"Please! I did no such thing," he caught his breath, and checked his lip for blood. "We dabbled in college, but I was never addicted. I came here and started working with the needle exchange. Then she joined in and she started using . . ."

"Look," I replied, feeling a rush of guilt and disgust. "I don't want to hear it. I just want my sketch pad and that's it."

"Can I buy the sketches from you?" he asked hesitantly.

"Hell no!" I shot back. "No fucking way."

"Fine, come on." I followed him a few blocks to a renovated yet crappy tenement. He silently opened the heavy metal downstairs door. I accompanied him up the smelly, narrow stairway to his cramped flat on the second floor. When he opened his old wooden apartment door, I knew this was where Rita had lived. Pictures of the two of them embracing were placed on cabinets and shelves.

Along the walls in his living room in new, customized frames were all the frantically completed sketches I had churned out in the middle of those feverish nights together. In one room toward the rear, I saw a stack of boxes.

"Was this her room?" I asked. He nodded yes.

Without asking, I entered. A pillow was sitting on a box. I picked it up, and inhaled deeply. There she was.

"So she died in . . ." I couldn't talk.

"I found her in there," he said, dismally pointing to the floor. "I'm just grateful that she wasn't on the street, in some hallway somewhere."

"And how exactly . . ."

"It was a bad mixture. I think she went quick. Her eyes were open. She looked peaceful, like she was in no pain."

"I just can't believe this whole thing happened." I plunked myself down into a chair.

"I tried to protect her. I had all these friends who I worked with telling dealers not to sell to her. I wouldn't give her any money."

"I gave her two hundred dollars," I confessed.

He looked at me for the longest time. He couldn't make me feel any worse than I already felt.

"It was just a matter of time," he finally, mercifully, said.

"This is how life works," I decided. "You meet the love of your life and she's a crazy fucking heroin addict." Considering she was his girlfriend I probably shouldn't have said that. "I mean, she was really cruel. She said she could have stopped if she wanted to, but she never did."

"There was a reason," he finally said.

"Oh, that's right," I chuckled remembering her ridiculous *reason*.

259

"She was sick with some mysterious illness and heroin was the miracle cure."

"Two years ago she was diagnosed with acute lymphoblastic lymphoma. A-L-L."

"All?" I remembered her telling me she was dying of it all. I thought she was just being poetically cute.

"It's a brain tumor. Treatable in children. Fatal in adults. It's pretty symptomless. Your gums bleed, you bruise easily."

"A brain tumor!"

"The neurologist gave her six to eight months, a year tops. Since she started shooting heroin, she hit two years. She firmly believed the heroin was mysteriously keeping her going."

"So she only started shooting after she was diagnosed?"

"Not entirely. First she snorted it, then she became a weekend shooter. You do a bag on Saturday and Sunday and have little colds on Monday and Tuesday. Cold turkey cutlets, she called them. We both did it, but it was mild. Nothing we couldn't handle. She was attending graduate school at the time. It wasn't till she got diagnosed that she started seriously getting into it."

I smiled. It all made sense. Here she was dying of a terminal illness. Why should she worry about AIDS or heroin addiction? In another year or so she would be dead anyway. It was a wonderful little "fuck you" to death.

"It seems like if you only have a year or two to live," I said to Lou, "you'd go on a trip around the world or something."

"She did her trips around the world, with her family. She did everything and went everywhere," he replied. "I think she was trying to go somewhere she had never been before."

"But who would want to go into hell?" I asked myself aloud.

"I don't know if anyone plans on it. She just sank deeper and deeper, and she started changing."

"What did her family do?"

"Her mother was heartbroken by the whole thing. She tried to help her, but Rita just pushed her away. They knew she was shooting up. They'd send me an allowance for her, but I didn't give her any cash. Soon she was taking things from around the house. After she sold the VCR and TV, she started with the prostitution. When I realized this, I told her I'd pay for her habit, but by then I think she got into this whole weird role—you know, becoming someone she wasn't. I caught her hooking a couple of times and tried stopping her. That's when we got into terrible fights."

"I saw her bruised up pretty badly," I recalled. "I thought you were smacking her around." I smiled. "She gave me this impression you were some big mean black or Latin asshole."

He chuckled. "She was taller and probably stronger than I was. She broke a bottle over my head once." He pointed to a scar on his forehead. "The only bruise I ever gave her was when I tried to restrain her, to keep her from going out. She'd always come back." He started weeping softly.

"I did it. I gave her the money to kill herself," I said morbidly. "I should have done what you did, but I was greedy, I wanted her with me, I wanted her love." He looked off in one direction and I stared off in another. I envied all the time he had with her.

"She said her day-to-day search for heroin was a full-time job." He composed himself. "It replaced her fear of death. I just wish I didn't have to see her at her ugliest. Scrounging for food. Begging for cash. Hustling."

"I wish I knew her before she got into all this," I replied. "But she probably wouldn't have anything to do with someone like me."

One of the sketches on the wall that I had drawn showed her naked, twisting her body around feverishly, searching for an uncollapsed vein.

"I'm so glad you did these sketches," he said, surveying them. "I look at them at night. You really captured her." He began to gently remove them from the wall, stacking them neatly for me. "The way

261

she moved, her expressions—you caught so much more than any camera. When she initially showed them to me, it was the first time I saw her excited about something in so long."

He had framed them beautifully in plain, unfinished pine, and they were spaced so evenly around the house, it was like being in a little museum. It was obvious that the works were much more than just a commodity. They helped him deal with her death. If art ever had a greater function than that, I couldn't imagine it.

"Stop it," I said, as he struggled with the back wire of one picture. "They're yours."

I got up to go. It was time to move the headstone.

"Hold on," Lou said. "Want to see what she was like before all this?"

He pulled a photo album off the shelf and started flipping through the vinyl pages. The photos looked at least ten years old. Images of Rita as a lanky teen leapt out, laughing, swimming, skiing, arm wrestling. I couldn't stop smiling back at her.

"Here." He took a photograph out of the album and handed it to me. In it she was making her signature I'm-so-glamorous expression. It was perfectly her. We shook hands and I left.

Twenty-four

A lifetime had passed, and when I finally returned
home, I was dead inside. All desire and interest vanished, leaving
me in a kind of mental desert. Though I was in denial, this was definitely grief. It required tremendous will power just to walk up the
stairs. Relentlessly, I'd push away the recurrent thought that I would
never see Rita again. The grief stymied my brain, and stuffed me as
though it were an enormous yet tasteless meal. It seemed too much
to digest even for a lifetime.

I looked at the mural I had done of Rita, struggling between the
two hells. Now and forever she'd be stuck there.

I took out paints and started working on swimmer images, but my fuse kept short-circuiting. I'd wake to the fact that I had just paused for ten or twenty minutes staring off at the mural of Rita. Then I'd reset myself and start painting again. Laboriously I pushed my brain into an avoidance mode, trying to build a fortress with cold, hard thoughts: I wasn't really close to her. I barely knew her. She never trusted me with her secrets. She wouldn't have anything to do with me before all this. She never really cared for me. She just used me. She was a typical prostitute. I never should have even talked to her. She only said she loved me so I'd keep giving her money.

Then I realized I'd never see her again and all the intricately placed ideas would tumble down. The door opened behind me and I heard noises.

"Can you believe what's going on with this fucking election?" I heard Lynn's voice, but I couldn't take my eyes off of the image of Rita's face.

"You okay, Or?" Lynn came over slowly.

"The girl who modeled for this just died." I explained, stuck before the mural. "She was only twenty-five."

"This was the girl you were seeing?"

"Yeah."

"How'd she die?" Lynn asked softly.

"Bad heroin." Lynn hugged me for a while. "Also, she might've been HIV and we had unprotected sex."

"Shit, Or, you're kidding!"

"No, but I loved her."

"Do you think that if you were HIV, she'd have unprotected sex with you?" I didn't answer, but she added, "If I were HIV and I cared for someone I wouldn't let them have unprotected sex with me."

"What can I say, I never loved someone so much?"

"Was it really her you loved?"

"Why are you asking me that?"

"I just know a little about falling in love with an idea, as opposed to the thing itself."

"I can't imagine never seeing her again."

Lynn held me until the doorbell rang. She buzzed the intruder in.

"Today's the big day to deliver your sculpture, isn't it?" she asked.

"Yeah, I finished last night." It was then I realized it was time to go. The doorbell must have been one or all of my reluctant buddies downstairs to help me move the colossus. I washed off my palette, and dropped my brushes in water.

"You're done!" she said excitedly, clapping her hands, "That's just wonderful. Are you going to take some photos of it?"

"I don't have time."

"Do you want me to do it right now? You should have some pictures for your portfolio. This is the kind of stuff that's really useful for getting future commissions or applying for grants."

I smiled at this because I couldn't even remember all the art I had made and sold without ever knowing where it ended up.

"Sure," I said, accepting her offer. After all, for better or worse, this was my first and hopefully last sculpture. She grabbed her camera and dashed out.

In a moment, Pablo entered. His right eye was swollen, his right nostril was inflamed, and his lip was split.

"Is anyone else out front?" I asked.

"Not as far as I know."

"What the hell happened to you?"

"Bush." He smiled dismally.

"Bush hit you?"

"I got into a fight with Cecil."

"When?"

"Let's see, some time before they filed their final count in Broward County, but after they officially ceased the recount in Miami Dade."

"You're kidding!"

"Yes, I'm kidding. It was last night, you idiot!" he shot back. "Just after you left." He looked off dismally. "Fucking Nader didn't even get his five measly percent."

"I guess Cecil isn't coming," I deduced.

"Probably not," he replied as we started walking down the stairs. I needed this day to be over with. It was after one and no one else was in sight.

"I'm sure more people will show," he tried to comfort me.

"It's just that I'm running on a tight schedule. I got a guy on the other end with a hoist who's going to help me unload this hernia inducer."

"Why don't we just see if we can budge it?" he suggested.

I ran up and got my hand truck, which I brought down to the base of the outside stairs. Lynn had just finished photographing the piece. She helped as we each grabbed a corner of the little stone carton and attempted to lift it. After a lot of grunts and curses, we were only able to shove the monolith a few inches. The two-by-two-foot piece of alabaster was deceptively heavy. It felt like two bathtubs folded neatly on top of each other. After a few more minutes of heaving and hoing, we only hurt our backs. Even if we angled it off the top step, it probably would've toppled over and killed us. Lynn wished us good luck and had to dash off to work. Pablo and I decided to wait downstairs for more friends. To fully utilize the time, Pablo helped me unload all the crap I had stashed in my van over the years. We relocated it up to Shade's loft.

After taking three boxes of paint supplies upstairs, I discovered endless sketch pads filled with drafts and deframed canvases of years gone by that I had painted and stored away. We shuttled load after load after load upstairs. I was astounded by the sheer volume of paintings and sketches that I had produced and thought I had either lost or sold. Most were studies of New York City, the remains of various groupings that I had painted over the past decade. Works I barely remembered doing, which, like old friends, I was happy to see again. Altogether they formed an impressive and cohesive chronicle of a living, shifting city: views of different skyscrapers in the changing seasons and light. Bikes chained to posts. Homeless sleeping in cardboard encampments around City Hall and in the now-demolished New York Coliseum. Various paths in Central Park surrounded by distant buildings. Winter commuters crammed together in rush-hour trains, and so on.

As we ferried stuff out and up, Pablo revealed that Cecil wasn't the only one who hit him last night. He explained that after the disappointing evening, he had gotten into a fight with his unexploded blonde bombshell. It turned out she wasn't Croatian but Serbian, and she felt Milosovic was a goddamned national hero. Upon getting into a big screaming match, she smacked him across the mouth, splitting open his lip.

"Yesterday was certainly not your day for politics."

The van was empty, so the engine had no weight other than me and the sculpture to haul. I was grateful that Shade was not around. I knew he'd never forgive me if he knew I had wasted the whole advance he gave me only so that Rita could eventually die on bad heroin.

"Fuck this," Pablo blurted out as we hauled the last hand-truck load of canvases and books upstairs. "How much money you got?"

"Would you greatly mind if I paid you later?" I asked. "I'm a little short."

"Just tell me how much you got."

I wasn't sure if he wanted to start his own political party or buy someone's services to help us. It didn't matter. I counted out all the paper I had in my pocket, six twenties, three tens, two fives and six single dollar bills. That was everything.

"Come on," he said, and out we went. He had a bright idea but wasn't ready to share it. I followed him to one of the many mini-loading docks, where we saw a Chinese guy sitting in a front-end loader chewing gum.

"Speak English?" Pablo asked.

The guy just stared. Pablo pulled out some of the smaller bills and waved them at the driver. "Twenty bucks."

"What you want?"

"Twenty bucks, you come help for five minutes." Pablo extended his five fingers.

"No." He returned to his off position, just chewing his gum.

Pablo dashed to one of the next improvised truck bays that dotted the area. One guy was operating a hand-held forklift, also known as a pallet jack, as it lifted the wooden pallets holding the supplies.

"Want to make some cash?" Pablo asked him. The guy ignored him.

"We need a forklift for something this size," I told Pablo as we kept moving. Again we found another illegal who had just finished hoisting and transporting a large wooden pallet of Saran-wrapped supplies.

Pablo waved twenty-five dollars in small bills and said, "Just three minutes. You help now. This is yours."

"How much?" the guy asked.

"Twenty-eight dollars." Pablo counted it out for him. "Three minutes."

"Fifty dollar," the guy spat back. Capitalism transcended all barriers.

"Get your van," Pablo said to me counting out the cash. "We'll meet you at your place."

I dashed off three blocks east and two blocks west to where I was parked, sped back to the Jarmulovsky's Bank, and parked in the tow-away zone.

Pablo and the guy with the Nissan loader were waiting.

"Bush is going to round up all illegal aliens," Pablo explained to the immigrant. "You wait and see."

"Bush bad?" the Asian man asked. I sensed his vocabulary didn't exceed ten words, much like the new president.

"Yes, Bush bad."

"No, Bush good," the guy replied, and laughed heartily.

"Give it a break," I muttered, and opened the large metal doors that lead to the back of the building. The fellow scooted his vehicle like a bumper car, heading down the narrow corridor that ended at the stairwell. He lifted the forks to eight feet, which thankfully reached the first landing where the statue sat. Then Pablo and I shoved the piece back, balancing it on one corner as the Asian driver inched forward, slipping the two large forks underneath. Once it was set firmly on the front-end loader, he reversed it back out. On the street, though, my van was tightly wedged between two postal trucks. It was immediately clear that he couldn't angle the takeout carton into the back door.

"You're going to have to pull out for him to slide it in there," Pablo said the obvious.

"Actually," I realized, "if he puts the stone in the back, all the weight is going to be centered in the rear. The back tires might go flat and it could conceivably slide out when I go up a ramp or something. If he puts it up here," I pointed to my roof rack, "it'll be better centered and I'll get better traction."

"But your roof will cave in," Pablo replied succinctly.

"No, no. It's reinforced," I explained, "Those steel girders are fastened to the chassis. It used to hold bathtubs and water heaters simultaneously." Pablo conceded that it was worth a try.

The forklift operator drove on the sidewalk right up to the middle of the van, then slowly elevated the sculpture to the very highest he could, roughly twelve feet in the air. The bottom of his steel forks just scraped the roof of the vehicle.

"Hold on," I called out before he could lower it. On the sidewalk I found a filthy old wooden pallet that someone had discarded. I angled the wood under the sculpture to center the weight between the steel beams. As the front-end operator lowered the forks, the wooden boards snapped in half and the roof slowly sunk inward, as did the steel girders—but it held.

"It looks like a square egg in a wooden nest," Pablo commented, "but it appears to be securely in there."

"I just pray it holds," I said under my breath.

"And you got someone on the other end who's helping you get it down?" Pablo confirmed.

"Yeah, hopefully."

While he watched the vehicle, I dashed off to the hardware store and bought what seemed like ten thousand feet of heavy duty rope. We both spent about a half hour lassoing the inverted pyramid and lashing it down. When we were done, Pablo asked several fateful questions. "Do you really think your van will make it all the way up to Long Island?"

"She's been traveling pretty well lately."

"Don't you think it'd be better to drive it late tonight, when the road is empty?"

"I have to get it there by late afternoon, if the guy's going to help me get it down."

"I'd just hate for that to be *your* headstone," Pablo kidded, then stepping up he asked, "Do you want me to come with you?"

"Yes," I replied, "but the van can't carry any more weight."

I thanked him for all his kindness. I thought I was going to be on the road by one thirty. It was now around two o'clock. Hopefully, if I didn't get too lost, I'd be pulling into the cemetery by three. Then I could still get Marty to help me unload the monster.

"So when you return how much money will you have?"

"Around six grand." For a moment, I allowed myself to fantasize about Cali's van, and after paying Shade off, I'd still have enough cash to pay off my parking-ticket debt. A new life was waiting for me when I got back.

Inspecting my old Chevy one last time, I realized that it was sitting completely flat on the chassis. The shocks were squeezed into four tight fists, and the old tires were bulging at the bottom. I turned the key and put it into first gear. Slowly I touched the pedal, and the van started grinding forward. As I headed up Orchard, the engine responded like a geriatric. Here we go again, it seemed to say in its mechanical creakiness. I turned on Delancey and sped up to thirty miles an hour. All seemed fine. If traffic on the Williamsburg Bridge caused me to lose any momentum, I knew I'd be screwed. Despite the fact that four lanes were merging into two, I saw a tight line of cars moving in steady procession, like a slow conveyor belt over to Brooklyn. I was able to keep my foot on the gas and head up onto the back of the steel dinosaur to Williamsburg.

Every pothole, every rut, every seam between the large metal plates and the roadway would cause an incredible thump from the roof. As I got onto the bridge, I was able to accelerate until about a third of the way across the East River. Then I hit one preposterous bump. Behind me I heard an incredible crunch. It was as though God's hand had reached down and squeezed my van like an aluminum beer can. Traffic slowed to a crawl. Then I heard a horrific screech, and was suddenly aware of a new angle of light cast over the dashboard. Looking up, I realized that the roof had ripped open. I peeked up into the blue sky. The weight of the stone had crushed it. It had cut a three-foot triangular gash through the metal ceiling, slicing right through the painting I had done of the train's undercarriage. The more bumps we hit, the further the stone slipped. Soon I feared that it might drop down. If it did, it would go right through the floor and snap my transmission in two.

That was when the second unthinkable event occurred. Still puttering uphill, the car about ten feet in front of me came to a full halt. Right then and there I knew that if I stopped too, that would be the end of it. With all that top weight, while still on an incline, I'd never be able to start again. I slowed down to a crawl and prayed as I moved closer and closer. Eight feet, six feet, five feet, four feet, three feet, two feet, and just at the moment of impact, he zoomed ahead. I hit the gas and slowly moved up, gradually gaining more speed. My little engine was putting up her last great fight.

Throughout the remainder of the ride, I never came that close, but

271

problems were always threatening. Upon various highways, I moved at a crawl, slower than cars around me. The one time traffic did stop, I kept moving along the shoulder, under the disgusted stares of my fellow drivers. With such a considerable weight I was afraid to hit the brakes. After getting a bit lost on the North Shore of Long Island, I finally ended up at that eternal resting place for Jewish restaurateurs and their patrons.

Once there, I checked the instructions again and drove around the swirling, grass-lined lanes of the graveyard until I saw it, a strange red tripod manipulated by a panel of short levers. I parked alongside it and checked the time. I was late and Marty the smooth operator was nowhere in sight. For ten minutes I tried pulling the black knobbed levers and pushing the red and green buttons. Nothing happened.

"You the fellow that I spoke to on the phone?" said a lanky lad in his mid-twenties, approaching from behind a mausoleum.

"Yeah, you know how to operate this thing?"

"Got the cash?"

I counted out my last hundred dollars. He slipped it into his shirt pocket and told me to park the van on the grass, right under the little crane. Apparently it didn't swing to the right or left, it only lifted objects up and down. Upon doing so, he climbed up onto my van and looked at the sculpture wedged in the roof.

"How the heck did you get this in there?"

"I'm just grateful it didn't fall through," I said, climbing up next to him.

After unknotting the miles of complex ropes, the biggest problem was widening the edges of perforation in my roof, and pulling out pieces of wood from the splintered pallet. Then, to protect the piece, we covered the sculpture in a tarp and finally threaded a net of chains down around it. He carefully linked all the chains to a single hook that was hanging down from the end of the little crane.

"That thing looks pretty nimble," I said, referring to his hoist. "Are you sure it'll lift it?"

"Let's find out," he replied. He slipped a key into the slot, started it up and pulled the levers. Slowly he lifted the sculpture out from the collapsed roof of my wounded vehicle. After I moved the van, he lowered it down. He spun and carefully positioned the stone on the holy site in line with the other headstones.

Initially, it looked odd, like a picnic basket in a graveyard. But slowly, as I took a couple of steps back, the piece seemed to lock into the landscape. The geometry and uniformity of other white stones framed it nicely. It belonged with the surroundings while quietly taking on a singular identity of its own. I knew it was wonderful, because I suddenly had a swell of pride.

Marty wheeled away his little crane. I thanked him and began my long descent back to the big city. It was early rush hour. I leisurely passed all the urban evacuees stuck in the bumper-to-bumper havoc on the opposing roads and byways. There was an odd victory to the whole endeavor, and yet it felt hollow. With no sculpture to work on and no Rita, I had neither purpose nor celebration. The idea that I would be getting a pile of cash and a newer, larger van to call home did not fill the overwhelming vacancy. As I slowly drove, I kept returning to Rita and what Lynn said about having fallen in love, not with her, but with an idea rising from her.

In a world of bland, fearful, uneducated pigeons, she was a peacock on acid. In all her self-entertaining egotism, and despite her begrudging eleventh-hour concession of love, I wondered if she ever really even noticed me. As I recalled all those quirky and suicidal decisions that were her, I found myself smiling. The sheer fact that I was still alive and didn't have to suffer for her left me feeling strangely energized.

The poor van, on the other hand, did not share in my renewed strength. The Triboro and the Tunnel charged a toll. The 59th Street

Bridge was at a standstill, so I headed south until I found myself steadily moving back up the trusty, rusty old Williamsburg. It was there the van started stalling. When I reached the steepest part, the engine revved, but now the gears didn't seem to be catching. Gradually the van came to a slow halt.

Horns honked behind me as I gunned the gas pedal and sent up a final coronary of black smoke. The old girl didn't budge. I put it into reverse and backed up about six inches, then threw it into first and gunned the pedal—nothing.

"Move that piece of shit, you asshole," said the asshole in the no-good, gas-guzzling SUV behind me.

"I'm stuck," I yelled back. "If you could just give me a bit of a—"

"No way I'm scratching my bumper on your piece of shit."

As cars circled around me, growling and glaring, I got out to try and push, but I could see what had happened. The front wheels were stuck in the three-inch groove—a gap where two parts of the roadway had actually drifted apart. It was as though the rut was designed specifically for vehicles like mine, those just operating on their last strength. Yet I was only a few feet away from the midpoint of the bridge, where the incline of the road turned into a decline. Already exhausted and in pain, I tried to push the van in a seesaw motion to free it, but it wouldn't budge. I had a twenty-dollar bill left, so I tried waving down anyone who would stop.

"Here's a hundred-dollar bill," I lied to the driver of a monstrous old dump truck. "All I need is a slight push, just one fucking foot."

The bastard wouldn't so much as make eye contact. Inevitably, there it was, the siren. A cop car pulled up. I could see his partner typing my license into their dashboard computer. I knew what he was going to find: a lottery ticket in unpaid parking violations.

"Oh boy," he said as the first cop got out, "did we hit the jackpot or what?"

"A tow truck has been notified," he explained. "You're going to have to pay two hundred bucks for that on top of the twelve hundred or so in back tickets you owe." As one of the cops started writing me up, the other guided traffic around my lane.

"Once you pay everything off, you can pick up your *ve*-hicle at the College Point Auto Pound," the cop instructed. "Want some advice? Let them keep it. The money you'll have to pay far exceeds the worth of your *ve*-hicle, but you'll have to pay your ticket eventually."

By the manic intensity of his scribbling, he seemed to be undertaking the great American novel. My van had been with me far longer than any girlfriends or apartments. Without knowing where my thoughts changed lanes, I found myself thinking about Rita. All the love I had for her never stopped her from taking whatever drug money she'd need. With June I fucked up, yes, but once she met her millionaire, never did a woman marry and get pregnant so rapidly, without looking back. As the cop scribbled a third page of citations, I started tensing up and stepping toward him, more than ready to knock him on his fucking ass.

The unbelieveable blast of a horn from a passing tractor trailer left me deaf for a moment. I awoke to the fact that hitting the cop would only get me killed or arrested. Brooklyn was a much shorter distance away. With no other reason to remain on that pointless bridge, I walked along the meridian against the traffic, along the inside rail, next to the elevated subway tracks.

About five minutes later, I dashed across the downward ramp and found myself on the grimy, carbon monoxide–laden streets of southern Williamsburg.

Twenty-five

The Pomegranate Gallery was shrouded in darkness when I happened to pass by it. I was heading for the L train, but since I was there anyway, I tried the door. It was locked but a faint glow was visible from the rear. When I tapped on the glass, thankfully Persephone appeared and let me in.

"Or, what are you doing here!" She opened her door.

"I figured since I was here, I might as well pick up the *Latin Fishermen*."

"Did you get my message?" She looked delighted to see me. She pulled me inside and closed the door.

"What message?"

"First, Moe just called. He loved the piece and he's giving you a five-hundred-dollar bonus." I smiled. "Also why didn't you tell me about the *ARTnews* story?"

"What are you talking about?"

She handed me the copy for the upcoming week. On its cover was a painting of a busy midtown street that I had done and had given to Cali at least five years ago. The banner announced, "New York's Best Hung Artist—Or Trenchant, by Klein Ritter."

I remembered that Shade had said Cali had given some of my work to Ritter. She must have orchestrated this. This also must have been what the scary critic wanted to speak about at the Elder opening the other day when I was harrassing Victor Oakridge.

"I'll be able to sell your Fishermen piece now," she said, "even with the center poked out."

I didn't think this one cover story would *make* me, but the article would undoubtedly put me on the map. Still, it wasn't as if I hadn't paid my dues. For years, rich and influential people had picked up my works for a song. Now, with my sudden inflated value, all those collectors pulled in a tidy profit. This was how business was conducted. It was never about the assessment of art, but buying cheap and selling dear. Not only was the artist expendable in the marketplace, his painful and premature death invariably boosted the price of his work.

Coincidentally, this would lift me back to Chelsea gallery status for a while. With all the miscellaneous pieces I had unloaded at Shade's loft, I was sure I'd have enough work for at least two if not three or four serious shows.

I thanked Persephone for the astounding news, and only wished I could share it with Rita. I pictured her standing alone forever on the far corner of Canal.

"You don't seem very pleased," she observed aptly.

"I didn't think I'd have to sacrifice so much."

"You're still young," she pointed out. "You know how many artists spend their entire lives waiting for that big writeup and never get it?"

I manufactured my best possible smile and left. As I passed a liquor store, I went in and bought a half liter of cheap vodka with my last twenty bucks. Slowly, as I headed west, I opened the bottle and began drinking. One resolution I passed then and there was that I was not going to buy Cali's van. I was done living in vehicles. Rita pointed out my own hypocrisy; even if I had to trade some of my artistic freedom for work, my own self-degradation had to end.

It was an unseasonably warm November evening. I felt calmer as the alcohol raced through my system. I walked through the empty streets until I reached the fence preventing passage that Bethsheba had taken us to when we had our romantic dinner. The river was on the other side of it. I walked until I came to the tear and slipped through. I went back to the area where I had sat with her.

On the rocky shore of the East River, I finished the last of the vodka while watching the night sky undergo the final throes of sunset. The New York skyline was beautiful and I felt warm all over.

As I looked beyond that flowing moat that separated me from the latter-day castle of Manhattan, I thought about the East River Swimmer as though he were alive. I considered how he might swim this slender channel of water.

Partly because of the liquor, partly due to the long walk, I found myself sweating profusely. I removed my jacket.

What was it about this particular series of Swimmer paintings that so consumed me? The last time I remembered being this obsessed was when I painted the underside of the subway trains—the death I had survived for no clear reason. God or fate had pushed me in front of that oncoming train, and that same faceless force had let me live. These paintings were different, though. The swimmer fought the waves and triumphed. The tons of steel had an intrinsic might and an intractable destiny—there never was a place for my own pathetic postpubescent will beneath the wheels of the train. In the waves, even though the odds were against me, I could still have a chance.

Dipping my fingers into the lapping current, it felt cold, but I was flushed and sweating. I simply knew at that moment that I needed to get into the water. I pulled off my shoes, pants, underwear, and shirt. Naked in a moment, I slipped in. Immediately I felt myself going numb and yet, I wasn't in pain. The cool water was perfect. I really intended to just dip in and get right out. In a flash, though, I started stroking outward. The East River was fairly narrow at that point. There was almost no current. I decided to just swim for a few minutes and turn back. But in no time at all I was halfway across, and the glory of swimming to Manhattan was irresistible.

With each slice of my arm and thrust of my leg, I found myself focusing on a chant: *If I didn't give her the money, she wouldn't be dead now. If I didn't give her the money, she wouldn't be dead now . . .*

About halfway across, the bone-gnawing temperature started really penetrating. The body chills seven times quicker in water than in air. The cold discombobulates the nerves and turns swimming into floundering. In fact, one is not supposed to swim at all in freezing water because heat is expelled through the extremities more rapidly. I kept thinking, *This isn't water, it's just a trillion tiny solid particles.* I knew I could still make it across. It was only cold if I *believed* it was cold, I thought and repeated to myself. Ironically, my greatest fear was being rescued. Either a J or an M train would be passing over the Williamsburg Bridge. If no one saw me, I could still be spotted from either Manhattan or Brooklyn.

Just as I passed the second span of the Williamsburg Bridge, a large tug passed. I dove under the surface. A massive wave from the boat's wake swept me up and propelled me the final twenty feet or so, face forward, right into that huge seawall that buttressed the park—*pow!* I was in Manhattan with a nose bleed. The north end of East River Park was a sheer concrete cliff with nothing to hold onto; there was no way to climb up onto the walkway. My teeth were chattering and my body was growing colder by the minute. I found a yellow rope tied around an old wooden piling on Twelfth Street, but I couldn't shimmy the additional five feet or so up to the little dock. My arms were shivering and my muscles were beginning to cramp and convulse: withdrawal from warmth. I splashed back down into the water and doggie paddled south along the wall.

Black iron moorings were posted horizontally every couple of hundred feet, but they didn't offer a way up either. Finally, I found a crack in the seawall. All sensory stimulation was gone, I could see and move my body but not feel it. As I wedged my fingers between the two slabs of stone, I wondered if I was digging them in too far. Was I crushing my bone and not knowing it? As I angled slowly up, trying to control the shaking, I felt like I had devolved into some amphibious creature. I only wished I had suction pads because algae slime made the ascent difficult. After about ten minutes, having struggled only about a third of the way up the seven-foot stretch, a huge wave from the rising tide caught me and I splashed back into the river.

"Help!" I wailed, praying I'd catch a jogger or anyone. But if someone passed, I didn't know. I couldn't see a soul. This was the place where I had spent the sweltering days of last summer painting all those Latin fishermen. Now they had all gone home.

Finally I spotted a small pipe protruding from the top of the seawall, but it was too high to reach. Below it was a green sign, "If you see discharge during dry weather please call NYCDEP."

As I slowly drifted south with the current, passing more pilings, I saw the rusted metal gates bordering the river. Parts of it were missing. A wooden picket fence was temporarily unraveled over the gaps. Still I saw no place to climb up.

Twice I heard, or thought I heard, voices going by, and through a locked jaw and clicking teeth, I coughed out for help, but to no avail.

The Domino sugar plant under the dark eastern sky and the World Trade Center towers in the west looked down at me like a gang of ambivalent gods. As the current carried me downstream, I felt like a disembodied head swirling in the clouds, trying to hold still while the city passed me by.

I had been in the water for about twenty minutes. My arms and jaw were trembling. I felt the cold like some monstrous mass literally sucking the life out of me. My fingernails and skin were turning blue. The only thing I could think of was to try and swim back to Brooklyn, but I knew I wouldn't make it. By the time I was pulled under the Williamsburg Bridge, I felt as though I were inhabiting a frozen body.

At the southernmost end of the park, just as the burning numbness was turning to a dull, tired ache, I went under, gulping water as I went down. But at that point the river wasn't very deep. It was only a foot above my head. I kicked the muck and slowly sprang back up. Reaching the surface, I started coughing up water.

"Holy shit!" I heard. "What 'chu doing down there?!" God sounded uneducated.

Looking up, I saw an older homeless guy bent over the rusted metal railing. He had a beanie and a beard. I couldn't determine either age or race. He vanished for a moment and returned suddenly, lowering a filthy blanket down to me. He wrapped one end around the rail.

"If you just pull it, it'll rip," he mercifully instructed. "Twist it."

I did as he said, and hand over hand, I yanked myself up slowly, scraping against the jagged concrete wall. I was shaking uncontrollably, but I didn't let go. When I was within clinging distance, he leaned over and grabbed my shoulder. When I was up to the gate that bordered the esplanade, he threw his arms around my naked chest and he heaved backwards. He pulled me right over the chest-high gate onto the cold, hard walkway as though I were a big fish he had just caught.

"What, you couldn't afford the subway!" he mocked.

I curled myself into a shivering ball on the ground, near the filthy

281

wool blanket, and tried to dry myself. He pitched in, wiping me down with an old newspaper. His filthy hand on my cold back felt like a red-hot poker.

I was lucky—it was a warm November night, about sixty degrees. Otherwise I probably would've died of hypothermia. Once I got some core heat back, I rose slowly to my numbed and stinging feet. I thanked the urban nomad and promised that I'd come back and reward him for saving my life.

"I won't turn it down," he assured me. Around his cheeks and the sides of his mouth, I saw symptoms of ancient drug use.

He let me keep the filthy blanket, something I would always prize. For a moment I considered trying to get a cop or an ambulance, but I quickly realized that I would freeze if I waited there. As I walked out of the park and through the streets, I kept wondering, if Rita were out there in the water with me, would she have simply let herself drown, or would she have tried to survive? With wet hair and bare feet, as I staggered the mile or so homeward across the Lower East Side, I couldn't decide.

The way she dealt with death at first appeared courageous, even defiant. But now, after I was forced to really struggle for life, her conduct seemed more like spite than survival. Existing in her netherworld, she was neither living nor dying. Ultimately she just seemed to be degrading life itself.

The closest I could remember to her ever showing anything as intense as love was a sorrow for being unable to show it. Only in those few minutes when she let her cynical guard down and stopped the whole spiteful-life act did she really seem to enjoy herself. In some ways, she had died long before I ever met her.

Careful not to step on any broken glass, I moved like a ghost through the benches of Allen Street where we had spent our last evening together. No one seemed to notice me.

Holding the blanket tightly around my chest, by the time I finally reached Mekong Delta, I didn't recall ever feeling so tired. Lynn raced from behind the counter, passing the line of homebound patrons who stared at me vacantly.

"What the hell—" Lynn grabbed me. She pressed me against her warm body, rubbing my frigid back and legs with her open palms. Her body heat felt like a transference of life itself.

"I'm sorry," I said, exhausted. "It's a long story."

"Where's your van? Where are your clothes?" She looked outside as if I was parked out there.

"Lost them."

She yelled into the rear of the kitchen that she'd be back in a minute. With her arms tightly around me, she led me around the corner into the bank building.

"What the hell happened?" She asked as we crossed the street.

"I swam the East River."

"Are you fucking nuts!" she asked angrily. Strangely, it felt good to be scolded.

When we got inside the building, I told her I was okay, she could get back to work. She ignored me. In a moment, we were upstairs in my apartment.

"Get into the shower," she commanded and turned on the hot water.

"I'm fine. Go back to work before you get fired."

She told me that she'd be back on her break with some soup and food.

"Thank you," I said earnestly. She gave me a hug, kissed me on the cheek, and left.

Behind her was the addict mural. In it I saw a defect in Rita's reasoning. She had felt that because nothing lasts, nothing really mattered. Now she was gone, but to the end of my life she'd be a part of me. That life, no matter how short and finite, was my own, private infinity. Forever didn't matter.

The long steamy shower didn't remove the sense of chill, but it left

283

me utterly exhausted. As I lay in bed, I glimpsed at the East River Swimmer sketches. These tormenting images were what had lured me into the water in the first place. I simply couldn't get past them. I had been unable to judge their authenticity. Now after having survived the insane crossing, I was finally ready to move on. With everything I had gone through, not a single added brush stroke could heighten the utter agony and fear I had just suffered. Nothing I could do would make them any more convincing or enduring.

Rita was right about one detail—Art was one thing and life was another.

ACKNOWLEDGMENTS

Dan "The Man" Mandel

Joelle Yudin, phenomenal editor

Brian Lipson

Jennifer Zeger

Susan Weinberg

Jennifer Hart

Heather Burke

Marie Elena Martinez

Brothers Burke & Patrick

Kim Kowalski

Pete Morse

Charles Small

Ken Dombrowski

Melissa Barberia

and all the other pagans in East River Park